"Lieutenant Franco, LAPD."

"Lieutenant Franco," the cop repeated, nonplussed. "Hold on." He picked up a phone, eyeballing her as he talked to Silvester. "Yeah, okay." He hung up. "She'll be down in a sec," he told her.

Frank nodded. About ten minutes later a trim woman in dark gray descended the stairs. The two detectives immediately made each other and as Silvester neared, she reproached, "You said you were gonna call."

"Happened to be in the neighborhood."

Silvester pursed her lips while they took each other's measure.

The detective was a couple inches shorter than Frank, late forties or early fifties, sharp dark eyes, salt-and-pepper hair cut below gold hoop earrings, wide mouth, generously lipped. She looked Mediterranean—Jewish or Italian, Frank guessed.

Tilting her head toward the box, Silvester asked, "This your evidence?"

"Yeah. So what did you find out?"

"Come upstairs."

As they climbed, Silvester asked, "You workin' this case indie, or what?"

"No. Not at all. Like I said, it's a long story and I don't have a lot of time. I'm just visiting for the weekend. Got a nine o'clock flight back home tonight."

"Oh." Silvester feigned concern. "Why didn't you say so? If I'da known that I'da had this case solved for you ten minutes ago."

"Look." Frank stopped to glare. "Enough with the attitude, okay? I come to you as a colleague with potential evidence and you're treatin' me like a snitch hoping to con a twenty outta you. If you can't be bothered with doing your job, find me someone who can."

Visit

Bella Books

at

BellaBooks.com

or call our toll-free number

1-800-729-4992

END *of* WATCH

Baxter CLARE

Bella
BOOKS
2006

Bella Books, Inc.
P.O. Box 10543
Tallahassee, FL 32302

Printed in the United States of America on acid-free paper
First Edition

Editor: Christi Cassidy
Cover designer: L. Callaghan

ISBN 1-59493-064-3

For those in and out of these rooms.

About the Author

Baxter Clare is a wildlife biologist by vocation and a writer by avocation. She never intended to write mysteries but the L.A. Franco character rented a room in her imagination one morning and has been there ever since. This is her fifth L.A. Franco mystery.

In a ceremony at San Francisco City Hall she married her lifetime partner, artist Ann Marie O'Connor. They live in the rugged La Panza mountain range of California's central coast, and Clare ventures regularly from chaparral wilderness to the urban wilds of South Central Los Angeles.

CHAPTER 1
Wednesday, 5 Jan 05—home

All right. Here goes. Mary says I should write, that writing will keep me honest, so here I am. She said, don't think, just write. Ten minutes a day. I've got my timer set. Nine minutes and twenty-one seconds left.

Christ, where to start? WWJD? What would Julie (Andrews) do? Let's start at the very beginning, a very good place to start.

Let's start with Mary since this is her brilliant idea.

I bitch, but she's a gem. Knocked on my door at six thirty the morning after I tried to eat my gun. Took one look at me and said, "Kid, you look like you've been eating rat poison and sleeping under rocks."

Which was exactly how I felt. I liked her right away. No bullshit. She's from Brooklyn. Left her husband with two little boys and ran to California, just like I did. Minus husband and kids, of course.

She was a terrible drunk. Now she looks like somebody's sweet old granny but evidently she did everything short of murder before she

1

sobered up. She's a retired dispatch operator from the sheriff's department. I can tell her things I couldn't tell a civilian—from the baby drowned in a bucket last week, to fucking up with Gail, all the drinking on the job. The blackouts. Eating my gun. No secrets. That's the deal. Got to tell your sponsor everything. She just nods and keeps knitting. She's fucking shockproof. She's kept me sober this far—sixty-one days—so I may as well keep doing what she tells me. Beats a bullet for dinner.

Six minutes left.

Got Stan Getz on. Moved the CD into the living room. Too many memories in the den. Easier to be out here. I've been going through new CDs like I used to go through Scotch. Hard to listen to the old ones. They remind me too much of wine, or Scotch, or beer, or ad nauseum . . . a drink for every song.

So I'm making new memories, sober ones, ones I can remember in the morning. I'm loving Getz's West Coast Sessions. He was a junkie. Amazing how many musicians were junkies or drunks—it either killed 'em or they kicked it. No half measures. Getz kicked it. Died sober. Good deal. One day at a time, right?

Which reminds me. I'm going to New York this weekend. Mary thinks it's too early, that I'm too vulnerable in my fledgling sobriety, but I'm afraid if I don't do this now I never will. Been putting it off a long time and I need to make peace with it. It's only a weekend. I'll be back on Monday.

Jesus. Gail just called. She got my letter. Wants to come by. She's going out of town tomorrow and wants to talk before she leaves. She sounds pissed. What could have pissed her off? This is what I wrote (I spent so much time on it I know it by heart):

Gail—
I'll keep this short—I know you're busy and probably don't want to hear much from me. I knew when I walked out on you that I'd made the wrong choice but wrong as it was, it was the only option I could see at the time. And I pursued that option as hard as I could until I was an ounce of trigger pressure away from ending up on one of your gurneys. I got some

2

help and have been sober a while. My head's clearing and I'm seeing the messes I made.

The worst is what I did to us. For whatever it's worth, I'm sorry. That doesn't change anything. It doesn't make it all better. It's just the truth. I was wrong—dead wrong—to walk out on you and I have to live with that. I hope it hurts me more than it hurts you, but when I see you at the morgue you look miserable. I hate what I've done to you and I'd do anything to take it back but I can't. Please know it wasn't about you, Gail. It was never about anything you did or didn't do—one of the things they say in AA is "no human power could have relieved us of our alcoholism." All our love combined couldn't have kept me from reaching for the bottle instead of you. I wish I could take that night back, but I can't. At least please know I loved you then and I love you now.

Always—F.

What's offensive about that? I can't see it. Oh, well. I guess she's going to let me know. Wonder if I should change clothes. Got my old academy sweats on. They're pretty gnarly. Shit. I wonder what she wants. I swear, it's easier taking down a rock house than waiting for my ex to knock on the door.

A drink sure would be nice. A couple drinks. Oh well. Not an option. Just gotta tough it out. Okay, okay. Ten minutes is up. I'm going to change my clothes. Later.

CHAPTER 2

The doorbell rang and Frank took a deep breath. She held it a second before opening the door. She thought she was ready but seeing the doc made her guts and her knees go quivery. Gail looked tired and pale, grim even, but to Frank she was still beautiful. Her heart felt like it was being squeezed in a giant fist and she wondered vaguely if that was what a heart attack felt like.

"Hi. Come in."

Gail stepped past Frank without looking at her.

"You coming from work?"

"Yes."

"Are you hungry? I can make you something. A sandwich? Soup?"

"No." Gail faced her. "I'm not staying that long."

"Okay." Frank motioned toward the couch. "Staying long enough to sit?"

Gail swept back her bangs with her knuckles and Frank followed her into the living room. Gail primly took one end of the long couch and Frank took the other. She waited for Gail to speak. The doc just stared, until her obvious frustration made her blurt, "Why did you send that letter? What could you have *possibly* been thinking?"

Frank was surprised. She thought the letter was plain, but she explained, "To apologize. You were right, I was wrong. I guess I didn't make that clear."

Gail snorted her disbelief. "I don't hear from you, except for an occasional nod and a 'hey' at work, for nigh on six months and then this letter drops out of the blue. And you're terribly sorry and contrite and sober, and just what the hell am I supposed to do with all that? Forgive you? Everything's fine now because you're sorry? Is that what you thought would happen? That everything would be *dandy*, that all would be forgiven if you just dropped me a little note? That I'd forget you left me for a bottle of Scotch?"

Gail's vitriol was another surprise, but a good one. Frank reasoned that she'd only be this angry if she still cared a lot. So Frank proceeded on tiptoe through the minefield of her reply. "No. I don't expect anything like that. I just felt the least I could do was apologize. You deserve that. You deserve a whole lot more and I hope you find it with someone who can be better to you than I was. I don't expect you to take me back. I don't even expect you to like me very much. I guess I just need to accept responsibility for what I did. I fucked us up in a big way. It doesn't change anything. I just wanted you to have the satisfaction of knowing it was all my doing. In case you had any doubt, which it sounds like you don't."

Gail retorted, "You're damn right I don't," but her wrath was cooling.

Frank continued her mollifying. "I'm sorry I upset you. That wasn't my intention. If you want to stay angry, that's fine. You have every right to. I can't change that, and if you want I'll never bother you again. I'm just trying to extend an olive branch. We still work together and I'd like to make that as peaceful as possible. If we can't get to peaceful"—she shrugged—"that's the way it is. I don't know what else to say. Tell me to leave you alone, never talk to you again, and I will."

Gail's green eyes burned. She looked near tears and finally thumped the couch with her fist. "God damn you, Frank. God *damn* you. I've spent the last six months trying to forget about you and in one fell swoop you obliterate all that effort. And you're damn right I want to be mad at you. I *hate* you. I hate your damn letter and your damn apologies! You can't just swoop back into my life like that."

"Then I won't," Frank answered gently. "I promise I'll leave you alone. I won't call or write or even say hello when I see you. Is that what you want?" Gail dropped her head and Frank pushed, "Is it? Just tell me. Say the word and I'll be gone forever."

"Damn you," Gail whispered. "Damn *me* for ever falling in love with you. All the red flags were there and I ignored each one." She shook her head, picking invisible things from her slacks. Frank waited her out. At length Gail admitted, "I don't want to hate you, but I don't trust you either. You scare the hell out of me."

"How so?"

"Because you're two people. The thoughtful, sensitive Miss Hyde that I fell in love with and the alcoholic Doctor Jekyll that I detest. I never know which one you're going to be."

Frank nodded. "That scares me too. I wish I could look you in the eye and swear I'll never drink again, but I can't do that. I've been going to all these AA meetings and I hear stories about people who were sober ten, fifteen, twenty years and then one day they start drinking again. Seems like the common denominator among them is that they stop going to meetings and stop working the steps. They stop being honest with their sponsors and themselves and eventually they drink again. So I know it happens." Scooting down the couch, close enough that she could reach out and touch Gail, she added, "All I *can* promise, and I promise this more for myself than for you, is to keep doing the things that will give me the best shot at staying sober. And that starts with telling the truth, being honest about where I'm at and where I've been.

6

That's why I wrote that letter. I need to admit what I did to the people I hurt. And I need to remember what I did because if I forget then I'm in danger of doing it again. And I don't want to do that, Gail. To you, to me or to anyone else."

Frank sat back. It was a long speech for her. It felt strange, talking so much, but it felt good, too. Awkward as it was to get into, the truth fit comfortably once it was in place.

So she continued, "Tell me what to do. Do you want me to leave you alone? I can do that, if that's what you want. Just tell me."

"I don't know what I want. I thought I did until I got your letter. It was beautiful. I cried when I read it." She half laughed. "Then I balled it up and threw it across the room calling you names you'd be proud of." Gail hated profanities and the two women shared a tentative smile.

"Look, if it's any help, I don't know what I want either. I feel all . . . disjointed lately. Like I have no idea who I am. I don't want to be the old Frank but I'm not sure who the new one is. So what do you say we go back to square one? Start all over. No expectations. Just try to be friends again. Maybe see how that goes."

"It's not that easy."

"Why?"

"Because." Gail's eyes searched the room. "Because I'd have to suspend my disbelief to be with you. I don't know that I can be in a relationship with you without expectations. And I'd keep waiting for you to turn into Dr. Jekyll, waiting for you to shut me out again. I don't know that I'm willing to do that."

Frank nodded agreement. "Yeah. I'd be scared too. Hell, I *am* scared. I don't *want* to be Dr. Jekyll again. I can't afford to be. The cost is too high. If I become her again I can only see two options—one really. Somehow I'd kill myself. Probably in a car wreck or with a bullet—but something bad'd happen and I don't want to go there. I've been close enough to that edge and I don't want to go back. That's all I can tell you."

"I know. I know you can't make any promises. But neither can I."

"Fair enough. How about we just try for civility and see where it goes from there?"

"All right," Gail yielded. "We'll try that." She looked like she had more to add, but stood up. "Thanks for letting me come over."

"Thanks for wanting to."

Walking her to the door, Frank asked where she was going on her trip.

"New York. I'm speaking at the NAME convention on Friday."

A grin spread across Frank's face and Gail interpreted it as confusion.

"Oh, sorry. NAME is the the National Association of Medical Examiners. I'm leaving early to see some friends and do some shopping. What are you laughing about?"

Frank was still smiling, shaking her head at the floor. "What are the odds?"

"The odds of what?"

"The odds that I'd be in New York this weekend, too."

"You're going to New York?"

"Yep."

"What for?"

"Take care of some business. Stuff I should have taken care of twenty years ago."

"Like what."

"More apologies, kind of. Amends. Very late amends. I don't suppose you'd let me buy you a cup of hot chocolate at Rockefeller Center? Tell you all about it it if you were interested."

Gail looked dubious. "We'll see. Why don't you call me?"

"Same cell phone number?"

"Yes." Gail actually chuckled. "It hasn't been *that* long. And I'll be staying at the Crowne Plaza. In Times Square. You can always leave a message for me there."

"All right. I'll do that."

"Where are you going to be?"

"I'm not sure yet."

"You don't have a room?"

8

"Nah. It's New York. I'm not too worried."

Gail nodded. All the fight had left her. She looked soft. Touchable. Frank wanted to stroke her cheek, just for a second, but sensed the timing was wrong.

"If I don't hear from you, I hope you have a great trip. It's a helluva city."

"Yeah, I'm looking forward to it."

They lingered by the door. Gail offered a small but earnest smile. "Maybe I'll see you there."

Frank returned the shy smile. "I'll call you. Be safe."

"Always the cop."

Frank chuckled. "I can't change *everything*."

"I hope not," Gail said. "So much of you is wonderful. I'll see you."

Instead of walking Gail to her car and watching her drive off, Frank closed the door and leaned against it. The smile crept back onto her face.

CHAPTER 3

Frank got to work Friday morning well before the rest of the LAPD's Ninety-third Homicide Squad. Her detectives trailed in around six—Johnny hungover, Darcy and Diego mute, Lewis and Jill cackling about *Survivor* and Bobby teasing the women, "You don't get enough on-the-job reality?"

"Yeah, but I don't have to clean up the shit on TV," Lewis shot back.

"Amen," Jill said, and the women high-fived each other.

"All right, let's get started. Fubar's going to be on call while I'm gone. Hopefully it'll be quiet. Looks like there's some rain coming in and killers don't like getting wet. Bobby's lead while I'm gone. Got any questions, ask him first. Bobby, run what you have to by Fubar, but try and keep it to a minimum or else you'll confuse him and he'll start making shit up. I'll have my phone with me so call if you need to. Jill, I want to read the Fuentes sixty-day on the airplane. Got it?"

"Got it." The redhead sighed. Johnny and Jill were chronically late with their sixty-day follow-up reports and Frank was tired of taking Foubarelle's heat for them.

"Johnny, I want—"

He raised a hand to stop her. "I know, I know. Valenzuela and Brown."

"And Acuña. That's only a week late."

Johnny didn't even protest and Frank hurt just looking at him.

He had gone through a department-ordered rehab and done pretty well for about a month afterward. Then he came in one morning with the bleary-eyed shakes, but Frank was in rough shape herself at the time and couldn't say much. She warned him that he was running out of chances. She kicked herself for being a hypocrite, but after she went to her first couple AA meetings she tried to get Johnny to go with her. He wouldn't. Said he didn't want to become a Bible-thumper.

"Oh, man," she argued. "It's not like that. Got nothing to do with banging Bibles. It's like *Cheers*, only in reverse. Everyone knows your name but they're sober. Come on. Won't kill you to check it out."

"Man, I had to do AA in rehab. I'm not into it. I'd rather be drinking than sittin' around talkin' about it. You go to meetings for both of us and I'll go drink for both of us."

Frank didn't argue. She couldn't have gone six months ago either—she hadn't been kicked hard enough yet. "All right. You know where I am if you change your mind."

"Yeah." He flapped a hand at her, managing the semblance of a cocky, old Johnny grin. "I never thought I'd see the day."

She grinned back. "Neither did I. But let me tell you. Beats eating a bullet."

Johnny had stared oddly at her before she'd walked away.

The phone on Bobby's desk rang and he answered. Everyone listened to see if they'd caught a case, but the big, black detective said in his shier-than-a-virgin-on-her-wedding-night voice, "Yeah, all right. Around eight or so." Rejoining the group, he offered, "That was Irie. Says he has a good tip."

"Yeah," Jill said of Bobby's informant. "And he wants a twenty in his pocket before the liquor store opens."

After the meeting Frank said to Bobby, "Let me know when you're going to talk to Irie. I want to ride with you, stop and talk to that clerk at the Circle Jerk."

"Roger that."

Frank tied up loose ends, talked to the duty sergeant and met with her captain until Bobby tracked her down, asking if she was ready.

She nodded. "Let's roll."

He checked out a muddy unmarked and Frank opened the door to see empty cups and cans and Burger King bags all over the floor.

She told him, "Go see who had this signed out last."

"Uh-oh."

"Yeah, uh-oh's right. Fuckin' pigs."

Bobby came back a minute later and handed Frank a scrap of paper.

Getting in on the passenger side she read the names, grunting, "Figures."

"Ha ha." Bobby chuckled, turning onto Vermont. "Remember when you found Nook taking naps when he was supposed to be knocking?"

Frank grinned. Watching a muscled young man loping along the sidewalk, she answered, "That was a while back, huh?"

A brand new LT, she'd inherited two old-timers who refused to change their ways. Nook was one of them. When she found out he was taking a nap every afternoon in a shaded lot she had Bobby and Noah sneak the jack out of his car. Later, after Nook parked and was snoring in the backseat, under a blanket no less, the three of them quietly jacked his vehicle onto blocks. After they'd slunk back to their car, Frank raised him on the radio. Through binoculars she saw Nook lurch from the backseat, fall out the rear door and stand staring in amazement. Frank kept calling him and he finally reached inside for the radio, answering that he had a flat and that someone had taken the damn jack out of the car.

"Tell me where you are," she responded. "I've got a jack."

"No, no!" Nook cried, pacing around his car. "There's no spare either!"

"Well, I'll come get you. Where are you?"

Nook stalled. "Repeat. You're breaking up." Frank repeated and he said, "Oh, it's okay. I got a cab here. We'll let the garage take care of this. What's your twenty?"

Instead of answering she approached on foot.

Nook was asking into his radio, "Do you copy?"

"I copy," she said, stepping into the shade.

Nook whirled. He stammered, "I just went into the store and when I came out—"

Frank held up a hand. "No more naps, Nook. Clear?"

"I just—"

"Clear?"

He shook his head and sighed. "Clear."

"Good. Here." She tossed him the jack.

His mouth dropped. "I was gonna call the garage."

"Garage is busy," she'd said, walking back to her car. "When you get it down meet us at Denker and Sixty-ninth."

"Oh, man." Bobby was still laughing. "That was a good one."

Frank nodded, missing Noah and wishing her old partner were here to laugh with them. They pulled into the Circle K and talked to a clerk. They worked him a solid half-hour but he maintained he didn't see the shooting that happened twenty feet away from him.

Back in the car, Frank said, "Keep an eye on him. Give him time."

"Yeah," Bobby agreed. "Time enough to have someone *he* loves get shot. Then we'll see how eager he is to talk."

"Oo-oo, Picasso. Your cynicism's showing."

"Am I wrong?"

"Wish you were."

"Then it's not cynicism. It's the truth."

"How can I argue with a double major in art and philosophy?"

13

On the corner of Slauson they found Irie hawking bags of oranges. He looked older than Moses—his skin, his hair, his clothes, all gray. His pants and shirt were frayed but clean and he wore gleaming white Reeboks. They made a show of pulling the old man over to the car. A couple dudes in a passing car hissed at them.

"Irie," Frank chided. "S'up wid dem shoes, mon?"

Without even thinking about it, Frank slid into Irie's vernacular—habit from years of dealing with people, from adopting their accents and dialect to help break down the huge wall between cop and civilian.

"Ya like dem?" Irie bragged in his thick patois. "I foun' dem. Four pair, lyin' in de street! Dem fit good, too! I keep two, give dem rest away." Irie's face was a topo map of wrinkles and old wounds. He rubbed a raised keloid on his cheekbone and said, "Ya wan' we talk 'bou' my feets or I tell ya somet'ing ya migh' wanna know?"

Bobby asked, "What do you have?"

The CI leaned against the car and squinted at the cops. "Fidelio Ramirez," he enunciated. "'Im de one."

"Him the one what?" Frank asked.

"'Im de one shoot Oscar Fuentes."

Bobby wrote the name down. "Where can we find this Ramirez?"

With a shrug Irie told them, "Dat ya problem dere. Street say 'im run away to Mexico, but 'im used to be livin' with 'is girl on Fif-eight Street."

"How'd you hear it was Ramirez?"

"Ya can't fuh to axe me dat," Irie snorted. "Chuh! I gots protec' meself. Ya know dat."

"Does Ramirez have any other names?"

"Mebbe Cuco."

"Cuco," Bobby repeated. "What else?"

"Why fuh ya axe what else? I fuh gotta fin' 'im and han'cuff 'im and bring 'im in fuh ya? Chuh!"

Bobby gave Frank a sheepish look. "Do you have a twenty?"

Frowning, Frank pulled a Jackson from the wallet in her back pocket. She slipped the bill to Irie, asking, "Irie, mon, how old you is?"

Tapping the fat scar under his eye, he calculated, "'Bout fif-tree, fif-fo'. Why fuh you axe?"

She shrugged. "You been 'round a long time. Known you since I was a rookie."

"Fuh true." He grinned. "A long time."

"All dat time and I'm still not for sure why you do this."

Irie flashed pink palms. "Fuh be good ci'zen. Fuh do right ting."

"Right," she responded. "Of course."

Grinning, Irie stepped back. "Ya have good day, office's. Irie be tankin' you."

"Dat bwoy." Frank shook her head as they drove off. "'Im I fuh shuh n'unerstan'."

Bobby asked, "You want to try and find Ramirez?"

Frank flipped her wrist over. "Naw, you better take me back. Been joy-ridin' long enough."

"Roger that."

CHAPTER 4
Saturday, 8 Jan 05—LAX

Alrighty then. Waiting to board my flight. Didn't write yesterday— didn't have time—so will write for twenty minutes today. Mary says if I found the time to drink I can find the time to go to meetings. Or write. Or whatever damn thing I'm supposed to be doing.

At any rate, here I am in the thumping, thriving heart of LAX. Haven't flown since the extradition to Miami. Not looking forward to sitting with my knees on my chin for five hours but I'm glad I'm getting this over with.

Gotta love this place. It's like a separate universe, got every race, religion, nationality, sexual orientation, etc. Can find every manner of relationship here—there's a creep that looks like a pedophile by the women's restroom, next to a girlfriend crying against her boyfriend. In front of them a toddler's banging into his grandmother's legs, the guy walking past could be a hit man, an adulterer, an extortionist or a guy who loves his wife and sells copy machines. Or a terrorist. You never know. And this is just one terminal. Incredible place.

There's the boarding announcement. I'll finish this on the plane.

Here we go. Fat guy on his laptop to my left, old lady reading on my right. Me stuck in the middle. Only five hours. And then what? Tonight won't be so bad. I'll find a room in Canarsie—they gotta be cheap in Canarsie. Not exactly a tourist mecca—and get a good night's sleep. That's one thing about being sober. I'm sleeping again. Took a while. First couple weeks were pretty rocky but now it's good. Pretty sweet to wake up rested instead of hungover. I'd forgotten what that was like.

So tomorrow, first thing in the morning, I'll take care of business then I have the afternoon free until my nine o'clock flight home. I hope Gail takes me up on Rockefeller Center. She probably won't, probably too much, too soon. Besides, she came to New York for a convention and to hang out with friends. She can see me anytime.

Look at me. I got Sunday over with before it's even started. What happened to "one day at a time"? Still Saturday, far as I know. Oh, great. Here comes the stewardess with the booze trolley. "I'll have three Scotches and a can of club soda, please. Oh, and don't go too far away with that thing."

That's what I wanted to say, but it came out "Coffee. Black."

The fat guy got a Budweiser and of course I had to pass it to him. The can was cold and wet like it just came out of a cooler. I wanted to rip it open, guzzle it down and pass it on like nothing had happened. I wonder how much alcohol they stock for a five-hour morning flight. Probably not enough to keep me going once I got started. That's the thing. Mary says you have to think the drink through—think that first drink all the way through to the end. One would be nice, two would be lovely and three even better, but how many would be enough? There's no such thing as enough. One drink doesn't even begin to satisfy the craving, just kicks it into over-drive and sets up the desire for more. More and more and more, world without end, amen. This is getting me nowhere.

Mary would ask why I want a drink right now.

Oh, many reasons, Mary. For starters I'm in a tin can a mile above the earth. The smell of the fat guy's Bud is crawling up my nose—no temptation there—not to mention I'm about to revisit the scene of my youthful and childish crimes. And atone for them. If I can. Other than that, gee, no reason.

This isn't very productive. Maybe I should get some work done. Think about what I can do instead of what I can't. Mary would say that too.

Jesus, I sound like a damn AA parrot. "Squawk, squawk, squawk." Okay. Time's up. On to reports.

CHAPTER 5

The fat guy ordered a second beer and when he snapped it open Frank tasted the tangy, malty spray through her nose. She took a long swallow of tepid coffee and focused on Johnny's sixty-day.

By the time the plane landed at JFK the fat guy had downed four beers. Watching him jerk out of a drooling, snoring sleep, she was glad she stuck to coffee. She made haste from the plane and followed the exit signs to the taxi stand. When her cab came she asked the driver, "You know the Canarsie Cemetery? On Remsen in Brooklyn."

"Yah, yah. I know whey ees," the cabbie answered.

"All right. I want a hotel near there. A Holiday Inn or a Motel Six, something like that."

"Yah, yah." He bobbed his head. "I know prace."

She sat back and the cabbie slalomed from the terminal. Frank lowered the window—no matter what coast she was on, cabs still smelled of rancid body fluids. The stale air rushed out. What replaced it was the muddy, dank smell of Jamaica Bay and she was instantly ten years old again. The gushing cold air ripped at her eyes but she kept her face into the wind. The bay smells mixed with truck diesel and the must from centuries of city living. A hunger pang stabbed her and she suddenly craved a warm onion bialy with a shmear. As the driver tore through the precocious dusk, Frank allowed a thin smile and rolled the window up.

She rapped on the Plexiglas divider. "I changed my mind. I want to go into the City. To the Times Square Crowne Plaza."

"You no want Brookryn?"

"No. Midtown. The Crowne Plaza."

"From Motey Six to Crowne Praza?"

"Yeah."

The cabbie shrugged and slid the window shut, veering north off the parkway a couple exits later.

Frank was at the hotel in under an hour. She carried no bags, only a toothbrush in her briefcase. Upstairs, stretched on the taut bed, she wondered which floor Gail was on. She clicked the TV on and roamed through channels. Nothing caught her interest. She knew there was a bar downstairs. Warned herself not to even think about it. She should think about food instead, and remembered her desire for the bialy. She dialed the operator, called Katz's Deli. They were open until nine. Frank thought about schlepping all the way down to the Lower East Side but decided she was more restless than hungry. Nor was she sure she wanted to go traipsing through her old neighborhood, seeing things she might not want to be reminded of.

Instead she took the stairs to the lobby. In the gift shop she popped for an outrageously priced pair of shorts and a T-shirt. She found the gym and worked out for an hour. After a shower she walked down Broadway, finally stopping in front of a kebab house. She'd passed the Italian restaurants knowing she'd want wine with dinner. Sushi was out because of the sake. Pizza because of the beer. But she couldn't associate Afghan food with alcohol, so she ate there. Mixed kebabs with spiced tea were good and after dinner she wandered Times Square back to the hotel.

It was eight thirty, too early to go to bed and still nothing on TV. She read the *New York Times* with her attention inevitably drifting to the locked minibar, whose key she had wisely declined.

She dropped the paper on the floor and laced her fingers behind her head, staring at the same ceiling that was there earlier. She wondered if Gail was in, imagined she was out dining with friends and colleagues, kicking up her heels in the Big Apple. She was sure the doc wouldn't be in her room staring at the ceiling. She'd be having fun somewhere, and her ability to play was one of the things Frank loved best about Gail. All Frank knew was drinking and working. Playing was something she'd have to learn about.

Not wanting to bother Gail on her cell phone, Frank called the desk to leave her a message. She scanned the room service menu while waiting for a machine to answer. She was surprised when Gail answered.

"Hey. It's Frank. I, uh, I didn't think you'd be in. I was just going to leave you a message."

"Well, here I am. I got in about thirty seconds ago."

"So what do you think about my offer of hot chocolate?"

"I think that'd be lovely."

"Okay, then." Frank couldn't believe Gail had said yes. "Lovely, it is. Uh, how about one?"

"That'd be fine."

"Okay. How about I meet you in the lobby."

"Sure. Where are you?"

"Well, actually I'm on the third floor."

"Here? At the hotel?"

"Yeah. Don't worry, though. I'm not stalking you. I was headed to a Motel Six in Brooklyn and I thought what the hell, why not treat myself? So here I am, about to order a hot fudge sundae from room service." Frank decided to gamble big. "I don't suppose you'd care to join me?"

21

"You're not playing fair. You keep plying me with chocolate."

"It's my new drug of choice. Better a big bowl of ice cream than a bottle of Scotch."

"What room are you in?" Frank told her and Gail said, "Order one for me, too. I'll be down in five minutes."

"Roger that."

"With extra chocolate."

"Roger again."

CHAPTER 6

Frank opened at Gail's knock and gawked. "You're running around the Crowne Plaza in pajamas?"

Swishing by in flannel pants and a shirt, Gail scoffed, "I have more clothes on than three-quarters of the women in the lobby. And in case you haven't noticed, sleepwear has become street wear. I'm sure I'm very fashionable."

Frank hoisted a brow and closed the door. "Make a cool *Post* picture. 'LA's Chief Coroner Traipsing Plaza in PJs.'"

"Since when did you become so priggish?"

"Priggish? Me?"

"Yes." Gail giggled. "You."

"Never. Never a prig. Just surprised, is all. Guess I'm self-conscious in such a fancy place."

"Then I suggest you not run around in your pajamas."

"I won't. I don't have any."

"How long are you staying?"

"Just tonight. I'm going home tomorrow. Sit?" Frank perched on one of the chairs at the small table. Gail took the other. "So how'd your speech go last night?"

Gail chuckled. "Oh, God, I was so nervous." In a quivering voice she said, "I sounded like I was driving down a bumpy road. But everyone told me I did a good job so I assume I was at least intelligible."

"I'm sure you were wonderful. Did you present anything else?"

"No. After the opening speech I got to relax and just be an attendee. Thank God."

"What was the best session so far?"

"Probably the one on forensic tox software. God, there's so much technology out there. Applications I couldn't even have dreamed about twenty years ago."

"Oh, yeah? Like what?"

Gail cocked her head and squinted at Frank. "You hate computers. Why do I get the feeling you are oh-so-adroitly deflecting conversation from yourself?"

Guilty as charged, Frank fibbed, "I don't know. Can't a girl be curious?"

"Not you. Not about software applications."

Frank had to grin. Gail knew her too well.

"My turn. Can I ask what you came here for?"

Stalling, Frank answered, "You mean the hotel or New York?"

"New York."

"Sure. You could ask."

"And would you tell me?"

Frank sighed. "I'd have to. That's what I'm supposed to do to stay sober. Tell the truth. Hide nothing."

"Wow," Gail said, crossing her long legs, tucking her feet under. "I shouldn't think that would be an easy task for you."

"I've had easier. You cold? Want a blanket?"

"No, I'm fine."

"It's probably gonna be a cold fudge sundae by the time it gets here."

"Any fudge is good fudge. And you're fudging."

"Busted," Frank conceded. "All right. Guess we should start from the beginning. I told you my mom was dead, right?"

Gail nodded. "You said she died of heart failure and when I asked from what you got vague on me."

"Sounds like something I'd do." Frank sighed again. Seemed that the truth required extra oxygen. "She died when I was twenty-something. Twenty-three, I think. I came back and took care of all the arrangements but I didn't have a funeral for her, just handled the business of burying her, paid for it and left. Never went to the cemetery where they put her. Never said good-bye. And I . . . I figure it's time to do that. I've waited long enough. Time to say good-bye, put an end to her—to us." She shrugged, wondering where the hell room service was.

"Why now, after all this time?"

"It's just one more thing I've been running from all these years. One more thing I don't want to face. And I have to. I have to put all these ghosts to rest if I want to stay sober."

When the knock came Frank jumped so quickly she almost tipped the table over. After holding her eye to the peephole she opened the door. A uniformed man smiled, hefting a tray. Frank watched him place the tray on the table and uncover the sundaes.

"Thank you," Gail gushed.

"You're welcome," the man chirped in a thick accent. Frank put two bucks in his hand as he passed. "Thank you, ma'am."

She closed the door and bolted it. "How is it?"

"Good. But hurry. It's melting."

Frank complied. She buried her spoon into the mound of ice cream as Gail asked, "Why didn't you have a funeral for your mom?"

Around a mouthful of sundae Frank snorted. "She's lucky I buried her."

"What did she do that was so awful?"

"She wasn't awful," Frank admitted. "She was just sick. She was a manic depressive and wouldn't stay on her meds."

"Did she have the radical mood swings?"

Frank stared into her bowl. "Yeah. More toward the end. And

25

to be fair, it wasn't always so awful . . . When I was little, before my dad died, they'd be getting dressed up to go dancing—they loved dancing—and my dad was shaved and he smelled like Old Spice and Scotch and he'd put me on his feet and dance with me. Sinatra or Benny Goodman. He loved those guys. Then he'd shoo me off and I'd sit in the bathroom on the john, watching my mother put on her makeup. She'd be humming and making faces in the mirror—putting her face on, she used to call it—and I loved watching her. She was so pretty. She looked like a queen in a fairy tale, or one of those Greek goddesses they were always trying to teach us about in school. And I thought, I mean I really *believed* she was magic. She'd make flowers appear in the window box in mid-winter, or she'd cheep at these tough little New York sparrows and they'd come flying into her hand. And there was a pit bull in the basement that would kill anything that came near it, but my mom would say, 'Oh, hush,' and walk up to it, pretty as you please, scratching his ears, rubbing his belly, and that dog would act the fool over her. Wagging his tail and rolling on his back, licking her cheek. I was sure he was gonna eat her one day, but she'd just laugh and play with him. He'd whine for her to come back when she walked away."

She took a bite of ice cream. When Gail didn't say anything Frank continued.

"I never knew which it was going to be." She gave a wry smile. "How the pigeons have come home to roost, huh? I'm just like her in that I never knew if she was going to be the fairy princess or the wicked witch. Was she gonna be high or low? Laughing or weeping? Dancing or sleeping? Toward the end, after my dad died, that's when she got pretty predictable. It was all bad then. Everything went to hell. I did what I could to try and make up for it, to try and keep her from spilling over into the lows, but it didn't matter. She always ended up in a depression. There'd be days, sometimes weeks, she wouldn't get out of bed. Toward the end I preferred that. At least I knew where she was. And I could take care of myself. All I really needed her for was to cash the welfare

26

checks. I'd drag her outta bed to the supermarket then I'd keep the cash they gave her and do all the shopping, pay what bills we could."

The ice cream didn't taste good anymore and Frank stirred it into soup. Gail was scraping smears of fudge from the sides of her bowl. The click of her spoon was comforting. Gail sitting across from her was comforting. Licking the tip of the spoon, Gail asked, "How old were you when it got bad?"

Frank did the math. "I was ten when my dad died. She held it together for a little while after that. She didn't get really bad until I was in my teens. My uncle helped out when he could. He'd come by once a month or so, slip her something. It was pretty embarrassing. My mom had been so pretty—I think he was crushed out on her even after my dad married her. She'd cry all over him and grovel and thank him. He had a wife and two kids so he never gave us much. And he must have been leaning on the landlord because I don't how else we paid the rent."

"What do you mean he leaned on the landlord?"

"He was a cop—things were different then. A civilian did you a favor, you did them a favor. So he probably helped the landlord with rowdy tenants, cruised by more often than regular patrols, who knows? At any rate, he did his best. I think it hurt him to be around us. He must've missed my dad something awful. They were best friends. I tried to stay at my uncle's as much as I could. I didn't want to be home, but my aunt was a bitch. She made it clear she didn't want me around, so I stopped going after a while. My older cousin had joined the Army by then and the younger one started fooling around with drugs. We drifted away. After I left for California my mom lost the apartment, started living on the streets. My uncle'd find her and take her into a shelter but she'd always leave." She dipped her spoon into the pool of ice cream, let it run off, dipped it again. "She died on the street. A shopkeeper noticed she'd been in the same spot a couple days in a row. Called the EMTs. She was frozen under a pile of newspapers. Had my number on her. Cops called me. That was that. Nice, huh? That's the kind of daughter I was. Let my own mother freeze to death on the street." Frank looked up to see Gail wipe at a tear. She glanced back into her bowl, quietly telling it, "I ran and I ran just like the Gingerbread Man."

Gail cleared her throat. "God, Frank. You were just a kid. Kids do that. It's a normal reaction."

"Nice try. I was eighteen years old. Hardly a kid. I knew better. I could have gone to school closer to home. I could have taken her to California with me. I could have institutionalized her. I could've done a lot of things. Truth was, I didn't want to be anywhere near her. She wouldn't stay on her lithium and I was gonna be damned if I'd go down with her. So I bailed."

"You may have been a legal adult," Gail argued, "and despite *acting* like an adult and taking care of yourself and your mother all those years, inside you were still a kid. You reacted like any kid would."

"Maybe." Frank dropped the spoon into the bowl. "Whatever. It's done. I did what I did, she did what she did, and I need to live with it all."

"Oh, boy. That is frighteningly stoic. Vintage do-or-die Frank."

Frank thought about that, allowing, "I'm willing to live with it but I never said it would be easy, or that I'd do it gracefully. I'm still mad at her. I'm mad at myself, too. I don't like what I did, but I'm willing to let it go. I have to. I'm tired of being mad, being such a hater. Doesn't get me anywhere but closer to a bottle. Or a gun. I don't know much but I know I don't want to go there. So it is what it is. Rocks are hard, rain is wet. I can't change any of it. All I can change is how I react to it. If that's stoic, then that's what it is."

"It's like when you left me," Gail mused. "It was so much easier to hate you than to admit how much it hurt. How much I missed you and wanted you back."

"I'm sorry about that."

"No. Don't be. I'm not saying it to make you feel bad. I just know how it feels to be mad at someone when all you really want

28

is to love them. Case in point, my father. I just wanted to love him but after all the broken promises it became so much easier to hate him and push him out of my life. I think now I love him because he's my father, but I don't like him and don't particularly want a relationship with him. I was always mad he wouldn't be the father I wanted him to be and could never accept him for the father he was."

"Yeah." Frank nodded. "You wanted the sober dad and I wanted the mom who lived between the highs and the lows."

"Did you hate me after you left?"

"No. I was too tired to hate you. Too busy drinking and getting numb. Hate would have interfered with the numbness. I just didn't think about you. When you popped into my head I pushed you out. Just like I've always done with anything that hurts. Push it out, cover it up with lots of booze or work and pretend it just doesn't exist."

"And now you can't do that anymore."

Tracing the pattern in the wood veneer, Frank echoed, "And now I can't do that anymore."

"I'm glad."

Frank looked into the cool and limpid green eyes, just like the song said, and she had to turn away. She hadn't earned the right to look there yet.

"Tell me about the night you quit drinking."

Frank shook her head. "You don't want to hear about that."

"Yes, I do. If you want to tell me."

Frank sighed, plunging into the short version. "I'd gotten off early. Fubar was on call. I had the whole night to get shit-faced and that's what I planned to do. I was buying Scotch by the case at that point so I settled in with a bottle the minute I got home. Watched TV and drank and drank and drank. Waiting for the booze to kick in, to feel the click that quiets everything down. But it didn't happen. I was well into my second bottle and stone-cold sober. I couldn't get the click. And I got scared. I'd been cleaning my guns. They were all lying on the table in front of me. Picked up the nine millimeter and put it in my mouth. If I just squeezed a little tighter on the trigger it would be quiet forever. Peaceful. Nothing would ever hurt again. So I squeezed a little tighter. I was daring myself to do it. I remember thinking, 'Pull, pull! Just pull, damn it!' and then the TV went black for a second, just a quick, two A.M. pause between infomercials, and I saw myself in that black screen—gun in my mouth, finger on the trigger, shaking—and I threw the gun across the room. Threw up all over. Couldn't stop shaking. I was crying. Managed to call Joe, my old LT. He told me to sit tight, he was gonna get help. I dozed off, sitting on the floor, wrapped in my bedspread. Phone woke me up. I thought it was work. It was Mary—she's my sponsor now—and she said, 'Joe called me last night and I'm taking you to a seven o'clock meeting. Get showered and get dressed. I'll be there in half an hour.' And that was that."

Gail shivered, hugging herself. "It sounds so harrowing."

"Yeah. Harrowing. That's a good word for it." Frank pointed at the raised flesh on her arms. "Still gives me goose bumps every time I think about it. But I don't ever want to forget it, either. If I forget I might go back there. So that's why I'm here." She gave Gail a tight smile. "Still on for tomorrow?"

"For more chocolate? You bet!"

"Good." Having had enough of talking, Frank got up and put the tray outside. Gail came up behind her. "Thanks for the ice cream."

"Thanks for the company."

"Call me when you get in tomorrow."

"I will," Frank said. "Good night."

"Good night."

Gail walked down the hall and Frank watched until she got into the elevator.

CHAPTER 7

Sunday, 9 Jan 05—Manhattan

Early. Still dark out. Dark as this city can be. Drinking awful hotel room coffee. Okay, still a day behind in this damn thing.

Had a nice time with Gail last night. Came down to my room and we talked. Made her cry. Yea! Way to go. Hell. Almost made myself cry. Sad story, yada, yada, yada. But today I'll put a period to this whole sorry affair. Who knows, maybe I'll even cry.

Ten minutes, huh? Want a sad story. I'll give you a sad story.

My uncle came over one day. This is after my dad died.

"Al," my mother says, gives him a hug.

She's got a wooden spoon in her hand. Dripping yellow cake batter all over the floor but she doesn't even notice. Why would she? She didn't have to clean it up. I digress.

"Al." She smiles at him.

"Cat," my uncle says, "how ya doin'?"

He had a deep voice like my father's. I wanted to cry every time I heard him.

My mother goes back into the kitchen. My uncle follows her. I did too, after wiping up the goddamned batter.

"I'm making a cake," my mother announces. Duh. "With chocolate frosting," she says. "Luce likes chocolate frosting."

Luce. She was the only one who ever called me that.

"That's nice," my uncle says.

He's staring at my mother's back, and she's whipping the batter like she's trying to churn it into butter. My uncle, he says, "I made arrangements for the funeral. I got him into Holy Cross," and my mother screams, "Holy Cross? You're putting him into Holy Cross? No, Al. No! I will not let you do that! I will drag him up to Central Park and bury him myself before I let him near a Catholic cemetery. Do you hear me, Al? He is not being buried in the church. I swear you'll have to kill me before that happens. I swear it, Al, I swear it! Do you hear me?"

She's fucking hysterical now. Berserk. She runs over to my uncle, starts pounding him in the chest.

"You bastard!" she's screaming. "Don't you dare bury him there. Do you hear me? I won't let you, Al. I swear I won't let you."

My uncle clamps her wrists like she's a two-year-old. "For Christ's sake, Cat, take it easy. Jesus. Calm down."

My mother only gets crazier. She's trying to get her hands loose, panting, "I won't let you! I won't let you! I'll kill you before I let you bury him there, I swear it, Al. I swear it."

My uncle says, "All right, Cat. We won't bury him there. Jesus Christ. I promise. We won't bury him in the church. Any church. Shh. I promise. Cat, I promise."

"No, no, no! No church! He'd hate that. I know he would. You know he would."

"Calm down, Cat. Calm down. No church, I'm telling you. We won't put him in a church."

"You promise?"

"Yes. I promise."

"Swear to me, Al."

32

He crosses himself. "On my mother's grave, I swear to you, no church."

"All right." Then my mother slumped down onto the floor like someone had pulled all her bones out. Very dramatic, and she says, "I want him buried in Woodlawn."

My uncle, poor bastard, he just laughs. "Jesus, Cat, that's impossible. We don't have that kind of money."

"We'll find it!" my mother says, suddenly coming alive again. "We've got the life insurance policy! That'll cover it!"

My uncle kneels down beside her, shaking his head, tells her, "Cat, honey, that's only ten thousand dollars. At Woodlawn that wouldn't be enough for a flower arrangement. We just don't have that kind of dough. You gotta be reasonable here. We won't bury him in the church but he ain't going to Woodlawn, neither. I'll look around. I'll find a public cemetery for you, I promise, but it ain't going to be Woodlawn."

"But it's so beautiful and so close," my mom pleads. "I could visit him every day."

"No. Not Woodlawn. But I'll get him as close as I can. I promise. I gotta go. Marie's holding supper for me. I'll take care of it, though, okay?"

My mother stood up and went to the cake batter. I heard her whisper, "I just want him close to me."

Yeah. No shit, Sherlock. Who didn't?

How's that for a sad story?

And all in ten minutes. Shit. Still owe another ten from Friday. I'll get to it tonight. Promise. But for now, may as well see if the gym's open.

CHAPTER 8

Frank popped for a cab to Canarsie. When it pulled up at the cemetery she paid the driver and got out. She stayed a long time on the curb. Shifting a bouquet of flowers back and forth, she held her face up to the weak sun. She'd forgotten how lifeless northern sun was compared to southern sun, yet despite its bloodlessness the warmth felt good. She knew she was procrastinating, but she had all morning. This had been waiting for over two decades. Another few minutes couldn't hurt.

After a bit she felt silly and finally stepped through the iron gates. Her mother had been buried next to her father, and Frank walked in the direction that memory took her. She remembered his grave being near a tall, bare tree at the far end of the cemetery. But there were dozens of tall bare trees. She meandered between headstones looking for her father's name. She paused at some of the more poetic headstones, impressed by the age of others. Almost surprised, she read a white marble slab inscribed "C. S. Franco 1932—1983."

For a second she was confused, wondering if there were two C. S. Francos in the same cemetery. She glanced at the stone next to her mother's.

Francis S. Franco
Born 1934—Died 1969.

Just as she remembered.

But there was a jar of cut flowers in front of her father's stone. And a devotional candle, its pale wax smudged and melted.

Frank wondered who could have left them. She felt like she'd stumbled upon a secret. She backed away from the graves to gain perspective, searching for a plausible explanation. Perched against a granite tombstone she began compiling a list of names.

Her mother's parents were both long dead. She had twin sisters that Frank never met. They'd lived somewhere in New England, maybe Rhode Island or Maine. She couldn't remember.

Her father's parents were also deceased. They had died when she was six. She remembered her father and Uncle Al flying home for the funeral, her mother crying in the airport and her father reassuring her he'd be back in a couple days. Not to worry. Telling Frank to take care of her mother, his cheek rough against hers when he kissed her.

Frank rubbed the back of her neck, bringing her focus into the present.

Al and her father were their only children. Al died not long after she'd moved to California and his wife had returned to Illinois.

Her cousin John had died of hepatitis, contracted from dirty needles. Her other cousin went to Illinois with his mother. Last Frank had heard, in a long-ago letter from her mother, he'd found God and joined a fringe Klu Klux Klan. Frank wouldn't have been surprised to see his name pop up on an FBI bulletin.

She tried to remember her father's co-workers, his friends at the bars. Her mother had known hundreds of people but Frank couldn't say she'd been close to any of them. She scanned nearby headstones, looking for similar offerings. There weren't any. Whoever put the flowers and votive here had done so deliberately.

Frank squatted in front of the candle. It had a paper picture on it, a kid dressed like a pilgrim. Santo Niño de Atocha. She reached for the glass, then pulled her hand back.

Someone would have left prints on it.

Frank studied the flowers. White chrysanthemums wilting at the edges. In an old mayonnaise jar stained with evaporation lines. The jar had been used before. She stood, peering down into the candle. There was water, about an inch collected at the bottom. Her heart was speeding. She wished she had a camera. She checked the headstones again, making sure she had the right ones. She calculated the odds of having identical headstones in the same cemetery, deciding they were slim to nonexistent in a place the size of Canarsie. She found two fallen branches and stuck them into the jars, inverting the glass onto the sticks so she could carry them without marring the prints.

Carrying the jars like flags, she walked to the corner deli she'd noticed on the way in. She asked a three-hundred-pound man for a phone book and he grudgingly slid it over the counter. Frank found the number for the Ninth Precinct and called on her cell phone.

"Sergeant-Jones-NYPD-how-can-I-help-you."

"Sergeant Jones, who would I talk to about a lead on a very old homicide?"

"Depends. How old we talkin'?"

"It's about"—Frank calculated—"thirty-six years cold."

"That's pretty icy. Where did this alleged homicide occur?"

"Ninth Precinct and last I heard, about twelve years ago, a detective from the Ninth was working it."

"What was his name?"

"Can't remember. He called out of the blue, surprised me that anyone was still working on it."

"Yeah, you think we're just sitting around drinkin' coffee and eatin' doughnuts, right?"

"Well, actually I'm a homicide lieutenant with the LAPD, so no, I don't think that."

"No shit?"

"Absolute constipation, Sergeant. So who would I talk to?"

"Seein' as how it's Sunday, that'd be Meyer or Silvester. Hold on a sec."

Frank waited until another voice came on the line.

"Homicide. Silvester.

The name came out "Silvestuh," in classic New York-ese. The voice was husky, but definitely a woman's.

"Detective Silvester, my name's Lieutenant Franco. I'm with LAPD homicide, and I got something that might help with an old unsolved of yours."

"Of mine?"

"Not yours specifically. Of the department's."

Silvester echoed the desk sergeant, "How old we talkin' here?"

"Nineteen sixty-nine."

Silvester whistled. "That's a mystery, all right. What sorta lead we talkin' about?"

"It's a long story, but I have some prints that should get checked out."

"Prints? What kinda prints?"

"Like I said, it's a long story and rather than tell it to every dick in the NYPD I'd rather just tell it to whoever's gonna look at this case."

The detective bristled. "Well, you know, we just don't go opening up old mysteries every time Jane Q. Public calls and says, 'Oh, I got a clue here's gonna blow this thing wide open.'"

Frank's temper surged like a dark tide, an unpleasant side effect of sobriety. Mary had assured her it was a phase and that it would pass, but until it did, Frank just had to ride it out, breathe through it. Mary said to pray through it but Frank couldn't do that. Instead she thought of song lyrics. *Tall and tan and young and lovely, the girl from Ipanema goes walking.*

"You there?"

And when she passes, each one she passes, goes, "Ahh."

"Hello?"

"Detective Silvester. We're both in the same business so I'd appreciate a little respect here. I'm not some mope off the goddamn street. I have a viable lead in an open case. You can deal with me here and now or you can deal with your supervisor after I get through with him. I'll leave it up to you."

After a long pause in which Frank wondered if Silvester was mouthing lyrics too, the detective demanded, "What's the case numbuh?"

"I don't have it with me. The victim's name was Franco. Francis Matthew Franco. The case would have been opened on twelve February, nineteen sixty-nine."

"Franco. So how are you related to the vic?"

"I'm his daughter."

"You're his daughter and you think you got a lead?"

"That's right."

"And you say you're with the LAPD?"

"Correct again."

"You got credentials to verify this?"

Oh, but he watches so sadly.

"Yes." Frank bit the hiss off the *s*.

The detective sighed. "Spell Franco for me."

Frank did.

"You got a number I can call you back?"

"Not right now, no," Frank lied. "How 'bout I call you in twenty?"

"Yeah, all right."

The detective hung up and Frank sneered at her phone. She snagged a cabbie and held up a finger. Back in the deli she asked the clerk for a box.

"A box?" He was mystified, as if Frank had asked him to pull a stealth bomber out from under the counter.

"Yeah, you know. Groceries come in 'em. They're square? Tan? Made of cardboard?"

"Yeah, smart-ass, I know what a freakin' box is. You gonna buy somethin' today or just see how much you can get for free?"

"Look, I'll *buy* the goddamn thing. Do you have one or not?"

38

The man gestured with pursed lips. "Over there," he said, indicating a door to the rear.

Frank found an empty candy carton, showing it to him as she passed the counter, slapping down a buck.

"Lower East Side," she told the cabbie. "Ninth Precinct."

"You know what street?"

Do I know what street, Frank thought.

The Ninth's arched entrance was branded into her memory. She still had dreams where she passed under the rounded alcove and stood before the massive duty desk, but instead of a cop behind the desk there was always a bad guy. Usually a junkie with black holes for eyes. Never a cop in sight, just junkies everywhere, shooting up, sprawled on the nod, vomiting, shaking, pacing . . .

"Fifth. Between First and Second."

The cabbie nodded and took off. Frank cradled the box in her lap. They crossed the East River and Frank accepted the water's flat metallic smell like the kiss from a loving but homely woman.

Being in the city was harder than she thought. Maybe Mary was right. Maybe it was too soon. She wondered if Cal's still stood next to the precinct. A couple doubles would feel fine right now. Absolutely fine. But thinking the drinks through to their logical outcome meant there'd be no hot chocolate with Gail in the afternoon. Frank checked her watch, wondering how long she was going to be at the station.

At home, Frank's schedule was unpredictable at best and as Chief M.E., Gail's wasn't much better. Between them broken dates had been the norm, so Gail shouldn't be too upset if Frank had to bail. Maybe she'd be as surprised as Frank was by this twist in events and be willing to let her make it up.

As the cab came off the Williamsburg Bridge, Frank averted her eyes. It was okay to look at the Con Ed yard and Fish Park glittering in its raiment of broken bottles, but she didn't want to look at the projects or tenements. Hurtling up Ludlow to First she couldn't help but notice the tony shops and trendy bars. The gentrification was a relief, yet at the same time she had to wonder where the poor were getting squeezed to. Seeing familiar names and buildings, her guts clenched. She cursed herself, wishing she'd listened to Mary and stayed home. The taxi rounded a corner and jerked to a stop in front of the Ninth.

Frank stared. The old station house looked cleaner than she remembered.

The cabbie twisted in his seat. "This the place?"

"Yeah." She paid him and got out with her carton, mustering the nerve to step inside, up to the desk. Squaring her shoulders she walked under the arch and through the door.

All these years the Ninth had loomed mythic in her memory but in reality the place was small, almost cramped. Frank almost laughed. She walked up to the desk, asking the duty officer where she could find Detective Silvester.

"In regard to what?"

"She's expecting me."

"Oh, yeah?"

"Yeah."

"Your name?"

"Lieutenant Franco, LAPD."

"Lieutenant Franco," the cop repeated, nonplussed. "Hold on." He picked up a phone, eyeballing her as he talked to Silvester. "Yeah, okay." He hung up. "She'll be down in a sec," he told her.

Frank nodded. About ten minutes later a trim woman in dark gray descended the stairs. The two detectives immediately made each other and as Silvester neared, she reproached, "You said you were gonna call."

"Happened to be in the neighborhood."

Silvester pursed her lips while they took each other's measure.

The detective was a couple inches shorter than Frank, late forties or early fifties, sharp dark eyes, salt-and-pepper hair cut below gold hoop earrings, wide mouth, generously lipped. She looked Mediterranean—Jewish or Italian, Frank guessed.

Tilting her head toward the box, Silvester asked, "This your evidence?"

"Yeah. So what did you find out?"

"Come upstairs."

As they climbed, Silvester asked, "You workin' this case indie, or what?"

"No. Not at all. Like I said, it's a long story and I don't have a lot of time. I'm just visiting for the weekend. Got a nine o'clock flight back home tonight."

"Oh." Silvester feigned concern. "Why didn't you say so? If I'da known that I'da had this case solved for you ten minutes ago."

"Look." Frank stopped to glare. "Enough with the attitude, okay? I come to you as a colleague with potential evidence and you're treatin' me like a snitch hoping to con a twenty outta you. If you can't be bothered with doing your job, find me someone who can."

Two cops squeezed past them on the steps, one of them crying, "Me-e-ow."

Silvester's jaw bottomed out and she took a step toward Frank. "Of all the freakin' *nerve*. You know how long it's been since I been home, Miss Hotshot California lieutenant? You know how long since my head's seen a pillow? I can't remembuh the last time I ate because Friday mornin' I got a eight-year-old whacked outta revenge and last night I get a fifty-four-year-old woman assaulted, raped and brained to death with her own broom and you got the freakin' *nerve* to stand there and tell me I can't be bothered with doing my job? If I had any freakin' strength left I'd kick your ass down these stairs all the way back to the airport!"

A passing man encouraged, "I got fifty bucks on you, Annie."

"Make it a hundred," Annie snapped without looking away from Frank.

When she walks just like a samba that swings so cool and sways so gently.

"Okay. I know you're busy. I know how it is to juggle a dozen hot cases at the same time and something like this is lower than low priority. I appreciate that. I do. I just want to get this evidence delivered through the proper chain of command as soon as I can—this case is nothing to you and with good reason, but this has been *my* case since I was ten years old and this is the first break I've ever had in it. Five minutes. That's all I'm asking you for."

Silvester shook her head and continued up the stairs, muttering darkly. Frank followed. Silvester pointed to a chair in front of a desk, ordering, "Sit!"

Frank did. Silvester took the chair behind the desk.

She glared at Frank while pouring a handful of espresso beans into her mouth. "How do I know you're who you say you are?"

Glad she'd pocketed her shield and ID card, Frank handed them to Silvester. She jotted down the numbers.

Silvester's phone rang and she picked it up, griping, "Swell. Probably another Miss Marple with more old clues. Silvester," she barked. She started scribbling furiously. "Yeah, okay. At ten-forty, you said? Uh-huh. And the neighbors behind the building? What time?" She made notes. "Yeah, okay. Thanks, Billy. Gimme twenty minutes, huh?" She banged the phone down, cursed. Yanking open a drawer, she extracted a handful of forms. Glowering at Frank, she snapped. "Whaddaya got?"

"Two items. One clear glass Niño de Atocha religious candle and a glass mayonnaise jar."

"Hold on," Silvester said, filling out a form. "How do you spell Atocha?"

Frank read off the candle. A thin, white-haired man strode into the room and when Silvester saw him she dropped her pen.

"Charlie, Charlie, Charlie," she purred. It came out "Cholly, Cholly, Cholly."

"Annie," he chortled from under a white handlebar moustache. "How are you, love?"

She stood to receive a big hug, chiding, "Aren't you supposed to be on vacation?"

"I am," he wheezed. "But we decided to drive home a couple days early. Supposed to be a big storm coming Tuesday and we didn't want to get caught in it."

"What are you doing here?"

"I heard you caught a couple while I was gone. Thought you could use a hand."

"Charlie Mercer, God love ya. There's a gold seat in heaven for you."

"Yeah." The old man chuckled. "Probably an electric chair."

Silvester pushed the forms toward him. "Come help our friend here from Los Angeles. She's got some evidence needs bookin'." Sliding her chair back, Silvester shrugged into a heavy coat.

"Which case?" Charlie asked.

Annie scribbled a note and handed it to him. "Here's the number. Be a doll and check it out for me, huh? I'm sure the lieutenant here'll be glad to fill you in on the rest." She stood on tiptoe to peck the old man's cheek. "Thanks, Charlie."

Grabbing a welter of binders and papers, she left Charlie and Frank staring at each other.

CHAPTER 9

Figuring it would go easier if Mercer knew he was talking to another cop Frank extended a hand and introduced herself. Mercer shook, asking, "Los Angeles, huh?"

"Yeah." Tipping her head toward the candy carton she explained, "I'm on vacation and happened to find these."

"What sorta case we talkin' about here?"

"Happened thirty-six years ago. A junkie killed my father. Ninth caught the case but never caught the guy. I come out to visit my father's grave. I find these. Thing is, everyone in my family's dead. There's no friends, no family that coulda left these. So who did? And why? If you're a cop, what's your first idea?"

The old man scratched his chin. Flakes of skin speckled his leather jacket. "You thinkin' the skel left these?"

Frank shrugged. "Or someone who knows the skel, knows what he did."

" 'At's a stretch, ain't it?"

"You never stretched a lead?"

The old man chuckled again, patting his chest and pulling a pair of glasses from a jacket pocket. After adjusting them he read the note Silvester gave him. He dropped it in his pocket.

Frank continued, "I want to print these. See what's on them. Can we do that?"

"Yeah, sure, kid. We can do that. But first things first." Mercer shuffled over to the coffee machine. He sniffed the half-full pot, made a face. "Murphy's Law, ain't it? You ever notice no matter what time of day it is the pot's either empty or old? I'm gonna dump this, make us a fresh pot."

"I'm good," she insisted.

"Well, good for you," he said. "I'm not, and I'm too damn old to drink bad coffee. Been doing it all my life." He carried the pot from the squad room, telling her over his shoulder, "Sit tight, kid. I'll be right back."

Mercer ambled down the hall, pausing to talk to everyone he knew, which sounded to Frank like everyone from the janitor on up to the captain. She heard him joking, showing off pictures of his new granddaughter.

Frank flicked her wrist, wondering about her date. Pacing the room she thought how homicide desks looked the same everywhere. Files, binders, scratched notes on scraps of paper, which turn into reams of scraps, all set off by institutional walls tattooed with memos, bulletins, wanteds, rules and regs.

She checked her phone, made sure it was on. No messages from Bobby or anyone else. Alone in the quiet room, Frank studied Silvester's computer. She leaned over and joggled the mouse. The screen saver disappeared and Frank zipped around the desk. Finding an Internet icon she Googled *Nino de Atocha*, quitting when she heard footsteps in the hall.

Mercer wandered back in, the coffeepot clean and filled with water. "Here we go." Dumping fresh grounds into the basket, he asked, "Now what did you say your name was?"

"Frank."

The old man peered over his shoulder in disbelief. "Frank?" he shouted.

"Yeah. Short for Franco. It's a nickname."

"Frank," he repeated. "I remember when girls were named Lucy or Kathy or Linda—now you're all Franks and Keyshondas, Sky and Brie." Mercer wagged his head. "My youngest daughter just had a baby. Named the poor kid Brie. How would you like that, huh? To be named after a cheese."

With the coffee burbling and trickling into the pot, Mercer reached into his jacket again, producing a stack of baby pictures. He handed them to Frank.

"That's her. Isn't she a cutie?"

Frank pretended to study each one. "Adorable," she told him.

"Nine days old today."

She passed the photos back and Mercer displayed the school pictures in his wallet.

"That's John. He's twelve. He's my oldest grandson. My son Richard's boy. And those are his sisters, Michaela and Kathleen. This is Cory and Eileen. Eileen's my oldest granddaughter. She's thirteen. No. Fourteen, now. Yeah. Fourteen in November. We went up to Schenectady for her birthday. That's where my boy Danny lives. Oh, his wife's a sweetie. We didn't think he'd ever settle down, but he finally did and thank God with Sue. She's been so good for him. This is my daughter Linda. She just had Brie. She has a boy, too, Michael. Got a Michael and a Michaela." He chuckled. "How 'bout that? I don't have a picture of Michael. He's a devil. Almost two and givin' his mother fits. Or is he two already? No. Almost. He was born in February, that's right."

Frank sang an entire Cole Porter standard while gulping her impatience. "Nice family. You're a lucky guy. Think we could get this evidence booked now?"

"Yeah, sure."

Padding to the desk he took Silvester's chair. He felt around, found a pen and said, "Okay. Whadda we got here?" She started describing the candle again but Mercer interrupted, "Speak up. I can't hear so good outta my left ear."

As she described the containers Mercer gave them a slow once-over. He did the same with her when he finished filling out the forms.

"So your old man, huh?"

"Yeah."

"How old were you?"

"Ten."

He nodded as if watching one's father get popped by a crashing junkie was a rite of passage for all ten-year-olds. Getting up stiffly, he poured coffee. Handing Frank a cup he tipped his head toward the pot. "There's cream and sugar there."

"Black's good. So how soon do you think we can get these printed?"

"No telling," he answered. "Old case like this. Could be a while."

"Any idea who'd handle it?"

Mercer shrugged, casting an eye around the empty room. "It's assigned to one of these guys. Even if it's thirty-six years old some-body's gotta submit a Five on it once a month." With pride he added, "We never close a homicide, even if it just gets stamped 'Negative Results' every month."

Frank nodded. "Someone from the Ninth called me about twelve years ago. He was looking into it but I couldn't tell him any-thing new. Then this stuff appeared. May not be anything, might lead to a clearance. Who knows?"

Mercer leaned back, picking at his chin with a long nail. "It's worth a try."

"So you retired, or what?"

"Yeah. They kicked me out two years ago, but I still hang around, keep my hand in, help out where I can. But those forty-eight-hour days? Kid, let me tell you, I don't miss 'em at all."

"They get harder, don't they?"

47

"Christ!" He slapped at air. "You don't know the half of it. You're still a whelp."

"Yeah," Frank allowed. The gulf between twenty-five and forty-five was rough enough; she couldn't imagine pulling a forty-eight at his age. "You know what, though? I'm in kind of a bind here. I've got to be back to work tomorrow morning but I'm afraid to leave this evidence just lying around. I've been waiting over thirty years for an answer to this case and right when there might be a clue I gotta leave it. So I'm wondering if you could do me a favor and pull the file for me, so I know who's in charge and who to contact about it. Could you do that for me?"

"Kid, don't worry about it. If it's on Annie's desk, it'll get taken care of. She's a stand-up cop. She's just got her hands a little full right now."

"Yeah, I know. And we got off on the wrong foot. My fault. This has just . . . I wasn't expecting this, is all. Just came out to pay respects to my father and I find this. After all this time . . . kinda rattled me and I took it out on her."

Mercer stretched and got up. "Don't worry about it, kid. Annie's good people. She'll take care of it for you. You got my word on that, okay?"

Frank stood, too. "I appreciate it."

Mercer nodded, lifting a hand as he left the squad room.

48

CHAPTER 10

Walking to Rockefeller Center, Gail asked, "How did it go this morning?"

"It was interesting. I'll tell you when we get to the restaurant. How about you? Tell me about your morning."

Frank listened to Gail, her eyes darting left and right, back and forth. Even on vacation she checked the crowd, tuning in to the pulse of the street. She did the same when they entered the café. There was one table available overlooking the rink, centered in a row along the window. As the waiter led them to it, Gail whispered, "Is this okay?"

Frank shrugged. She hated sitting with her back exposed but answered, "What the hell? Who knows I'm a cop?" Gail studied the menu and Frank gave it a short glance.

"Want to split a chocolate shake with me? I'm probably going to gain a hundred pounds before I get another AA chip, but my sponsor says I can do whatever I want in the first year as long as I'm not drinking."

"Have you got any chips yet?"

Frank made a peace sign. "Two."

"You're kidding?"

"Uh-uh."

Gail palmed her mouth, not able to stifle her laugh.

"What's funny?"

"I'm sorry. I'm just having a hard time seeing you standing up, saying, 'My name's Frank and I'm an alcoholic.' Not to mention accepting a chip. *Two* chips. It's such a contrast to your lone avenger persona."

"Tell me about it. I can't believe it half the time, either. But you know," she said, watching as a laughing mother and daughter sprawled on the ice, "it seems to be working, and that's all that matters."

"You're right. Something seems to be working. You look softer. Less rigid."

"Great. Soft's a good look in a cop."

"Don't worry. You don't look *that* soft. Just not so pinched, so tight."

"There's a line in *Cat on a Hot Tin Roof*. After Big Daddy realizes he's dying of cancer he tells his son he's been walking around his entire life like a doubled-up fist and by God now he's gonna have him some fun. I wouldn't say I'm having fun yet, but by God I think I'm starting to unclench."

Their eyes met and Frank looked away first. Gail graciously returned to the menu.

"Okay. Tell me about this morning."

"You're not gonna believe it. Three thousand miles from home and here I am working a homicide."

Frank explained the morning's chain of events and Gail mused, "Wow. After all these years."

"Yeah, wow. Pretty weird."

"How's that feel? I mean, it seems that you'd pretty much closed the door on his death and then to have it swing open again . . ."

50

"Yeah. Don't think I haven't considered a couple drinks today. Not that I'm gonna, but . . . I don't know. I was surprised. Still am. You're right about the door being closed. And it took me a long time to close it. It hasn't bothered me so much lately. I'd pretty much given up on ever finding the guy, but, man, when I was a kid I used to lie in bed at night thinking about him—his eyes, mostly. That's the thing with hope-to-die junkies. They've got black holes where they oughta have eyes. There's just nobody home inside. They got *Night of the Living Dead* eyes and I'd fall asleep thinking about those eyes on me. I'd dream about 'em—still do some-times—and I'd wake up terrified to look in a mirror because I was sure I had junkie eyes."

The waitress appeared. Gail ordered the lobster quiche and Frank a cheeseburger. The waitress swished away and Gail protested, "You come all the way to New York and order a cheese-burger?"

"I didn't come for the food," Frank replied. "Besides, sober lunches have become a pretty steady diet of cheeseburgers and milkshakes. A cheeseburger's about the only thing I can eat with-out thinking of booze to wash it down with."

"Oh," Gail said, appearing abashed. "I didn't think of that. Anyway, go on, if you want. You've never told me any of this."

Frank dismissed, "Not much to tell. I kept looking for him on the street. Everywhere I went. Walking to school, riding the bus, getting groceries—I was looking for him in every face. I saw a lot of those junkie eyes and sometimes I thought I'd found him, but then he'd pass me or turn a corner and I couldn't be sure. After a while, I guess I got so caught up in looking for him that I forgot to be afraid. And I lived around enough hypes to understand that the guy had no idea who I was, that he probably didn't even know he'd killed a man and if he did know he wouldn't care—because the only thing an oil burner cares about is fixing. Food, sex, homi-cide—none of it means shit to them—only the high. Chasing it and getting it. Then I started feeling *superior* to the junkie—like he should be afraid of *me*, because I remembered and was straight enough to do something about it. I was reading Trixie Belden and Nancy Drew back then. The Hardy Boys—even the little kids series. Remember the one with the twins? Flopsy and Mopsy or something?"

The waitress set down the milkshake and an extra glass. As Frank spooned it out, Gail laughed. "Flopsy and Mopsy were in Peter Rabbit. I think you're talking about the Bobbsey Twins."

"Yeah, yeah. That was it. The Bobbsey twins." Frank's smile was nostalgic. "Man, those kids were lame. I thought they were dumber than shit—sorry. I hated them for having such happy families and clean houses—I thought that was as fake as Bugs Bunny—but I loved that they always solved the mystery. So I went from harmless fluff straight into *In Cold Blood*. Somebody left it lying on a table at the library. The title hooked me so I picked it up and that was that. Then I discovered Joseph Wambaugh."

"Yikes," Gail interrupted. "Your mother let you read Joseph Wambaugh?"

"My mother wasn't exactly monitoring my reading habits. I think as long as I was home and taking care of things, for all she cared I could have been reading *Playboy*. I didn't understand a lot of Wambaugh, but I began to see that only two kinds of people made the rules—crooks and cops. I think the seed to become a cop was already in me but reading Wambaugh was like adding sun and water. *Helter Skelter* came out around then too. I read everything I could about Charlie Manson and the Tate-LaBianca killings. It fascinated me."

"Uck." Gail shivered.

"After being exposed to all that, and from seeing what I saw everyday in my own neighborhood I realized that the bad guys only had temporary power. They were only powerful until their next arrest, but it was *cops* that were at the top of the food chain. And that's where I wanted to be. At the very top, looking down on everyone else. That's where I went and never looked back."

"Until now."

"Until now," Frank agreed.

Their food arrived and Gail said, "It must be very exciting to have a lead after all this time."

"Exciting," Frank said around a fry. "I guess it's as exciting as popping a lead in any big case. There's the adrenaline thing. But I don't want to get too close to this, too excited. I mean, what difference is it gonna make after all this time anyway, huh, after all these years? And then if I don't find him, if this goes nowhere . . ."

Gail finished, "You don't want to be disappointed."

"No. I don't."

"Well, do you think these flowers are an isolated incident?"

"Who knows? There's so many questions. I'm thinking of calling Fubar, telling him I'm gonna stay out here a little longer. I want to make sure Silvester follows up on this. Doesn't drop the ball."

"Maybe it's been going on for a while and you've just finally stepped into the picture."

"Great. So I could have solved my old man's murder years ago but I was too self-involved?"

"That's not what I meant. There's a big difference between being self-involved and moving on. There are positive and negative aspects to every situation. Running from the pain of your father's death was negative, but accepting it and moving on is positive. The feat then becomes incorporating the two aspects into a vital, integrated whole."

"Jesus." Frank stared her. "I think you've been to too many lectures this weekend." Gail's smile was easy and Frank tapped the doc's hand with a fingertip. "You know what?"

"No. What?"

Tracing a line between freckles, Frank suggested, "I hope we can incorporate our negative and positive aspects into a vital and integrated whole."

Gail pulled her hand away. "We'll see."

Frank cleared her throat. "I took the opportunity while I was alone in the squad room to Google the saint on the candle, Niño de Atocha. Turns out that the Moors were holding a bunch of

Christians prisoner and were going to use them as slaves but weren't feeding them or giving them water. Then this little kid dressed like a pilgrim shows up. He's got a gourd of water and a basket of bread and for some reason the guards let him in to feed the Christians. Story is that the gourd never drained and the basket never emptied, so they decided he was Christ disguised as this kid from Atocha, doing his loaves and fishes thing. Ever after, the Niño de Atocha's been the patron saint of prisoners and those unjustly accused. Kinda interesting, huh?"

"I'd say so. What kind of flowers were they?"

"The ubiquitous white chrysanthemums you can buy in any grocery store. Nothing to work with there."

Gail declared, "I think it's a woman."

"Because of the flowers?"

She nodded. "And the candle. It just doesn't sound like something a man would do."

"No, probably not. So I'm thinking maybe the visitor is the perp's mom or sister. Maybe an aunt. His grandmother'd probably be dead by now. And a girlfriend or a wife would have found somebody else. Moved on, as you'd say."

"So now you just wait?"

Frank spread her hands. "What else can I do? I was thinking of going back to the station this afternoon and hanging out until Silvester gets back, or someone else who can pull the case for me. Until then, one thing at a time, right? So tell me, doc. You know how to skate?"

"No. And I'm not about to learn."

"Aw, come on. I went horseback riding with you. And hiking. I even tried golfing."

Gail giggled. "*Try* is the operative."

"So you owe me a sporting adventure."

"I'm too old," she protested. "The thought of falling on that ice. Ouch. No thanks."

Frank leaned over the table. "I won't let you fall."

Gail frowned. "You're flirting, Frank."

"Am I?"

"I thought we were just going to be friends."

"We are. What's a little harmless flirting between friends."

"Quit being so damned charming."

"Gail," Frank said seriously, "I'm not gonna lie and pretend I don't have feelings for you. Because I do. Very deep ones. If all I can be is a friend then I'll settle for that, but it's not all I want."

"You're pushing."

"I just want to put it out there. I want you to know exactly where I stand. Cards on the table and all that. And I promise this is as hard as I'll push. Just don't ask me to pretend I don't care. I won't do that. I'm trying to feel things, for once, and be honest about them instead of shoving them aside and pretending they don't exist. So I'm not going to pretend I don't love you." Frank sat back. "Ball's in your court. You gonna take a chance and go skating with me? Maybe have some fun."

"And maybe get hurt," Gail said, her implication clear.

"I promised you. I won't let that happen." Frank cocked her head. "Weren't you the one who gave me a lecture a couple years ago about how you have to live life to the fullest? That by blocking out the pain you blocked out all the joy too? Wasn't that you?"

Gail's dark bob swayed. "I think you're mixing me up with one of your other girlfriends."

Frank stopped a laugh. "That's right. I have so many of them."

"You promise you won't let me fall?"

Making an X over her heart, Frank vowed, "Cross my heart, hope to die."

CHAPTER 11

The Ninth's squad room echoed when Frank walked in, her cheeks still slightly numb from skating with Gail. The doc had been hopeless but Frank had fun holding her up. She looked at the clock on the wall.

Almost five. Two at home.

She called her captain. There was no answer on his cell, office or home phones and Frank wondered how her crew was supposed to get hold of him.

"Asshole," she whispered just before his machine picked up. "John, it's Frank. Something's come up and I'm going to be longer than I thought. I'll know more tomorrow. Call you then."

She hung up and dialed Figueroa. She asked the desk sergeant if he'd seen Foubarelle around and he snorted. "On a Sunday? You gotta be shittin' me."

"Anybody upstairs?"

"Hold on. I'll transfer you."

The phone rang and Darcy picked up. "Hey. You home?"

"Not yet. Might be a while. How's everything going?"

"Fine. Quiet."

"What are you doing there on a Sunday afternoon?"

"Catching up on sixty-days."

"I wish your work ethic would rub off on your colleagues."

Darcy grunted. "They have lives. When do you think you'll be back?"

"Don't know. Three thousand miles from home, and believe it or not I'm working a homicide. I'll tell you about it when I get back. How's Gabby doing?"

Darcy's pause told her his daughter's cystic fibrosis was flaring. "Marguerite had to take her to the hospital last night. She's home now. I might take off tomorrow if nothing's going on."

"Do that."

"Yeah. We'll see. Don't be too long out there. I don't want to catch something and have Fubar all over me."

"I'll do my best." She hung up, missing her crew and her routine. She found a phone book and the number she was looking for. She dialed it on Silvester's phone.

"Alcoholics Anonymous. How can I help you?"

"Yeah, I'm looking for a meeting tonight." Frank gave the man she was talking to the Ninth's address and the Crowne Plaza's.

"You got a couple to choose from. Any particular emphasis?"

"Anything but a men's stag."

"All right, get your pencil ready."

Frank wrote down half a dozen times and places. She hadn't planned on going to a meeting in New York, but then again there were a lot of things she hadn't planned on. She pocketed the list, thinking she'd need to find a cheaper hotel.

Seeing as no one was around, Frank took a seat in front of Silvester's computer. Because her computer skills barely exceeded turning the damned things on, Frank didn't have any luck searching for information about her father's case. She got up and rummaged through rows of gray file cabinets, snooping the

57

old-fashioned way. Hearing loud voices she slipped a drawer shut and posed near the coffee machine.

Hooting and hollering in the language of a successful collar, four detectives stomped into the homicide room. Silvester, long past her second wind and running on a third or fourth, was one of them. Calling one of the men "Lieutenant" she told him, "We got the little bastard. He was hiding under his grandmother's bed. He crapped his pants when we pulled him out."

"Nice job, Annie. How about the kid? How we doing on that?"

"We've got her nailed down to a mom-and-pop shop after she got out of school. There are a couple of mopes hanging around there that Vince and Billy are talkin' to. After I get this mutt processed I'm going to go home and grab a couple hours sleep, get a fresh start in the morning, huh?"

The LT nodded. "Yeah. Nice work. Vince and Billy gonna grab some shuteye, too?"

"Vince and Billy, too." Accepting the lieutenant's amiable pat on the shoulder, Annie turned and saw Frank. "Oh, spare me. Are you still here?"

"Charlie got the evidence booked but he couldn't tell me who was handling the case. Can you?"

"You're lookin' at her."

"You?"

"The one and only, Anne Marie Silvester."

Frank seethed, "Why didn't you tell me earlier?"

"Because I didn't have time to check you out. You said you weren't just some mope off the street but how was I supposed to know that? You wouldn't believe the nut jobs we get in here."

"Yeah, I would. We get the same fuckin' nuts in LA. So what do I have to do make you believe me?"

Despite her obvious exhaustion, Silvester's eyes sparkled. "Nothin'." She grinned. "Charlie already did it. I told him to call LA and check your shield. He says you're all right."

Shaking her head at the floor, Frank muttered, "That's why it took him twenty minutes to make coffee. Okay. So can I see the file now?"

"Dear, did you happen to notice with your brilliant detective skills that I got a suspect here? Your pop's been dead what, thirty, thirty-five years?"

"Thirty-six."

"Thirty-six. So another day's gonna matter? God willin', this mutt'll talk and I can get some sleep tonight. You come back in the mornin', seven sharp. I'll get you your father's book for you. Deal?"

Being in no position to argue, Frank asked, "You like bialys?"

Silvester patted her hips. "Don't I look like I like bialys?"

"Not really."

"Psh. Enough with the brown-nosing. With a vegetable shmear, huh?"

"See you in the mornin'."

Frank zipped her thin windbreaker and walked out into the frigid New York night.

CHAPTER 12
Still Sunday—PM—Manhattan

*Going to spend one more night at the Crowne Plaza. What the hell.
Called Mary, told her what was going on. She's worried about me but
I'm all right. Confused, maybe, but I told her I'm not going to drink over
it. I want a drink, hell yes, but not the consequences. She was happy I'd
been to a meeting. It was at Grace Church. I walked over. Forgot how
much I like walking. Never walk anywhere at home but you could spend
your life here without venturing more than ten blocks in any direction.
Amazed how much I still remember, too.*

*Passed St. Mark's, where A.T. Stewart was buried. They kidnapped
his body from there in the late 1800s and demanded a $200,000 ransom.
I think the widow bargained them down to $20,000 and got him back
but she didn't bury him in St. Mark's again. Commodore Perry's buried
at St. Mark's and Peter Stuyvesant. All that history in one block. I miss
that in LA. Everything's new and modern, ultra this and techno that. It
lacks a sense of place, perspective.*

Anyway. St. Mark's was cool but Grace Church blew me away. Beautiful little church, built in the 1800s. It's got some scaffolding up around the spire now, like they're working on it. When I got there, before I went in, I was standing outside admiring it and I almost started crying.

I felt small. The trees were taller than me and the church was taller and the buildings around it were taller still and above us all was the sky. I felt like I was such an infinitesimal part of things, but that somehow all the infinitesimal parts— including me— came together to make the whole picture. I felt like a dot in a Seurat painting. A pixel. Barely a speck on its own but together they make a picture. It just felt like at that instant in time everything was as it should be. A baby being born across town, and an old man dying in the apartment across the street. Someone getting married while someone else was getting knifed in an alley. Someone shooting junk while someone else is out on their first date. I don't know. It just all seemed to fit. Life going around and around, doing its thing.

I told Mary about it. How I just got filled up with the majesty of it and she laughed. Said that was gratitude and that when I was drinking I was too busy getting loaded or figuring out how to get loaded to feel it. Definitely a nice result of sobriety. Told her what a roller coaster day it had been. All the mixed feelings—surprise, anger, joy at being with Gail. Sadness. Seems everywhere I turn there's a memory, not always a good one.

Nice people at the AA meeting. Amazing how you can just walk into a room full of complete strangers and have this instant rapport with them. Mary said that's because we all have one thing in common that bonds us instantly, and that's the fact that alcohol's almost killed us and will likely kill us if we pick it up again. So right away you got a bond with everybody in an AA room. We've all come through the fire together. Lets you strip away the bullshit and cut to the chase.

Wish I had answers. Wish I had a match on the prints. Hate waiting. Hate the uncertainty. Gail asked how it felt to have this door open again after all this time and I got to admit it's damned uncomfortable. I gave up on ever having an answer and now the question's shoved back into my face. Who is the motherfucker? Where is he? Who's leaving this shit on my father's grave? Spent all this time trying to forget and now it's all pouring back in. Not liking this. But I gotta see it through. Woman at a meeting said when God wants something for you he rolls the red carpet out. I feel like this is my chance, that the carpet's rolling out and no matter how uncomfortable it is I have to walk it to the end.

One day at a time, right? Mary says this is all unfolding according to God's schedule, not mine. That my job isn't to force the unfolding but to follow along in the direction of the movement. She told me not to push it. Damn—been getting a lot of that lately. Said drunks are like five-year-olds. We don't have a lot of discipline. Want what we want and want it now. And the bottom line is, sometimes you just can't have it. Like Gail. At least not now. So you move on and take what you can have. Which in the World According to Mary is a good night's sleep, a decent meal and faith that tomorrow will bring what I need. Maybe not what I want, but what I need.

It's ironic. At work I know exactly when to force things and exactly when to sit back and let them develop. I can wait weeks on a stakeout or take a perp down in an instant. Flexibility makes me a good cop, so you'd think I could apply that logic to my personal life.

Whatever. Progress not perfection. And I'm Audi. My extra ten minutes is up. And you know what? Right this second, it's all good. New York is shining outside my window, I'm warm, I'm healthy, I don't have a hangover or the shakes, and I have a soft bed to sleep in. There's a hell of a lot of people out there who can't say that. So this drunk's going to turn the lights out and admire the view. I'm paying enough for it.

CHAPTER 13

By quarter to seven Annie Silvester was already in the squad room, chatting with a man shaped like a fireplug. She raised an eyebrow in Frank's direction, her glance taking in the bag Frank held out. Reaching for it, Annie plunked the bag next to a fresh pot of coffee and introduced her to a detective from the Fourth Precinct. Extracting a bialy, she told the cop, "Detective Franco here's from Los Angeles. She visits her father's grave to pay her respects and finds something that may or may not be of interest to us. An old case of ours, thirty-six years old, to be exact. Her pops was shot by a junkie on East Ninth and Second. The lieutenant here was the only witness. She and her pops were walking home from the deli. Junkie popped out from a doorway. Shook her pops down. Pops resisted, junkie capped him. Pops was dead before he got off the sidewalk. Not even a hint of a suspect." Biting into her bialy Annie asked Frank out of the side of her mouth, "How'm I doin'?"

Frank was impressed by her blunt grasp of the details. "Light bedtime reading?"

"Naw." Annie winked at her. "First thing this morning. Much better than the *Post*." Annie turned back to the squat detective. "Billy found the little girl's backpack last night, ripped open and dumped into a trash can three blocks south. I was gonna run it over to the lab with the lieutenant's things while he and Vince track down our mopes. There's a couple places we want to check today. While I do that"—she turned to Frank again—"the file's over on my desk if you want to look through it. Maybe something fresh'll come to you, huh?"

Frank doubted she'd have a sudden brainstorm after thirty-six years but answered, "Sure. Thanks."

As the rest of the detectives sauntered in they fell on the bialys like crackheads on a loose rock. One of the detectives, who turned out to be Vince, came up to her and said around a mouthful, "I got a sister in LA. She works for Fox Studios. Says you couldn't pay her enough to come back to New York. When she visits—you know, Thanksgiving, Christmas—all she says is LA this and LA that. Me? You couldn't pay me to *leave* the city. Best place on earth. You can't get a bialy like this in LA."

"You can't," Frank agreed. "Or the right hard rolls or bagels either. Must be something to do with the weather because San Francisco's got sourdough bread that doesn't taste right anywhere else. Everyplace has got something, I guess."

"Yeah. LA's got earthquakes, floods and fires."

"Don't forget the mudslides," a Hispanic detective chimed.

Vince waved him down. "That goes with floods."

"They're totally different," the other detective argued.

Leaving them to it, Frank wandered over to Annie's desk. She saw the file marked "Franco," the case number. She returned to the coffeepot and poured a cup. After making such a big deal about getting the file, she was suddenly reluctant to touch it. She sipped her coffee and listened in on the squad room chatter.

Annie was conferring with Meyers, her partner. One of the

detectives was reading aloud from a newspaper to a cop ignoring him, while Vince and the Hispanic swapped natural disaster lore. Maybe if she was alone, or if it was quiet, she could have picked up the folder, but the room was too noisy and distracting.

It was a good story, Frank decided, but she felt that even if the room were empty she'd still hesitate to open the folder. She groped for the bottom line and the bottom line was dread. It was one thing to describe that night to another cop, but something else entirely to relive the details.

She debated the wisdom of picking at the scab of her father's death. After all, it was her mother she'd come to make peace with, not her father. The man had been dead nearly four decades with no resolution in all that time. Was the sudden urge to find one now just because she was a cop? And where would these leads go anyway, besides straight into the circular file like most leads? Why was she wasting Silvester's time on some wild-ass goose chase?

Frank's arguments sounded hollow even as they occurred to her.

There was no statute of limitation on murder. If she had a possible lead in a case, no matter how old and forgotten, it should be checked out. That was the law. That's how justice supposedly worked. She couldn't ignore the evidence because it made her uncomfortable. She had to see it through. She was a cop. That was what cops did. Not only was she a cop, she was witness to a homicide. She had a moral duty to cooperate with solving a man's death.

Cop and witness. Frank was fine with both roles. It was a third role that kept her from the folder. She stared at the floor, not wanting to go through with it. She heard Mary's words from the night before, telling her to have faith that tomorrow would bring what she needed. Not necessarily what she wanted, but what she needed.

Frank walked back to Annie and asked, "Is there somewhere quiet I could read the file? An interview room or something?"

"Sure." Silvester picked up the folder. Frank followed her down the hall to another room. Annie opened the door, motioning her into an office. "This is Lieutenant Jacobs' office. He won't be here today. Take all the time you need."

"Thanks."

Annie handed her the thin folder, shutting the door behind her.

Frank put her father's folder on the wide, clean desk. She thought to return to the squad room and fill her coffee cup. She squinted at plaques and framed pictures, family photos on the desk. Her father's file stared in blind accusation.

Settling in the LT's chair she swiveled a few times, fingered the middle drawer. It was locked and she idly tried another. Locked too. She crossed her legs, studied the hem of her Levi's. She'd have to buy an extra set of clothes today. She'd find a cheaper hotel and then go shopping.

Frank squared the chair to the desk. Centering the folder, she drew in a long breath and flipped it open. At the top of the folder was a stack of DD5s, the detectives' progress reports, all dated consecutively throughout the years. All concluded NR—Negative Results.

She sat back before going deeper into the file. By the time she got back onto a plane for LA the file's latest DD5 might also read Negative Results. Frank decided that would be a bitter pill but she still had to see this through. There was no going back. She owed her father at least that much.

The sudden sanctimony didn't sit well and Frank jumped up to pace. She hadn't been to the man's grave since she left home and she'd done her best since then to drown his memory. The pacing worked her conscience, helping her realize that her sense of obligation was real enough but that it stemmed from atonement rather than righteous vindication. That was a more comfortable reason to continue and she settled to the folder again.

It was like thousands of homicide cases she'd read over the years and not remotely like any of them. With a detachment bordering on an out-of-body experience she pulled the original DD5s. She did the same with the ME's report and the responding officer forms. She arranged a crime scene sketch next to the reports but left the pictures inside.

Picking up the responding officer's report, she checked his name. Wolinsky. Frank matched the name to a blurry face. Wolinsky was indistinct then and had become more so with time. She wondered if he was still on the Job, guessing he quit long ago or retired. Could even be dead.

He must have been the one who had lifted her off her knees. She was kneeling next to her dad. He was slumped forward over his legs. He held out a hand for her. She took it. It was wet and sticky.

"Frankie," he whispered. "S'gonna be okay."

When her father had dropped to his knees he'd told her to call the police. She'd fled to the deli they'd just left. She couldn't remember what she'd said but a man followed her back to her father. She heard him talking to the tiny crowd, the words "shot" and "bad" buzzing above her head like angry bees.

Then strong hands around her waist lifted her from her father. The second she was freed she shoved her way back between the cop and her father. The cop smelled like cigarette smoke and wet clothes. He asked her father, "Who did this, pal?"

"Don't know," her father wheezed. "Junkie. Fuckin' hurts."

"A junkie?" the cop asked.

Weak nod from her father.

"A junkie." Frank intervened. "He jumped out from there"—she pointed to a covered stoop—"and told my father to give him his wallet."

"That right?" the cop asked.

Her father gave a small nod again.

"Did you get a look at him?"

Her father tried to hold up his hand but it fell to the sidewalk.

The cop stood up and Frank scooted closer to her father. She picked up his hand. It was cold and she held it between hers. Her fear ratcheted to terror. Behind her the cop was talking into his radio. She heard "eta" and "ambulance," "backup" and "homicide."

Her father's face was bent to the ground and she peered into it. His eyes were almost closed and his lips were loose. She squeezed his hand. "It's okay, Dad. It's okay."

"Tell 'em," he slurred. "Al. Uncle Al. Ninth Preesing."

His voice scared her. As the cop knelt again she blurted, "My Uncle Al works at the Ninth Precinct. Albert Franco. He works at the Ninth Precinct. He was in Cal's a little bit ago. You gotta get him. He lives at—"

She couldn't remember. She could see the apartment building. On Lafayette. But couldn't think of the building address. Or the cross street. Only Lafayette would come to her.

"Okay, honey. Don't worry. Look. Why don't you come over here—" The cop was directing her from her father with one large hand but she pushed his arm away.

"No!"

"Look," the cop insisted. "He's gonna be all right. Don't worry 'bout it."

They both looked as the siren cut the corner. An ambulance jolted to a stop in front of them. Two men jumped out with a stretcher and Frank was pulled aside. The men lifted her father onto the stretcher.

"Dad?" she called.

He didn't answer.

"Dad!" she screamed, running to follow but the cop caught her. Wolinsky.

Frank opened her eyes.

She was a homicide lieutenant with the LAPD.

She was a forty-five-year-old woman, not a ten-year-old watching her father die.

Frank closed the folder and left the room.

CHAPTER 14

Annie looked up from her computer as Frank carried her cup into the squad room. Frank noticed one of the other detectives still reading his paper. That wouldn't play in her squad room. She balled up the empty bialy bag and tossed it in the trash. *That*, however, was just like her detectives—rip through the food then leave the empty containers lying around like bones. The *Times* sports section was next to the coffeepot. Frank skimmed it. Looked like the Pats were going to the Super Bowl again, a dynasty in the making. No mean feat in an era of salary caps and free agents. More steroid scandals and basketball fights. Still no hockey.

Glancing around the room, she found Annie staring at her.

"Ya finished already?"

Frank shook her head. "Just needed more coffee."

She trudged back to the lieutenant's office, took the chair again. She ran her fingers over the glossy wood grain, wondering what she needed to read that she didn't already know.

They'd turned onto East Ninth. She'd been walking next to him, a bag of groceries cradled in his right arm, her hand in his left. When he walked with her or her mother he always kept himself between them and the street. He'd explained it was an old custom from the days of runaway horses in the streets. But that night the danger came from the entrance to an apartment building. Boing! Like a jack-in-the-box the junkie had popped out and landed in front of her father.

Wielding a short, ugly pistol, he demanded, "Gimme your wallet!"

Her father dropped her hand, pushing her behind him. "Take it easy," he said.

Frank peeked around his waist.

"Gimme your money!" the junkie yelled, dancing and jabbing his gun close at her father.

"All right! Jesus Christ, hold on! Let me put my food down."

"I don't care about your fuckin' food!" the junkie screamed.

"All right, all right, I'm getting it!" her father soothed. He groped for his wallet. Frank watched the junkie's feet. Tennis shoes with holes in them, dancing at the end of skinny legs, dancing close to her father's feet.

"Come on, man, hurry up!"

Her father pulled his wallet out.

"Give it to me," the junkie mumbled. "Give it here."

Her father dropped the groceries as his body swung forward. The junkie jumped back, swearing. Her father swung a roundhouse left at the same time Frank heard the pistol shot. Her father fell onto a knee then tipped over.

"Oh, shit," the junkie said. "Oh, shit."

Frank had a clear look at him before he bolted down the street. His eyes were round and black. Greasy hanks of hair hung in his face and his skin was gray.

"Frankie," her father said in an awful voice. "Go back to the store. Tell him to call a cop. Get 'em here quick. Get an ambulance."

70

"An ambulance?"

She turned to her father, saw his shirt darkening around his hands, staining through his jacket.

"Dad?"

"Frankie. Go!" He breathed hard. "Now. Run."

And she ran.

She ran and she ran like the Gingerbread Man.

There was a knock on the LT's door and Silvester poked her head in. "I talked to my Loo. You wanna ride over to Queens with me?"

Frank pushed a hand through her hair. "Yeah. I'd like that."

"Let's go."

Frank scooped the papers into the folder, passing it back to Annie as they walked down the hall.

"Anything?"

"No," Frank said. "Nothing."

Annie dropped the folder on her desk. "Here." She handed Frank the jars and their paperwork. "You're deputized. Let's go sign out a car. Maybe we can even get one with tires and a steering wheel. Psh. The crap they make us drive. Half the time they break down in the middle of rush hour and the other half they don't even start."

They got a plain brown Buick that choked to life, shaking like a wet dog.

"Cross your fingers," Annie muttered.

Leaving the lot she dug a pack of espresso beans from her purse and held them out to Frank.

"No, thanks."

Annie popped a handful, smirking, "Legal speed."

"Need somethin' on this job."

"Tell me 'bout it." She chewed, her dark eyes roving the street. "Franco? Is that Italian?"

"Nah. Spanish. Spanish-German on my father's side. Norwegian-Dutch on my mother's. You?"

"Eye-talian. True and true."

71

Frank deciphered "true and true" as through and through.

"I been called everything—guinea, dago, wop, greaser—I didn't know my name was Annie until I was six. My father's side of the family is from Naples and my mother's from Salerno."

"Ever been?"

"No." Annie grew wistful. "I've always wanted to go, but I've never had the time. You know how it is. Kids, the Job." She shrugged. "You got kids?"

"Nope."

"I got two. Ben and Lisa. They're good kids, despite me. Lisa's at NYU—wants to be a *lawyer*. Can you imagine? My own daughter. Her brother's a chef. You ever heard of Gramercy Tavern, up on East Twentieth?"

"Uh-uh."

"Oh, it's a nice place. Very fancy. They got foie gras and quail, salmon cooked in salt. They got eighty-five types of cheeses. My son's the grill chef."

"Quite an accomplishment."

"Let me tell ya, he didn't get his talent from me. That's for sure. I cook outta a box. If there weren't Kraft macaroni and cheese my kids woulda starved to death. Musta skipped a generation, cause my mother's baked ziti? To *die* for!"

Grizzled clouds spit snow, the flakes melting as they hit the windshield.

Jutting her chin skyward, Annie said, "Supposed to be more of this."

"I heard. Guess I better pick up a real jacket somewhere."

"You stickin' around a while?"

"Yeah. At least until we get the print results back. Then . . ." Frank flipped a hand, checking Annie's profile. "What about talking to someone at the cemetery? If you don't have time, I could do it. Ask around, see if the groundskeepers have seen anyone at the grave, if there's been things left there before? If so, how often? Stuff like that."

Annie nodded, covering the street. "I got this kid I'm workin'.

That's my priority, but maybe we can take a run out there when this breaks. Or you could ask on your own, let me know what you find out."

"All right."

They drove and watched, keeping one ear on the street, the other on dispatch chatter.

As the snow accumulated Annie said, "It's starting to stick. Bet you wish you were home now, huh?"

"Nah, I like it. I miss the city. I think it's prettier than LA."

"Prettier? New York? Come on."

"You're right. Pretty is for flowers. New York isn't pretty. It's . . . good-looking. It's handsome. Makes you stop and stare, you know? I like that no one smiles here. Until they know you. In LA everyone smiles. Until they know you."

Annie chuckled. "If New York was a woman it'd be Madeline Albright."

"Yeah." Frank thought. "If LA was a woman it'd be Britney Spears."

Annie banged the wheel and laughed. "How 'bout this? If New York was a dog it'd be a pit bull. Straight outta Harlem."

"If LA were a dog it'd be a papillon."

"Oh, yeah, yeah. One of them butterfly dogs, right? Always prancing and yapping? My neighbor down the hall has one. Makes me nervous as all get out. I'm afraid it's gonna get loose and I'm gonna step on it and she's gonna sue me for a broken heart. Okay, how 'bout this. If New York was a flower it'd be a rose. Beautiful, but it'll stick ya."

Frank countered, "If LA were a flower . . . it'd be a hothouse orchid—gorgeous but forced."

They went on like that, comparing the cities to vegetables, furniture, cars, even guns (New York was a Tech Nine, LA a nickel-plated twenty-five) until Annie asked, "Why stay if you don't like it?"

"Never said I didn't like it. I like the heat, the ratio of sunny days to cloudy days, the mountains—when you can see them—and

I get enough of the streets to keep me honest. Shoot me if I ever get transferred to a white-collar division."

"I hear ya. My last assignment was the Two-Oh. Upper West Side. I can take crap offa someone who's been *gettin'* crap all their life, but when these rich muhwhozuhs start beefin' at me, I can't help it. I wanna smack the snot out of 'em. They had to get me outta there. I was a liability to the department."

"That's why you got a cherry assignment like the Ninth."

"I don't mind. In fact, I prefer it. Here you're dealin' with a spade, you know you're dealin' with a spade. Up there. Psh." She waved a hand. "I ain't got time for politickin'. The city wants to pay me for that, they should make me mayor, not detective."

Frank smiled out the window, glad to be on the street with Annie. Hell, she'd probably be glad to be with the Son of Sam if that's what it took to get her out of that lieutenant's office. But Annie was good company. A little talkative, but at least they had mutual ground.

Frank asked, "How long you been working homicide?"

"Nineteen years, cookie. There ain't a cause a death I ain't seen. And I'm ready to throw in the towel. Nine months, I pull the pin and I don't look back. And I'm ready. I couldn't a said that before Nine-Eleven." Annie crossed herself. "But since then, it's all been different. I used to love my work. Now? I still love it but it's different. I'm different. I'm tired. I'm ready to let someone else clean up the messes. I done my share."

"I'd say so."

"You?"

"About fifteen."

Annie nodded grimly. "You seen plenty, too."

"Plenty," Frank agreed.

CHAPTER 15

After they dropped off the evidence Annie's cell phone rang. She answered while veering around a plumbing van and Frank braced herself against the dashboard.

"Vincent. Whaddaya got for me?" Annie listened. "Excellent. I'll meet you at the station as soon as I can. Keep him uncomfortable, okay?" Hanging up, she asked Frank, "You want to go back to the station or I should drop you somewhere?"

"There a good hotel near the station?"

"Let's see. There's the St. Marks over on Third. For forty bucks you can have the room two hours, no questions asked."

"Nice. But I'd like to stay a little longer."

Annie laughed. "Let me tell ya, there've been times I've popped for it. Just for the pure luxury of stretching out on sheets for an hour and forty-five then a hot shower. Um-mm. There's a HoJo at Forsyth and Houston. Sohotel on Broome. Used to be the Pioneer. I think it's pretty cheap. There's Hotel Seventeen up

Third. I can tell you it ain't the Crowne Plaza but it's not a Super Eight, either. It's clean and cheap. I think you gotta share a bathroom, though. Madonna stayed there."

"Madonna shared a bathroom?"

"Yeah, imagine? You open the door to go and there's Madonna on the can. 'Oh, excuse me. Bu-ut, as long as you're here, maybe I could I get an autograph?'"

Frank smiled. "Just take me back to the station. I'll figure it out from there."

When they arrived at the Ninth, Frank trailed Annie inside to use a phone book. She asked, "So I'm not gonna be steppin' on your toes if I canvass the cemetery tomorrow?"

"Aw, hell, no. Go for it. But," Annie warned, pointing a lacquered fingernail, "you tell me everything you find out. Even what you *don't* find out, *capiche*?"

"*Capiche.*"

After checking in with her squad, and talking to a very unhappy captain, Frank decided to try Hotel 17. Walking up Third Avenue, she passed the St. Marks Hotel, pleased that Annie Silvester was the detective on her father's case. She was also pleased when she got to the hotel and saw that the Hazelden Rehab Center was right next door—if things got bad she wouldn't have far to go for help.

Frank's room was small and funky, but cheap, as Annie'd said. Willing to compromise on lodging, but not on what she wore all day, Frank hiked across town to Macy's. Her long legs ate up the blocks as she hunched against the intermittent snow, warm from her exertion. A memory detached itself as she approached the monolithic department store—shopping there with her mother, having Coke and a grilled cheese sandwich for lunch, a small Macy's bag propped on the table between them.

The recollection stung. Frank found indignant comfort in her sad memories, but being back in the city of her youth revived happy memories for which she had no ready defenses. She realized that she'd been so busy resenting her mother that she'd forgotten how much she had once loved her. She stepped into Macy's, assaulted by the warm, perfumed air. The smell hadn't changed in forty years. Frank quickly bought a change of clothes and when she was done, ate lunch across the street. But the large Macy's bag propped defiantly on the table couldn't hide the little bag in Frank's memory. She couldn't remember what had been in the bag but her mother had beamed at it as if it held a queen's riches.

Then came darker days when Frank was towed through the store in her mother's manic wake, her mother stockpiling merchandise with delighted cashiers, only to leave empty-handed at closing time with barely enough money for bus fare. During the ride home to whichever project they were in at the time Frank had seethed in shame and anger.

The waiter delivered a carafe of wine a few tables down. Frank looked on as the man poured, reminded of a Ray Bradbury story where time was used in place of money. Some saved time, others spent it. The poor sap in the story was down to a few hours in his account. He'd rushed frantically about town, begging for time, but no one would lend him any. He ran out and died.

Frank paid her bill, thinking that was how her drinking was. All done, all her passes used up, none left. Pull the plug. On her way back to the hotel she walked Broadway all the way down to the Strand. For the last year, year and a half, she hadn't been able to read anything not related to work. Now, with lots of empty hours to face, she thought it might be a good time to try again. For the better part of the afternoon Frank lost herself in paper and ink, finally leaving the store carrying a Strand bag larger than the Macy's bag.

Dusk had become night by the time she returned to the hotel. Seeing the shared bath was empty, she warmed herself with a quick, hot shower. Ducking across the hall wearing only a towel made her think of Gail running around the Crowne Plaza in her pajamas. She wanted to call Gail, hear her voice. Instead Frank picked a book from the bag and snuggled under the covers. She wasn't ten pages into it before the phone rang. She jumped up, hunting for the cell phone hidden in her jacket. It showed a local number.

"This is Franco."

"Franco. Annie Silvester."

"Hey. What's up?"

"You wouldn't believe it if I told you."

"Try me."

"*Chi di spada ferisce di spada perisce.*" Annie laughed. "'He who lives by the sword, dies by the sword.' We're interviewin' my mope, we get a call about a homicide. The vic turns out to be the mope's friend, the *other* guy we're lookin' for. The little girl's father shot the *crap* outta him. Mope looked like a friggin' colander by the time he got put outta his misery. You should see the blood. Someone's gonna make a fortune cleanin' that apartment."

"Congratulations. Double-header."

"That's not the best part. We take a Polaroid of the vic, show it to my mope and ask if he knows him. I swear, Frank, he turned whiter than me. I thought he was gonna toss his cookies all over the box. I tell him the vic gave him up while he was bein' shot, that he told the father where to find him, and I kid you not, he starts talkin' faster than I can listen. Figures his chances are better with a New York jury than the girl's father. And he's right. Only I didn't tell him we had the father in custody."

"Sweet."

"Yeah, no kiddin', huh? What are you, my good-luck charm? You blow into town and *bada bing*, I close two cases. So I was thinkin' while I'm on a roll here, I should head out to Canarsie with you tomorrow. How would that be?"

"That'd be great."

"Good. Where you stayin' at?"

"Hotel Seventeen."

"I'll pick you up around ten."

"See you then."

A few pages later the phone rang again. This time Frank recognized the number.

"Hey," she answered.

"Hey yourself. How was your day?"

"Okay. Took the evidence to the lab with Annie, found a place—"

"Who's Annie?"

"She's the detective handling my dad's case. Annie Silvester. Did that, then I found a place to stay. It's funky, but like Annie said, 'It ain't the Crowne Plaza' but it'll do."

"Sounds like you and Annie are getting pretty chummy."

"Chummy." Frank tasted the word. "Makes it sound like we're going to the movies and hanging out together. We're workin' a homicide."

"I see. How's that going?"

"Well, we got the candle and the vase delivered, so now we wait. Tomorrow we'll go out to the cemetery and see what we can turn up there. No pun intended."

"How old is she?"

"How old is who?"

"This Annie."

"I don't know. She's going to retire in nine months. She looks like she's maybe early fifties, give or take a couple years."

"Hmm. How long do you think you'll be staying here?"

"No telling. I talked to Fubar. He's pissed. Told him it could be a couple more days, maybe a couple weeks. I don't know. It all depends on what we get back from the lab. Or don't. How about you? Going back tomorrow?"

"Yeah. From Manhattan to the morgue."

"Sounds like a true crime title. So what are you going to do with your last night in the Big Apple?"

"I'm going to a play."

"Alone?"

"No." Frank waited for an explanation, but Gail continued. "I'm finally going to see *Phantom of the Opera*. I've waited so long I hope my expectations don't exceed the reality."

"Who you going with?"

"A woman I met at the convention. She's nice. We've had fun together."

"Nice." Frank couldn't resist. "Sounds chummy."

Gail giggled. "A little."

"So, where does this woman live?"

"Minnesota."

"Good."

"Why good?"

"Don't know. Nice place, Minnesota."

"Have you ever been there?"

"Nope. You?"

"Not yet."

Her jealousy kindled, Frank quizzed, "Plan on going?"

"Maybe."

"To see your friend?"

"Maybe."

Gail sounded distracted and Frank asked, "What are you doing?"

"Painting my nails."

Frank let the silence stretch out. "You never paint your nails."

"I do sometimes."

"This for your big date tonight?"

"It's not a big date."

"All right. Your little date."

"It's not a date at all. It's just a play."

"Whatever." Frank sulked.

"My, we sound jealous."

"Oh, no," Frank answered too quickly. "Not at all. Should we be?"

"I don't know. You're the one who left, remember?"

"Of course I do. You remind me every time we talk."

"Well, given whose idea it was to walk I'm not sure how your rather high-handed inquisition is justified."

Frank bit down on her lip. Talking to Mary one evening Frank had called herself an asshole. Mary had corrected, "You're not an

80

asshole. You're just *behaving* like one. Now. Do you want to keep doing that or would you like to stop?"

Frank said, "Look. I hope you have a wonderful time. I hope the play's better than you can possibly imagine. You deserve to have some fun."

"You're damn right I do. And I'm having it. Would you like to know why I called you?"

"Love to."

"Well, I was wondering, before you started your interrogation, if you'd like to have dinner when you get home."

Frank cringed. She made a circle with her thumb and forefinger, flapping the other fingers in the universal gesture for a flaming asshole. "I would love that."

"Okay. Call me when you get back."

"Promise you won't be in Minnesota?"

"This jealousy, Frank, is it a trait peculiar to sobriety?"

"I wish. I've always been an asshole. Forgive me?"

"As long as I don't have anything to worry about with you and Annie."

"You care that much?"

"Let's just say I still have a proprietary interest."

"I like that. I'll call you when I get home."

"Okay. Good luck with your dad."

"Thanks. You have fun tonight. And be safe, huh?"

"I will, copper. You, too."

Frank hung up and tried to resume her place in the book, but Maggie haunted her. Frank's jealousy had caused her first love to walk into the middle of an armed robbery and the petty squabble had cost Maggie her life. Frank would carry that scar to her grave, yet here she was, acting the same way with Gail.

A steady *bump-bump* issued from the bar downstairs and Frank thought how easy it would be to slip out of her harsh skin and into a few soft drinks. That would certainly shift her perspective.

And so would an AA meeting. Frank sighed and got dressed. She passed the bar on her way next door.

CHAPTER 16

The first thing Annie said to Frank was, "So? Did you see her?"

"See who?"

"Madonna. D'you share a can with her?"

"Nah, I think she's moved up in the world."

"Psh." Annie slapped the air. "Forget about her."

As she drove, Annie scrutinized the sidewalks. Frank silently watched the road for her. Each time she was about to call out a warning Annie stepped on the brakes or twisted the wheel. Frank's stomach heaved and she wondered if the cop drove like this all the time.

At First Street Annie smashed the brakes. Frank started to complain but Annie growled, "Well, hello, kiddo. I knew you'd surface sooner or later."

Frank saw the two male blacks Annie was looking at. Both late teens or early twenties, one in a red Hilfiger jacket with black shiny jogging pants, the other in a navy ski outfit. The taller wore a red ski mask and the one in navy's head was shaved.

Annie drove past, averting her gaze to Frank. "I've been lookin' for that mutt for three months. I can take him in right now on parole violation." She drove around the block. "I want to take him, but if I call for backup he's gonna bolt. You up for a collar?"

"Sure. I don't have a weapon."

Annie whipped the wheel around. "What we'll do is get a backup en route, no sirens. Damn." She jerked to scan the backseat. "Check the glove compartment. See if there are some plastic lock-ties in there. I don't got cuffs with me. We shouldn't need 'em, but just in case."

Frank produced a handful of ties.

"Good. Take three or four. He's big."

Annie turned onto First Street. The two men were still talking by a cluster of garbage cans. Frank asked which one she wanted.

"The tall one in red."

"Why's he not gonna bolt when he sees you?"

"He might." She grinned. "But look at me. Would you?"

Annie requested backup and double-parked. Annie's mope made the women as soon as they got out of the car.

He started walking but she called, "Irvin, I just wanna talk! Don't make me haul you in on something as stupid as parole violation."

"What I do?" He stopped, indignant. He watched his friend keep walking. "Damn!"

"Other than the parole violation, you tell me." Annie planted herself under his chin, arms crossed. "We need to talk."

"Talk? 'Bou' what? I don't even *know* you."

Flashing her badge, she told him, "Now you do. I'm Detective Silvester and this is Detective Franco. I hear you might know somethin' about who capped Dread Knowledge."

The mope became agitated, dancing, claiming, "I don't know *nothin'* 'bout that nigger. Ain't nothin' I can tell you."

"That's too bad. Then I guess I have to take you in on PV."

"Yeah, right." He laughed. "Ain't goin' in."

"You can come in, talk with me and leave, or you can come in wearing cuffs and not leave. What do you want to do?"

83

"Neither one."

The mope turned away. Frank stepped in front of him. As he moved around her Annie grabbed his arm, twisting it into the small of his back. But the mope wrenched his arm loose, taking his eyes off Frank to swing at Annie. In that instant Frank's knee connected with his crotch. The big man gasped and went down. He must have hit Annie because she was recovering from a stumble. Yanking her 9 millimeter free she whacked his elbow with the grip. It made a solid crack and he cried out. Annie yanked his arm back to lock the tie on and Frank jerked his other arm around, getting a twist on it. Annie was ready with a third and zipped the ties together.

The perp was curled on the sidewalk, trying to breathe. Annie bent toward his face. She panted, "Dumb, Irvin. Very dumb. You just bought a trip to jail for resisting arrest and assaulting an officer." She tapped his head. "Very dumb."

When she straightened, pushing the hair back from her face, Frank saw her chin was swelling. "You okay?"

Two men in uniform ran up to them. Annie dabbed her chin. "Ouch. Dumb, Irvin. Very dumb." The cops yanked the mope to his feet and Annie told them, "He's all yours, fellas. We tied him up all nice and neat for you, just like a box of cannoli."

"Yes, ma'am."

Both cops were young and white. They glanced at the older women as they hustled Irvin into their unit.

"Sorry," Annie said, heading for her car. "Your interview's gotta wait."

Frank got in and buckled up, asking again if Annie was all right.

The bump on her chin had doubled but Annie grinned. "I'm gonna be sore tomorrow, I can tell you that. My chin stopped him but I took it all in my neck."

Annie gave her attention to the road and Frank relaxed. "You sure know how to show a girl a good time."

"Fun, huh? Crap, this hurts like a mother. I better get some ice on it."

"Pull over," Frank insisted.

Annie double-parked again and Frank darted into a deli. She got back into the car, tossing Annie a bag of frozen corn.

"Thanks." Annie held the vegetables against her chin.

"Shoulda got one for your neck, too."

"Yeah, no kidding. Hey, that was nice work out there."

Frank shrugged. "I like the elbow trick."

"Yeah. An old-timer taught me that. I was trying to wrestle this mope off a chain-link fence one day and this old fart from the backup unit walks up, goes whap-whap with his nightstick and that's that. He looks at me, disgusted, tells me, 'Go home, little girl, leave this to the men.'"

"Yeah, I had a couple like that."

Because she had nothing better to do, for the next five, almost six hours, Frank watched Silvester and Meyers interview their man.

Meyers started off shaking his head. "Look what you did, Irvin. Hitting a woman. You oughta be ashamed a yourself. Didn't your mama teach you better than that? Huh? And then to let two ladies take you down like that?" Meyers chuckled. "Oh, man. I wonder what your boys are saying about that?"

"They ain't no ladies," the perp declared.

Silvester let herself in. She carried a soda and slid it across the table for Irvin. "No hard feelin's, huh?"

Irvin looked at the soda like it was a bomb.

"All right, honey. This has gotten way out of hand. I just wanted to talk to you. Word is you know something about Dread Knowledge. I was gonna go easy on your PV, I just wanted to talk, but you pulled a dumb on me. Now *I* know you ain't dumb, and *you* know you ain't dumb, so the smart thing to do is just answer my question. If you can do that we'll go easy on the charges. I just want you to help me fill in a couple details about Dread. We've got a possible suspect and you might be able to help us pin him down. Is that so hard?"

"Who ya suspect?"

Annie said, "You know Alphonse Kincaid. Where was he the night Dread got popped?"

"Alphonse Kincaid?"

Annie nodded and Irvin was off.

Kincaid was a rival for Irvin's turf and at the time of Dread Knowledge's untimely demise he was being booked on a larceny charge. Apparently Irvin didn't know this because he took the bait, firmly placing Alphonse at the scene. In painting the lie he admitted his presence at Dread's murder. Over the next couple hours Meyers and Silvester probed his inconsistencies, agreed with Irvin and questioned him so deftly that he believed he had the detectives fooled.

When Irvin admitted he'd been packing a Walther PPK at the murder scene, the lieutenant watching with Frank murmured, "Beautiful."

"That your weapon?" Frank asked

He nodded, grinning at the glass. "That Annie. She's whipped cream with a cherry on top. But under all that sweetness?" He slapped his palms together. "A fuckin' bear trap. Christ, I could use a couple dozen a her."

Two hours after the Walther admission, the perp was signing a murder confession. Closing the interview door behind her, Annie danced into the squad room waving the signed paper. Frank clapped and Annie executed a low bow. She had sturdy, well-turned legs and the deep grace of her bow made Frank wonder if she was a dancer.

"You're good."

"You're damn right I am, cookie."

Placing a small bottle of Advil on Annie's desk, Frank said, "Take a couple of these tonight. They'll help your neck."

Rubbing under her hairline, Annie replied, "Tonight, hell. I'm taking one now." Dry swallowing a pill, she added, "Thanks."

"Just trying to make sure you don't call in sick on me. Want to try the cemetery again tomorrow?"

"You bet. I'll pick you up at nine."

"Okay."

Frank made to leave, but Annie called, "Hey. Thanks again for the collar."

"No sweat. It was fun."

"You California girls got weird ideas a fun."

CHAPTER 17
Tuesday, 11 Jan 05—East Village

Oh, yeah. We're having some fun now. Got to help Annie nail a perp today. Fucker took a swing at her when she tried to cuff him and I jammed him in the balls. Dropped like a coconut and six hours later squealed like a pig. I watched her work him in the box. Very impressive. We were on our way out to the cemetery when she saw the mope, so will try again tomorrow.

So surreal to be at the Ninth. I keep thinking I'll see Uncle Al come around the corner, then we'll go next door to Cal's and he and dad will empty a pitcher.

I took a stab at the case folder. Way harder than I thought. This whole fucking thing's harder than I thought. You'd think after having this monkey on my back for thirty-six years I'd be kind of resigned to it. I'd pretty much accepted the idea that I was never going to find out who killed him. Especially after I became a cop and realized the odds of closing stranger-homicides. Eighty percent of the time there's a link between the vic and the perp that helps seal the deal, but when a stranger kills a vic a lot of time there's nowhere to go except around and around in circles. That's what I did for years after he died—mad-dogging every lowlife on the street, wondering if he was the one, waiting every day for Uncle Al to knock on the door and say, "We got him!" And it just never happened.

Then I became a cop and had to deal with shell-shocked kids just like I'd been. Had to break ugly news to wives just like my mother and after a while I tuned it all out. I learned to say and do the right things, but I didn't feel it anymore. I couldn't—it'd make me psycho to take on all that pain. So I pushed it away. And it got just as easy to push my own pain away. To drink it away and work it away. So now what? Now what do I do with it?

At first I was hooked in an abstract, professional way. "Gee, here's this thirty-six-year-old cold case and isn't this an interesting break?" Then I realized, holy fuck, this is my thirty-six-year-old case. This was me. My whole life. So I'm reading through the case file this morning and bam! I'm ten years old again. What a pain in the ass. And just like when I was ten, I want to find this guy. I want to look him in the eye and I want to hurt him. I want to smash him. Thing is, the bastard's probably dead. I mean he was a hope-to-die junkie, right? What are the odds he's still alive? So here I am, almost four decades later, still chasing ghosts. When's it gonna end?

Maybe when I find out who's been leaving that shit for him.

Maybe not even then. I don't know. Feel like I've opened Pandora's box. Should have just left well enough alone and now it's too late to slam the lid shut. Christ. Oh, well. One day at a time, right? Done all I can do tonight. Wonder how Gail is. I'd love to call her. Hell, I'd love a lot of things—to catch a killer; solve a mystery for Annie; have a glass of wine with dinner; have my lover back. What I got is a warm bed and a pretty good book. Need to break down and buy some reading glasses. Damn print's swimming all over. Gotta hold the book halfway to my knees to get it into focus. Life's a bitch and then you die. Had a vic once had that tattooed across his back. Thought it was funny at the time. Now I'm wondering how much that tattoo cost.

I'm tired. Going to bed. How can I be tired? Didn't do anything all day. Maybe making up for all those lost nights. Anyway, mañana, with luck.

CHAPTER 18

Buckling her seatbelt the next morning Annie informed Frank, "I gotta stop and talk to a witness first. Make sure she's gonna be in court next week. I'll only be ten minutes."

"Whatever."

"Whatevuh. Listen to you. Miss Patience. Couple days ago ya had ants in ya pants. What happened?"

Frank lifted helpless hands. "What am I gonna do? It's your case, right? We work it on your schedule, not mine. I know you got dozens more important cases to be working, so I'm glad for whatever you give me. I appreciate it."

Annie shot Frank a dubious look. At the light she pondered, "Thirty-six years and you're still lookin' for the mope that whacked your pops. He musta been a good guy, huh?"

Frank nodded.

"If it was my old man," Silvester agreed, "I'd be lookin' too. To give the mope a friggin' medal. Then to kick his ass for not shootin' the son of a bitch before he had me. My pops, he shoulda been thrown in the East River the day he was born."

"Not so nice, huh?"

"He was an oiler, my old man. Couldn't hold down a job if you gave him a hammer and a box a nails. Drank away every paycheck he ever had. Never mind he had five kids to feed. My mother"— Annie crossed herself—"she's a saint. Raised us basically by herself. Throw in my old man and she was taking care of *six* kids. Sent three of us through college, workin' fourteen, sixteen hours a day. She'd come home some nights cryin', her feet hurt so bad. I'd rub 'em for her. Put liniment on 'em. I hated seein' her like that. Then she'd get a couple hours' sleep and be up before we were, making our breakfast, lunches already in little sacks she saved from work. A saint. A friggin' saint."

Annie checked the rearview mirror, the side mirrors. She scanned through the windshield and started the visual circuit all over again.

"She still alive?"

"Yeah. She lives with my brother Anthony over to Queens. His wife's a doll, God bless her. Took my mother in like she was her own. Yours?"

"Nah. Dead a long time."

"I'm sorry."

"Don't be. Like your dad was to you, my mother was to me."

"How old were you when your dad died?"

"Ten."

"Well, *that* I'm sorry for."

Frank nodded. "Here we are anyway. Despite the odds. Two old broads carrying guns and badges."

Annie smiled. "We done all right, huh?"

"Pretty good. I wonder if we'd be here without them. Our pops, I mean."

Annie dropped another look on Frank. She shrugged, resuming her scan. "Maybe better, huh?"

"Who knows?" Frank used her hands to weigh her words.

"Good guy, bad guy? For a while, it coulda gone either way for me."

"You serious?"

"Yeah. The bad guy was quick, immediate gratification. But I saw who always got to go home at the end of the day and kept my sights on that. There were times, though, I wavered."

Passing Tomkins Square Park, Annie pointed out the corner of 11th Street. "Back in the Seventies—I think it was 'seventy-two—BLA ambushed two cops there. Foster and Laurie. Both of 'em not even twenty-five yet. Foster was black, Laurie was white, but both of 'em was blue."

"I know. Word spread around the projects faster than fire in a meth lab. I kited a bus up after school the next day. Kinda morbid, I know, but I wanted to see where it happened. I remember how quiet it was. Too quiet. Only people on the street were junkies lookin' to score. Everyone else was inside lookin' out."

Annie was incredulous. "You're from around here?"

Frank found her answer out the window. "Spent some time here."

"Whereabouts?"

"Started off in the East Village, then after my dad died we moved to the Lower East Side. We were in the Towers when Foster and Laurie got killed."

"The projects, huh? That musta been tough for a white girl."

Frank shrugged. "I did all right. My dad taught me how to take care of myself."

After squinting at a couple parked cars, Annie asked, "Any other white kids there with you?"

Frank grinned. "There were a couple of us. We stood out like maggots in a shit pile, but I was the only blonde. They used to call me 'Yella.' It wasn't so bad."

Frank squirmed. The projects weren't physically bad. She got knocked around a time or two, frightened sometimes, but nothing terrible happened. The bad part was what had happened to her on the inside. The projects taught her to rely on herself and herself only, to trust or care for no one. But as they passed two kids skipping hand in hand with their mother she remembered that wasn't completely true. She'd gotten a lot of bloody noses defending kids who couldn't defend themselves. She hated the way the strong preyed on the weak, the trickle-down economics of the ghetto where the father beat the mother, the mother beat the kids, and the kids took it out on anyone smaller. Frank wasn't always bigger than her adversaries but she was always angry and her anger found outlet in perceived injustices. Injustices she could control.

A shriveled man hunched on a stoop brought Frank back to the present. "So your case with the little girl. Where'd you catch her father?"

"That's a helluva note." Annie rooted in her purse for a pack of coffee beans. "A unit picked him up on the sidewalk. He knew we had the other perp and he was on his way home to blow his brains out. Poor bastard."

"I had a case like that. Couple years ago. Perp raped an eight-year-old so hard he killed her. Internal bleeding. The girl's father found him before we did. Tied him up in the machine shop where he worked and sliced the bastard's dick off. Choked him with it. Felt kinda bad cuffin' him."

"Yeah, I know, huh?"

The women continued swapping stories, making the drive to Canarsie cheerful despite traffic and brooding clouds. They found a parking spot on Remsen and headed for the cemetery office.

"Good morning," Annie greeted the man inside, flashing her badge. "NYPD Homicide. I'm Detective Silvester, and this is Detective Franco."

The man bowed his head nervously. "Good morning," he answered in a rich Indian accent. "What can I do for you?"

"We need to talk to your groundskeepers. It won't take long," Annie assured.

"Yes, yes." He nodded. "I get them for you."

He darted from the office and the women looked around.

Annie asked, "You thought about this yet?"

"About what?"

"You know." Her hand circled the room. "What you're gonna do."

"Not really." Frank frowned. "I think I got a little time left."

"Ain't you the cocky one? How do you know some mope ain't gonna whack you tomorrow? Or God forbid"—she crossed herself—"we get in a car wreck on the parkway? You of all people," she chided.

"Why me of all people?"

"Bein' a homicide cop, for Pete's sake. Seein' what you seen. Of all people you should know there ain't no guarantees."

Frank had shaken hands with her mortality half a dozen times but had never considered what would happen next. "What are you gonna do?"

"Buried," Annie proclaimed, jabbing a finger at the ground. "Mahogany coffin, the works. I'm goin' out like a Viking, you know. In the most comfortable ship I can find, only not on fire."

Frank smiled. "You're somethin', Detective."

"Ya got that right, cookie."

The man returned, apologizing that the groundskeepers would be just a minute.

"No problem," Annie soothed. "Thank you."

"May I ask what you're investigating?"

"An old case. Thirty-six years old. See, the NYPD nevuh quits." She winked.

"Manny and Robert." He bobbed his head. "They will help you, yes? Please sit. They'll be soon here."

"Thank you." Annie was effusive in her praise, her charm wooing wits and perps alike.

They sat on the couch and Frank gave her an elbow. "You're good."

"You noticed." Annie sniffed.

Two men, one Hispanic, one Asian, both in work clothes, entered the office. Annie made the introductions, then they followed Frank to her father's plot.

Weaving around headstones Annie asked, "How often do you clean up the flowers left on graves?"

Manny, the Hispanic male, shrugged. "Depends."

"Depends on what?"

"On how bad they look," Robert answered. "When they start gettin' brown we throw 'em away."

Annie looked around. "I can see the place is very clean, very professional. I should be so lucky to be buried here."

From her comment about "the works" and Viking funerals it sounded more like Annie had Forest Lawn in mind. Frank murmured, "On a cop's salary you *should* be so lucky."

"Amen. So tell me, Robert." She interrupted herself. "May I call you, Robert?"

"Sure."

They were standing at Frank's father's grave. There were no flowers, no candles. Just two headstones maintained by indifferent strangers. Frank concentrated on Annie and the groundskeepers.

"All right, Robert. So tell me, how often do you throw away flowers from this grave?"

He hefted his shoulder. "Not that much. Someone comes and changes them. There's usually fresh flowers. I don't know, about every two weeks?" He appealed to his colleague.

Manny dragged on his cigarette with self-importance. The detectives indulged him. He nodded. "Something like that."

"You say someone. Who's the someone? Male? Female? White? Black?"

"I don't know." Robert shrugged again. "They must come durin' the weekend. We don't work weekends."

"When was the last time you saw someone at this grave?"

"Oh, man, I don't know. I couldn't tell you. There's a lotta people come and go from here. I don't notice 'em, you know? I'm workin'."

"There's a lot people come and go," Annie repeated. "But you never noticed anyone here?"

"No. I might have seen someone but I wasn't payin' attention,

95

you know? I never seen anyone cryin' or sittin' for a long time like some people do, you know? You, Manny?"

Manny shook his close-cropped head. "Nah."

Frank came back to the frequency. "So there are fresh flowers about every two weeks, is that right?"

"About that," Robert agreed. "Sometimes I've had to throw 'em away but mostly whoever brings the new ones throws away the old ones."

"The candle, too?"

"Yeah, I guess. Some a them you gotta toss 'cause they look old, you know? They're all peelin' or faded. They look messy. I've tossed a candle from here a couple times. Once or twice."

"What type of candle?"

Robert held his hands about ten inches apart. "The glass ones, you know? Religious candles?"

Frank nodded. "Can you remember what picture was on the candle?"

"No. There's too many. I can't remember 'em all."

"Manny?"

He flicked ash on the grave. "I don't know. There was one time, though." He stared at the horizon like a Clint Eastwood character about to divulge the secret tragedy that turned him into a brooding vigilante. "I saw a priest here. Had the white collar and black coat, whole nine yards."

"When was this?"

Manny pursed his lips. "A long time ago."

"Ten years? Five years? Six months?" Annie prompted.

"Maybe like a year, year an' a half ago."

"What was he doing?"

"Changing flowers, I think. Something like that. I wasn't paying much attention. But a priest, the collar and all, it catches your eye."

"And you're sure he was at this grave?"

Manny shook his head, "Nah. Maybe. Coulda been, but I ain't sure. It was somewhere around here."

Frank asked, "You ever seen anything else here, besides flowers and candles?"

The men answered with head shakes and Annie told them, "All right, fellas, we appreciate your help, huh?"

The groundskeepers walked off, leaving Annie and Frank staring at the grave.

"So you got no family that coulda left the flowers?"

Frank wagged her head.

"No old friends? No war buddies?"

"Doubt it. My father and his brother both served in Korea but neither one of 'em ever talked about it. I asked my father once and he told me it was nothing I needed to know about. After they were discharged they moved here from Chicago. All their friends were back there."

"They didn't make friends here?"

"Yeah, they had bar buddies but they were each other's best friend. I'm tellin' you, it's someone linked to the perp. Gotta be."

"Frank, I hate to be indelicate here, but what if, let's say, your pops, he had someone else in his life that you didn't know about? Someone special, huh? I mean, it's a possibility. Anything's possible and how would a ten-year-old know such a thing, right?"

"You mean another woman?"

"It's possible." Annie hefted her shoulders.

"Nah," Frank denied. "Not my dad. He was crazy about my mom. Yeah, sure, it's possible, anything is. But probable? Nah. I can't see it."

"Can't or won't, my friend?"

Frank stared hard at Annie before starting for the car. "We're done here."

CHAPTER 19

Annie unlocked the car and as they slid in, she pressed, "I know it's not a pretty idea but you have to consider all the angles. Come on, you know that. And look what we got here—flowers, candles—it screams female. You gotta admit that."

Frank couldn't speak around the rage in her chest. As a cop she saw the potential of what Annie was saying. As a daughter, she was furious. Betrayal and logic silently warred as they crossed the East River. Coming into the city Frank allowed, "Well, whoever it is visits on a regular basis."

"Yeah, but I hate to tell you, we haven't got the resources to leave a man at the cemetery all day until whoever it is shows up."

"Don't have to. I'm gonna do it."

"Whaddaya mean you're gonna do it? You gotta get back to LA. You got a job, don't ya?"

"Yeah. With years' worth of accrued vacation time. People take two-, three-week vacations all the time. Why can't I? It's winter, it's slow. I got a good crew that knows what to do without me. And

98

if our mystery visitor shows up as regularly as it sounds like, then it shouldn't take more than a week or two. Maybe three, tops."

"I don't know," Annie worried.

"You gonna stop me?"

"No-o. But if and when this person materializes, are you gonna handle him—or her—like a cop or a daughter?"

"A cop," Frank snapped. "Just a cop."

Lifting a placating hand, Annie calmed, "All right, all right. I had to ask. I'm sorry I brought this up but it's a possibility you gotta look at."

"Yeah, all right, I know."

"I can't have you goin' off on whoever's leavin' this stuff."

"I'm not going off on anybody. Whoever I find I'll treat 'em like I'd treat any other wit."

"And of course you'll let me know the minute you find someone."

Frank nodded.

"And you don't confront this person. You can tail her, or him, or whatever, but leave the questions to me. You don't talk to her. You got it?"

"Got it."

Pulling into the station lot, Annie asked, "You got friends here?"

"What?"

"You got friends here in town? Anybody to hang out with?"

"No."

"You got no friends, no family. You're dealin' with your pop's murder and if I may ask, how much are you spendin' a night at the hotel?"

"About eighty bucks."

"Eighty bucks a night for one, two, maybe even three weeks." Nosing into a spot Annie put the car in park, declaring, "That's stupid. I live fifteen minutes away in Tribeca. I got two bedrooms sittin' there empty since my kids left. You're gonna come stay with me. End of discussion."

"Nah, I can't."

"Why ya can't?"

Frank got out of the unmarked.

Annie asked over the top of the car, "You mad about what I said back there?"

Frank sighed, tracing a line through the grime on the hood. "The cop in me wants to slap myself silly for not thinking of that, but the daughter in me wants to slap *you* silly. I just . . . it's hard to take in, is all."

"I can see how that would be." Coming around to Frank's side of the car Annie told her, "You just go and keep an eye on the cemetery, huh? Let me worry about the case. You shouldn't have to do that. It's your pops, not some stranger. It's hard to be objective with your pops, huh? Let me do that. That's what the great city of New York pays me for. That's what I got commendations on my wall for, huh?"

"Yeah." Frank stared at the ground. "I'll go be your eyes and try not to think too much."

"That's a girl. And meanwhile, you're comin' to stay with me."

"I can't do that, Annie."

"Why? Why do you keep sayin' that?"

"You don't even know me. How do you know I don't snore and steal loose change?"

Annie grinned. " 'Cause I'm a detective, cookie, remembuh? Besides, I got ear plugs and can spare some loose change."

"I don't want to put you out."

"How are you puttin' me out? I'm never there. You're gonna be squattin' on a headstone in Canarsie all day. You should have a nice place to come to at the end of the day, not some hotel room."

"It's a nice room."

"Yeah, a nice eighty-dollar room. You come stay with me for nothin'."

Entering the station house, Frank insisted, "I couldn't impose on you like that."

"What impose? You're not listenin' to me. I just said I'm never there. I may as well be payin' a mortgage for a reason. And to tell

100

you the truth, I miss the kids. I don't like comin' home to an empty apartment."

Knowing the feeling too well, Frank asked, "What happened to Mr. Silvester?"

"Psh. He left when Ben was six and Lisa was eight. I never met a man yet that could live with the Job being first, so I stopped lookin'. I was busy enough with the kids anyway, who needed another one? The one good thing, and I gotta say this for him, is what he did to that apartment. It was a loft in an old manufacturing building when he bought it. Let me tell ya, it was fallin' down. Don't think I didn't give him a few choice words about it, either. But, God love him, he fixed that place up nice. You'll see. And never said a peep about giving it to me and the kids, after all that hard work he done . . . So it's just me rattlin' around the place all by myself. Come on, do me a favor. Come stay. If you don't like it I'm sure they'll be glad to give ya your room back at the Seventeen. Whaddaya say?"

Frank was the kind of drunk who liked to be alone, who crawled off into a hole to lick her wounds and feel safe. As uncomfortable as the idea was, she knew it would be healthier to stay with Annie than alone in a hotel room above a bar.

"You sure?"

"Naw," she chided. "I'm mentally deranged and I just changed my mind. Course I'm sure."

Frank trailed her up the stairs. "That'd be nice."

"Good. I got an extra key in my desk. You can let yourself in."

After checking out of the hotel Frank did just that.

The apartment was a flight up in a renovated loft building on Franklin Street. Turning to lock the door behind her, she was startled by a child-sized statue of the Virgin Mary beside the door. Rosary beads hung from an almost life-size wooden hand and candles encircled the base. Checking out the rest of the apartment, Frank wondered what she'd gotten into. But everything else seemed normal enough. Honeyed wood floors warmed the rooms and high ceilings with big windows made the place feel cozy rather than cramped. Framed photographs and studio portraits hung everywhere and Frank easily spotted family resemblances. She scanned the titles on a bookshelf, amused they were all romance novels.

Despite the Virgin Mary lurking by the door, Annie's crib was a lot nicer than the hotel. And Frank didn't have to worry about running into Madonna in the bathroom. After stashing her few things in the guest room she found Annie's phone book in the tiny kitchen, using it to figure out subway lines to the cemetery. Done with that, she looked for coffee and made a pot. She filled a china cup and carried it back to the living room on its saucer.

She was intent on taking another look at her father's file, but the statue caught her eye. It was about four feet tall and appeared to be carved from a solid block of wood. Frank wondered how much something like that cost. Sipping her coffee she moved around it. Its imploring eyes followed.

"So?" Frank suddenly asked. "Is it another woman?"

She waited for a sign. When none came, she shook her head and paced the living room. Her briefcase was on the coffee table. Frank popped it open. She pulled the file out and paced some more, finished her coffee. After refilling her cup, she settled onto the couch and opened the folder.

She flipped through years worth of DD5s, past her own statement, the deli clerk's statement, pausing at a list of evidence collected on and around her father's body. The list was short. Khaki slacks, navy T-shirt, navy cardigan, brown leather jacket, white crew socks, leather work boots, white shorts. Eighty-three cents in change, one gold Timex watch, one gold wedding band, a single-bladed pocketknife, a key ring, a pack of Winston cigarettes and a Zippo lighter.

Each item conjured a memory but the last was the most vivid. In the still apartment Frank could hear Frank Sinatra under bar chatter, the *click-snap, click-snap, click-snap* of her father's Zippo as she opened and closed it. Over and over, while her father and Uncle Al talked and smoked and drank. She waited for them to pull fresh cigarettes from their packs so she could fire up the Zippo. *Click-snap, click-snap, click-snap.*

She scanned the autopsy report.

"What the hell?"

The coroner had described her father's liver as "mildly cirrhotic." Cirrhosis was a nutritional ailment. She'd had autopsies done on kids whose livers looked like fine pâté instead of sleek, dark organs. Cirrhosis in those cases was caused by severe malnutrition but in most adults it indicated degrees of alcoholism.

"Christ."

Frank pitched the folder onto the couch. She'd never seen her father drunk but he drank every night. He and Uncle Al would put away pitchers at Cal's and knock back occasional shots. At home her parents always drank wine and beer, martinis and champagne on special occasions. Her father's tolerance for alcohol was prodigious. Just like her own.

She laid her head against the back of the couch. A familiar and comfortable anger welled inside her. She wanted to hold it and warm herself with it, but at this delicate stage of sobriety anger was an indulgence she couldn't afford. Instead she found her cell phone. She was relieved when Mary answered, "Hey, kiddo. How's it going?"

"I'm sober."

"Well, that's good. What else?" Frank told her sponsor about the trip to the cemetery. "When Annie suggested maybe it was another woman visiting the grave I wanted to punch her in the mouth. And I wanted to punch me too. Here I am a homicide cop, right? And I haven't even considered another woman. I still don't think it's true—I don't want to think it's true—but I guess I have to accept it might be. Then on top of that, I'm going through his autopsy report and I read he's mildly cirrhotic. He was a drunk, just like me. And a womanizer. I'm telling you, Mary, I'm not liking this. Not one little bit."

"Aren't you putting the cart a little ahead of the horse?"

"You mean the other woman?"

103

"Yeah! You have the poor guy drawn and quartered already! And even if he was involved with someone else, how does that affect how he treated you? Did it make him any less of a father? Did it make him love you any less?"

"No," Frank admitted.

"So get off your pity-potty about this womanizer business. One, you don't even know if it's true, and two, if it is, it doesn't change his love for you, which you were damn lucky to have. Now. So what that he was a drunk? I know some pretty nice people that are drunks." When Frank didn't answer, Mary probed, "It sounds like you've had him pretty high up on a pedestal."

Frank hid a sigh. As it so often did lately, her rage transformed into sadness. Tears replaced her clenched fists.

Mary continued, "That's an easy thing for a child to do. I'm sure this will come up as you work the steps, but for now just know that your father loved you. That's what you need to hang onto. In the end, love is really all that matters. And he loved you. Right?"

Frank caught the Virgin's sorrowful gaze. She closed her eyes and a tear slipped down her cheek. Mary was silent. Frank wiped the tear away, clearing her throat. "I hate how much I still miss him. Being here, at his grave . . . I didn't think after all this time it would be so hard. I didn't think I still cared so much."

"Oh, Frank, honey, of course you care. You have a huge heart. And this is a huge wound that you've never let heal. It scares me that you're doing this so soon in sobriety but I gotta tell you, kiddo, I think you can do it. I think you're ready to open up this scab and air it out, to really let it heal this time instead of just putting a Scotch Band-Aid over it and pretending it's gonna go away. It hurts to scrub out a wound, but that's how to heal it."

Frank had no reply. She'd just have to take it on faith.

"It's gonna be all right, kiddo. You're gonna get through this and you're going to be stronger for having done it. You go ahead and have a good cry. I'd say you're due."

Frank wiped her nose with the back of her hand. "You think?"

"I certainly do. I just wish I could be there with you."

"You absolutely are, Mary. You're here with me right now. Thanks for letting me blow."

"That's what I'm here for, honey. And I'm so happy you called me. You been to a meeting today?"

"No. I'll go tonight."

"Good. You need to stick close right now. It'd be too easy to hide out and crawl into a bottle for a little relief."

"Yeah, I thought about that. The cop I'm working with offered to let me stay at her place and I turned her down. Then I thought it probably wasn't such a good idea to be hanging out alone in a hotel room listening to the bar down below, so I took her up on it."

"Good girl! Where's she live?"

"Got a loft in Tribeca. It's nice. She's a nice lady."

"Well, good for you. I feel better you're with someone. And you know, this *will* end, Frank. One way or another you'll get through to the other side. Pain doesn't last forever."

"That's what I hear." Frank wasn't sure she believed it, but this too she was willing to give the benefit of the doubt. "Thanks for listening, Mary. You're an angel."

"Oh, honey, I'm just so glad I can be here for you."

"You are. Christ!" Frank slapped her forehead. "I'm so busy thinking about myself I completely forgot to ask how your grandson's surgery went."

"Oh, it went fine. They pinned his ankle and he'll be playing second base as good as new. Thanks for asking."

After she said good-bye Frank was left staring at the Virgin.

"You know what?" she told the statue. "I'm hungry."

CHAPTER 20

Annie came home, dropping to her knees in front of the Madonna. She crossed herself and mumbled for a minute. Standing, she saw Frank leaning against the kitchen wall, watching her.

"What? You never seen anybody pray before?"

"What do you pray for?"

"In the mornin' when I leave I pray for a safe day and at night when I come home I give thanks that I made it back in one piece."

"You Catholic?"

"No, I'm Jewish. Whaddaya think? Course I'm Cat'lic."

"Hey, for all I know, you could be. I never studied world religions, okay?"

Annie smirked, slipping out of her coat. "My mother wouldn't say I'm Catholic. She walks in here, she gives the Virgin a wide berth. She thinks it's idolatrous."

"Is it?"

"How should I know? I'm a cop, not a priest. It's Mary. How idolatrous can it be?"

"I took the liberty of making some spaghetti. You hungry?"

"Am I hungry? I could eat the sofa. You're a doll."

"I'll get it for you."

While Annie changed clothes Frank broiled garlic bread and tossed a salad. Dinner was waiting on the kitchen table when Annie returned.

"You cook *and* clean up after yourself," she marveled. "A miracle."

"And your loose change is still around."

Annie laughed, producing two glasses and a bottle of red wine. Frank watched her put the glasses on the table and pull the cork. It made a familiar *pop* and as Annie tipped the bottle Frank laid a hand over her glass.

"No, thanks."

"You don't drink?"

Frank shook her head, admiring the carnelian stream Annie poured into the other glass.

"Only three reasons cops don't drink. They're health nuts, they've found Jesus or they're drunks. Which are you?"

"You're the detective. You figure it out."

Annie grinned, corking the bottle. The wine's scent tickled every cell in Frank's body. Each one leaned toward Annie's glass like eavesdroppers in the old E.F. Hutton commercials.

"All right, Miss Hotshot LAPD lieutenant. You can't be a vegan else you wouldn't a made spaghetti sauce with meat, and it tastes like real butter on this bread. Plus, I saw the dressing came out of a bottle. Too many chemicals for a health nut. So I don't think it's that. Still, it's a better shot than the Jesus freak. A Jesus freak wouldn't a asked if praying to Mary was idolatrous. And I've heard what comes outta your mouth. No Jesus freak talks like that."

Frank grinned.

Wiping spaghetti off her chin, Annie went on. "And the way your hand shot out over that wineglass makes me think you don't even want to be tempted to drink. How'm I doin'?"

"I think you should get promoted."

"How long you been sober?" Annie asked around a mouthful.

"Couple months."

Annie lifted an eyebrow toward her glass. "This bother you?"

"No," Frank lied. As the silence unfolded she added, "I appreciate your letting me stay here. You're right. It's a lot nicer than a hotel."

"Heck, I'm the one who's glad. This is delicious."

"Glad you like it."

"Who's the lucky person you cook for at home?"

"No lucky person right now."

Annie nodded. "It's hard to keep 'em around. Men expect you to be secondary to their careers, but turn the tables and their egos can't handle it."

Deciding to extend the candor, Frank admitted, "I get around that by dating women. Been lucky so far. Been with cops and an M.E. They know what the job demands so they aren't pissed off— well, too pissed off—when they don't see you for days on end."

"Smart." Annie tapped her temple with a fingertip. "Why didn't I think a that?"

" 'Cause your mother would've really had a fit."

Annie laughed, choking on her spaghetti. Washing it down with wine she sputtered, "Oh, God forbid! Bad enough I'm a cop, huh, but a lesbian? She'd come unglued. She would just come unglued. God bless her, she'd starve to death, she'd be so busy lighting candles for me. I guess you didn't have to deal with that, huh?"

"Nope. Advantages to dead parents. They'd have probably been all right with it. My mom for sure, and probably my dad, too. They were pretty laid back."

Frank asked if Annie had caught any more bad guys and she answered, "Thought I'd take a break. But I gotta say, you're my good luck charm. You show up on Sunday and by Tuesday I got three collars. I ain't lettin' you go home."

"I've seen how you work. You make your own luck."

Annie deflected the compliment, asking, "What did you do today besides make a gourmet dinner?"

"Hardly gourmet. Not much. Figured out which subways to Canarsie. Read. Took a little nap."

"Nice." Dabbing the napkin at her mouth, she sat back with her glass of wine. "You know, my son's car is sittin' in the garage being a home for rats and spiders. Use that instead a the subway."

"Why isn't your son using it?"

"Kid thinks he's from California. He had to have a car when he turned sixteen so I bought an old beat-up Nova from a dealer owed me a favor. He drove it six months and realized what a pain it is to drive in the city. I keep it as backup. It's a great surveillance car, but for the most part it sits around gettin' rusty. You take it tomorrow."

Frank was uncomfortable with so much generosity. She fidgeted, asking, "You sure?"

"I'm sure. Wait'll you see it. You might want to take the subway. But if you're sittin' there doing surveil all day at least it'll be a little warmer. Supposed to keep snowing through Thursday, maybe Friday."

Frank nodded. "Okay. But I'm not sure how I can repay all your generosity."

"Are you kiddin'? Way I look at it, you're workin' for me for free. Repay me by helpin' me close your father's case. That's my payment."

"Deal." Checking her watch, Frank told Annie she was going to an AA meeting.

"Oh, yeah? I got a cousin goes to AA. He's a different man since he stopped drinkin'. Got a beautiful wife, an adorable three-year-old and a baby on the way. Couple years ago, I was sure I was gonna have to escort his mother to the morgue. But he's got his act together now."

Frank nodded. "You like ice cream?"

"Doesn't everybody?"

"I was gonna get some on my way back. What flavor you like?"

"Aw, get whatever you like. I'll be in bed by the time you get back. I'll see you in the mornin', huh? We'll go down and see if Ben's car starts."

"Okay. Sleep well." Frank stopped before she left the kitchen. "I really appreciate all this, Annie."

"Psh. It's nothin'. Get outta here."

Frank walked north, through the snow. Along the way she passed bums clumped together with bottles, huddled under cardboard tents or curled in tattered sleeping bags. Hunched against the sharp wind, she was glad she wasn't among them. And well aware she could be.

CHAPTER 21

No stranger to surveillance, Frank thought it the most physically challenging of all police work. For days, sometimes weeks on end, a surveillance team sat in the front seat of an unmarked sedan. They stayed there hours at a time, unable to stretch protesting muscles. They ate junk food, drank too much coffee and then spent most of the shift wondering when they could take a leak.

If the surveillance went down at night, there were no lights; in winter, no heat; in summer, no air conditioning. The detectives had to stay alert, focusing only on their subject and the street. They couldn't distract themselves with magazines, books or crossword puzzles. Or at least shouldn't. Frank rode with an old robbery cop who read the newspaper while she was on the eye. When he was done reading he'd do the daily puzzles. To his credit, he usually spotted their target before she did.

By comparison, setting up on the Canarsie Cemetery was a cakewalk. Frank's biggest concern was nosy neighbors calling the cops about her daily presence. To avoid a police scene, Annie notified the 69th Precinct of Frank's surveillance. They clamored for part of the action until Annie explained it was a long-shot setup on a homicide almost four decades old.

Frank found a parking spot on Remsen Avenue. It was a couple cars behind where she'd have liked to be, but by sitting on the passenger side she had a good view of her parents' plot and its approach. She locked the car and walked to the plot. There were no fresh flowers. No new footprints in the snow.

She returned to the relative warmth of the car. Annie was right about the Nova—it was perfect for surveillance. Dented and rusted, windows cracked, it looked like a small-time hustler's car. The upholstery was held together with duct tape and the dashboard was split like a busted lip. But it ran and the heater blew hot air. Even the radio worked. Frank turned it on, pouring a mug of coffee from the Thermos Annie had filled for her.

Her briefcase was on the floor of the passenger seat. She hadn't looked at it since reading her father's autopsy protocol. She knew she should plow through it, scrutinize it as closely as she would any other file, but she couldn't psych herself into thinking this was an ordinary homicide. Maybe it would be best to avoid reading it altogether. As Annie made clear, Frank didn't have any objectivity on the case. What was there to gain by poring through it?

But she had to try. It was only fear stopping her and she was tired of letting fear have its way with her. Yanking the briefcase up into the passenger seat she snapped the latch and pulled out the folder. Her statement topped the thin pile of supporting documents. Slipping it from the folder, she approved of the detective's neat typing. Homicide reports were always so coolly removed from the gore of their subject, all black ink and white paper, straight lines and precise edges. Clean, tidy and nicely sanitized.

She remembered Detective Heller. He was thin and young, maybe early thirties. He'd been patient with her but not overly kind. Having done it herself so many times, Frank surmised it had probably been hard for him to interview her. He had just kept his distance, trying not to get involved in her grief and pain.

The amount of detail in the report surprised her. She'd forgotten the suspect wore a black sweater with holes in it; the hand holding the gun was scraped; a long cut under his right cheekbone looked infected; he was missing an upper tooth; he was using a piece of yellow rope for a belt and he wore frayed black high tops—all useful at the time, but none of it relevant today.

She'd said the junkie had a little bit of an accent. Heller noted he had repeated the suspect's demands, as stated by the witness, in various accents but that said witness hadn't recognized any of them. Frank remembered how confused she'd been. Heller hadn't sounded anything like the junkie, but he kept trying and she kept shaking her head, looking to Uncle Al for help.

After Heller cut her loose she and her uncle drove through the pre-dawn streets. She was the one person who could identify the junkie. They searched alleys and corners, stoops and shooting galleries. They searched but failed to find. Long after the sun had struggled up, with her mother sedated and snoring, Frank took that failure to bed with her. And had every night since.

"Christ," Frank whispered, fighting back an avalanche of tears.

She remembered a burly, tattooed marine at one of her first AA meetings. His mother had been killed in a car crash when he was only eight years old. Tears cascaded down his face as he told the group his story. When he'd started crying at the funeral his father had taken him aside and told him to stop. That men didn't cry. So he never had. Started drinking when he was nine. Quit almost thirty years later after his second heart attack. The marine had wiped his tears away, smiling as he said, "Now I cry whenever I want to and I don't give a fuck who sees me."

Frank figured if a marine could cry she could too. She let them come. They were embarrassing but no one could see. She cried for her crazy mother, her lost father and the kid who'd tried to make sense of it all when there was no sense to be had.

She let the tears run dry then looked for something to blow her nose on. There wasn't anything. Opening the door, Frank did the Okie blow onto the street. It was gross and messy but she pulled the door shut with a smile. If anyone was watching it looked perfect. What better cover than an aggrieved woman crying outside the cemetery?

Oddly serene, Frank dried her cheeks with her palms. She got out of the car and stretched. Keeping her father's grave in view she walked the graveled roads within the cemetery. She read the headstones, their names heavy and familiar—Gosline, Voorhis, Schenk, Van Houten, McCrodden and Knutsen. Dozens of graves held veterans, from the Civil War all the way through Vietnam.

The cemetery's history was compelling. From old history lessons she knew the city of Canarsie went back to the Canarsie Indians. The natives were routed by the Dutch, who were displaced by English, and then George Washington kicked everyone out so that anyone could come in.

Frank's tour woke a nostalgia she didn't know she had. She thought she'd cut her ties to the past but its roots seemed to be thriving beneath her consciousness. Even her body betrayed her, reacting instinctively to familiar sights and smells and sounds. Despite decades in southern California, even the New York winter was welcome. She wanted to make snowballs and pitch them at unsuspecting pedestrians, like she and her cousins used to do. Or fall backward into a drift pile and make snow angels.

Shooing the memories with a shake of her head, Frank ambled back to the car.

She poured the last of the coffee and took *The Da Vinci Code* from her briefcase. Propping it just below her line of sight, she settled against the door, delighting in the simplicity of her stakeout. Before turning a page she scanned the cemetery. She read like this, indulging in the pure pleasure of it for almost two hours.

After using the cemetery restroom, she leaned against the Nova and called Figueroa. Diego picked up and she said, "Hey, Taquito. Let me talk to the great Picasso."

She heard Diego grunt to Bobby, who answered in a voice softer than rose petals.

"Picasso. How's it going?"

"Good. We closed out all our old pendings and are just sitting around waiting for the phone to ring."

"Damn. I shoulda done this a long time ago."

Bobby chuckled. "It's pretty quiet. We caught a domestic yesterday, but the guy was right there in the apartment when a unit responded. Easy slam dunk."

"Sweet. What else?"

"Remember that guy Irie told us about? Fidelio Ramirez? We traced him to a friend's house in Phoenix. Phoenix PD are looking for him. He's got three priors we can hold him on—one possession and two assaults—and if Phoenix finds him I was thinking of sending Lewis and Darcy out to get him. Is that okay?"

"Sounds fine. Do you have the paperwork ready?"

"No, I was going to call you about that."

Frank walked him through an extradition and clarified a few other things. After a little chitchat, she hung up. Despite her nostalgia, she missed her squad and was eager to be home.

The rest of the day passed dreamily. It was hard on Frank's ass but she was grateful for the down time. The cemetery had a fair trickle of visitors. Frank perked up when a few got close to her father's site but none lingered. When the gates closed, she meandered back to Tribeca by way of Dean and Deluca's. The prices were vulgar but considering what she'd pay to eat out she indulged. Plus, when she complained to Mary about how many doughnuts she was eating or how much she was spending on lattés, Mary always assured her that she could do whatever she wanted in the first year of sobriety.

"Worry about diabetes and bankruptcy later," she said. "For now, just focus on stayin' sober. If it takes doughnuts and lattés, so be it. It's better than drinkin'!"

With that in mind, Frank wheeled past the wine display, dropping two pints of Cherry Garcia and a bag of cookies into the cart. What the hell, she thought, adding another bag. A woman had to have *something* to do during surveillance.

CHAPTER 22
Thursday—13 Jan 05, Tribeca

I still got it.

Made a spectacular dinner. Pork loin roasted in black currant and apple glaze, surrounded by roasted butternut squash and potatoes, accompanied by autumn fruit chutney and sautéed chard with pignoli and red currants. Washed it all down with sparkling pear juice—okay, so pear juice doesn't have the panache of a Fumé or a Chard, but still and all it was damn good. Especially for a woman who didn't think she'd ever cook again.

Bought everything at Dean & Deluca's. I've wanted to shop there since I was a kid. Insanely expensive but worth it to see Annie's face when I served her dinner. She's fun to cook for, grateful, and it makes me feel useful. And I'm hungry. Really hungry. Maybe it's the weather, but I actually enjoyed cooking for the first time since I quit drinking. Maybe because I was in a different kitchen. No memories or empty liquor cabinets to haunt me.

Maybe I should move. Rent the house out and get an apartment closer to work. There's too many memories at home. Leaving that house would really be leaving Maggie. Maybe it's time. Leave Maggie, the booze, all the old hurts. Make a fresh start. I feel like I'm starting a whole new life—someone said in a meeting that the only thing that changes when you quit drinking is everything. And I'm starting to see that. How old habits and ideas have to go. Like holding onto my pain. It's all got to go. It's stuff I have to look square in the eye and say good-bye to, no matter how difficult or painful.

Cried at the cemetery today. Embarrassing as hell but it felt good. Like lancing an abscess and letting all the pus drain out. Felt clean when I was done. Raw, but clean.

This sobriety is a trip. Got to admit it's kind of interesting to see where it's going to take me next. Hell of a lot more interesting than sitting on my couch with one hand wrapped around a liter and the other around a 9-millimeter. Hey, I'm a fucking poet! Christ, what a life that was. Fucking sad. And crazy. Apple doesn't fall far from the tree. Mildly cirrhotic like dear old Da, and mildly mental like dear old Ma. Yeah, okay so maybe I fell close to the tree, but I landed on a hill, baby, and I'm rolling. Watch me—

CHAPTER 23

Frank put the pen down when her phone rang. The number on the screen was Gail's.

"Hey," Frank answered.

"Hey yourself. How's it going?"

"It's going. No match to the prints but we talked to the groundskeepers at the cemetery and they say the flowers are changed about every two weeks, so I'm staking the place out."

"Did they know who was leaving the flowers?"

"Nah. Whoever it is apparently comes during the weekend when they're off, so I still don't even know if it's a man or a woman. To show you how unobjective I am about this, Annie suggested maybe it was an old flame and I about came undone. In a normal case that probably would have occurred to me in five minutes, but here? No way. Still don't like the idea but I've braced myself for it. Promised Annie that if and when I see whoever it is, I won't talk to her. Or him. Just tail our mystery guest and let Annie do the interviewing. Least I can do, right? It's her case."

"Well, maybe you'll find him or her this weekend. Then you can come home."

"Maybe. With any luck."

"Would you like me to pick you up when you come in?"

"That'd be wonderful, if you have time."

"Let me know when and I'll see if I can swing it."

"You got it. Thanks. How you doing?"

"I'm okay. Tired. Wish I was still on vacation. Did you hear about Rodney Bentley?"

"The old anchor for KABC?"

"Yeah. During the last storm he called nine-one-one claiming his wife and two kids were trapped in a car that had gone off the road into the LA River. He said she'd called on her cell phone crying that they were being carried off by the current. Two hours later CHP retrieved the car with everyone dead inside. We did a routine autopsy but there wasn't any fluid in the wife's lungs, plus she has markings around her neck and petechial hemorrhage inconsistent with drowning. So it looks more like triple homicide than accidental death and the media's in a feeding frenzy. I even had a reporter waiting outside my apartment when I got home last night."

"Who caught the case?"

"The Sheriff's Department. Did Bobby tell you about the domestic you had?"

"Yeah. Said it was a slam dunk."

"How are they getting along without you?"

"Surprisingly well. Seems I'm completely expendable."

"Not completely."

"How so?"

After a long pause, Gail said, "I probably shouldn't say this, but I miss you."

"You do?"

"Yeah. A little."

"Only a little?"

"Don't push it."

"Yeah, I'm bad at that, huh?"

"You certainly are. But I had a good time with you. You were fun and easy to be with. Like the old Frank, but better."

"I had a good time, too. I almost called you a couple times but stopped myself. Don't want to push."

"A phone call's not pushing."

"No?"

"Um-um."

Gail sounded soft and willing. Frank wanted to reach through the line and hang on to her. To touch her, smell her, kiss her, make love to her . . .

"Are you there?"

"Yeah." Frank opened her eyes. "I'm here. How was the *Phantom of the Opera?*"

"Oh, my God, it was fantastic! It was so worth waiting for."

Frank couldn't stop herself from asking, "Did your friend from the frigid north enjoy it?"

"Yes, she did. Then we both went back to our respective hotels. Speaking of which, where are you staying?"

"Uh, I'm at Annie's. She's letting me stay in her guest room."

"My. That's convenient."

"Yeah, it is. Beats a hotel."

"I'll bet. Talk about chummy."

Gail didn't sound sweet anymore and Frank was happy that she cared enough to be worried about another woman.

"Is she a lesbian?"

"No. Not at all."

"What does she look like?"

"Annie? She's Italian. Thick salt-and-pepper hair. Conservative cut. Dark eyes. Great features. A little thick around the waist but fairly trim." Gail didn't say anything so Frank added, "She's handsome, but not nearly as beautiful as you."

Gail remained silent.

Frank looked at her phone, saw she was still connected. "You there?"

"I'm here," was the cool reply.

120

Frank couldn't resist teasing Gail. "So, this jealousy of yours. That a particular trait of sobriety?"

"Oh, please. Why would I be jealous? You're not even my girl-friend anymore."

"We could change that."

"I wouldn't want to interfere with you and *Annie*."

"There's nothing to interfere with. You gotta know my heart belongs to one gal."

"Hmph."

Frank chuckled, thrilled Gail cared so much. "Can I call you tomorrow?"

"If you're not busy. With Annie."

"I won't be. Try and get some sleep, okay?"

"I'll do my best."

" 'Kay. Good night."

"Night."

Frank hung up, trading phone for journal, smiling as she wrote.

CHAPTER 24

Gail just called. She misses me. Tadow! And she's jealous of Annie. Excellent. Means I'm still in the game. Like Robert DeNiro said in The Deerhunter, *"One shot, Nicky. Just one shot."*

That's what I've got. One shot to make this work. But if I'm patient and aim carefully, one shot is all I'll need. Maybe I ought to kneel down and talk to Annie's statue. Get a little extra mojo going on. Call Marguerite James and get a juju bag. Went to a meeting tonight and someone said getting sober's like listening to a country-western song in reverse—you get your car back, you get your job back, you get your lady back. No shit. You get your life back. The one you're supposed to be living if you aren't busy horking your guts up over a toilet or sucking on a barrel.

Go figure. Anyway. Shouldn't get too excited yet. But missing me is good. Very good. Big step. Christ, I hope I'm not wrong about this. I want her back in the worst way. I want a second chance. May not deserve one but that won't keep me from wanting it. That's an interesting thing, wanting. I've never let myself do much of that. Too disappointing when I don't get what I want. But here I am, wanting Gail, wanting my dad's killer. Even weirder, if I don't get either one, I'll still be okay. It's like nothing can ever be as bad as the Beretta in my mouth. Or picking up a drink. Nothing can ever hurt me as badly as that. Weird. I love her and I want her but if she says no, this isn't gonna work, than I'll be sad but I'll be okay. I'm not going to flip out. Still, I hope it's yes.

Christ, I hope it's yes.

CHAPTER 25

Friday evening, as Frank opened the apartment door Annie was slipping her key into the lock.

"Oh! You scared me," Annie said, hand over her heart.

"Sorry. I was just heading out to dinner. Care to join me?"

"Where you goin'?"

"I don't know. Thought I'd wander around until I saw something that looked good."

"There's a great chop house couple blocks from here. It's expensive but good, and what the hell, it's Friday, right?"

"Sure. Your call."

"Terrific. Just give me a minute to change, huh?"

"Take your time."

Annie put her purse down and knelt for a quick, mumbled prayer. Frank discretely waited at the window. She watched the street while Annie changed clothes.

"Ready," Annie called behind her, fussing with her purse. She was wearing a tunic sweater over slacks with pearl studs and a necklace. She'd touched up her makeup, too. She reminded Frank of someone but before she could put her finger on who, Annie told her, "Oh, hey. I got the report back on your prints. No match for 'em, I'm afraid."

"Damn." Frank sighed. "Oh, well. Guess I keep waiting."

"I guess so. Sorry."

"That's okay. At least the company's good."

They walked in the cold night and Annie asked, "Quiet out there today?"

"Couple funerals, handful of visitors, but nobody at the grave."

Annie puzzled, "What are you gonna do if this person don't show? You can't stay forever, right?"

"I was thinkin' of hiring a P.I. Know any good ones?"

"Sure. Charlie Mercer. He does private work. He'd probably do it for you."

"You're not just being biased?"

"Cookie, what you and I know together don't match what Charlie knows. Don't underestimate him just 'cause he's old."

"Just asking."

"I'll give you his number. You can talk to him. Cross here."

Annie cut through a knot of double-parked cars. Frank followed. As she squeezed between two sedans, a huge pit bull lunged from a front seat. The beast gnashed at a half-open window, growling in a frenzy of slobber and teeth. Frank spun, searching for her gun. It took a second to realize she didn't have it and another second to realize she didn't need it. The dog slavered at the air outside the window, but it was safely behind the glass.

Annie laughed, "Holy cannoli! He scared the *crap* outta me!"

Frank stared at the salivating brute.

"Hey." Annie tugged her sleeve.

Frank didn't move.

"Frank? Hey. Whatsa matter?"

Tearing her gaze from the dog long enough to glance at Annie, Frank answered, "Nothing."

"Nothing? You're white as a ghost. What's the matter with you? You afraid of dogs?"

"I'm okay."

"Come on." Annie pulled at Frank's arm again. "Look at you. You're shaking."

Frank crossed the street, wondering if her legs were going to hold her up. She felt queasy and stopped to lean against a building. She rubbed her right forearm.

"Did it bite you?" Annie asked.

Frank shook her head. "Long story." She took a couple deep breaths, willing the nausea away.

"You want I should get a cab?"

"No. I'm okay. Just . . . give me a sec. Catch my breath."

Frank tested her legs. Annie walked close beside her.

"I'm okay," Frank assured. "Not gonna keel over on you."

"You sure about that?" Annie was still peering at her. "For a minute there I thought I was gonna have to do CPR on you."

"Nah, I'm okay."

"Well, at least your color's back. You just drained, my friend. Looked like Dracula'd got hold of you."

"Sorry. Didn't mean to scare you."

"Don't worry about it. I been scared worse."

The restaurant was at the end of the block. Annie opened the door for her and the first thing Frank saw was the bar. Under the aroma of seared meat the scent of liquor set her cells aquiver. She concentrated on the other patrons, eyeing them as if she'd have to write them up in a report. The hostess asked if they had a reservation.

Annie said, "No, hon, but we're just two. And my friend here needs to eat or she's gonna faint dead away."

After glancing at Frank, the hostess must have believed Annie. Grabbing two menus, she announced with a worried smile, "This way, ladies."

They settled at a table and Frank studied the menu. She couldn't help but pair each entrée with the perfect wine and contemplated ordering dessert for dinner. But she'd been running on doughnuts and cookies all day so decided on sensible food, telling the waitress, "I'll have a dozen oysters on the half shell, the beet salad and onion rings."

"Very good," the waitress said. "As dinner or as appetizers?"

"Dinner."

"And to drink?"

A bottle of Chardonnay, Frank thought. Better yet two. "Water," she answered.

Annie ordered and after the waitress had brought her a glass of wine Annie asked, "So what's the story with the dog?"

Frank tore her eyes from the glass. "Weird case. We had this Santería priestess who we knew was offing people. First time I interviewed her she warned me about a red dog. I just laughed and forgot all about it. Couple weeks later this pit bull got loose near the station and latched onto my arm." She pushed up her sleeve to show Annie the scars. "Ripped into an artery and did some nerve damage. My thumb's still numb."

"Was the dog red?"

"Yep."

"Creepy."

"That wasn't even half of it. Got weirder. I had this like . . . vision while the dog was chewing on my arm. Of me and this Mother Love character. It was like we were adversaries doing battle in a different time and place. Very strange. I dismissed it as a by-product of shock but then it happened again. A couple times. Just this same vision of us dueling to the death. It was really vivid. And to tell the truth, it scared the hell outta me. At the same time, I had a witness in this case I was working against the Mother. But he was terrified to talk. He was sure she'd hexed him and that he was gonna die if he went against her. So to get him to testify we persuaded him that another priestess could undo Mother Love's hex, could turn it around so that he'd be protected from her. After I got him worked on by this priestess, she looked at me and said, 'I see Mother Love's hand all over you.' I laughed then, too."

Annie sipped her wine, distracting Frank. It was only her second sip. Frank would have been working on her second glass by now.

"And?" Annie prompted.

"And then I started having these visions all the time. I called Marguerite back—the good witch, we called her—and I let her do this cleansing ceremony on me. What the hell, right? Maybe there was something to it. Long story short, I was stupid and Mother Love ended up getting me alone in her warehouse. Had me strung up by my heels, ready to slit my throat and sacrifice me to one of her gods. Marguerite had said the Mother and I were in mortal combat and that the only way to beat her was to pray. Hanging there like a side of beef, you bet your ass I prayed. Strange so far, right?"

"You could say that."

"Gets better. I'm strung up there, totally helpless and I'm praying to this friend of mine, old partner. The other cops used to tease us. Said we had a Vulcan mind-meld thing going on. We knew each other so well we could usually anticipate what the other was going to do. So I'm calling him, trying to get him to feel my vibes, right, and come save my ass. I'm praying to Mickey Mouse, the spirit of Houdini, anybody who can get me outta this jam, and in busts my new detective. His ex-wife is the good witch. He knows all about this Santería jive 'cause of his wife and growing up in Louisiana. But he's got a gift too. Told one of my other detectives where to find a forty-four she'd been looking for. Sure enough, it was in a fridge just like Darcy'd said it would be. Anyway, he comes in, big shootout, I guess—I'd passed out by then—and later in the hospital I ask him how the hell he knew where I was. See, I hadn't told anybody where I was going. No one could have known where I was. He said he just kept seeing the Mother's warehouse and had this overwhelming feeling that I was in trouble."

Frank sat back as the waitress brought their meals. Patting her napkin over her lap, Annie observed, "You sound like one lucky kitten."

Frank smiled. Annie didn't even know about the 9-millimeter.

"If I were you, I'd light a candle, making your guardian angel work overtime like that."

Slurping an oyster, Frank needled, "You believe in angels? They come with the Madonna?"

Annie jabbed a finger. "Let me tell *you* a story." Between bites of steak, she narrated. "When I was sixteen we went upstate for a vacation in the Catskills. I'm swimming in this lake. I love swimming. It's late afternoon, everyone else is either napping or eating another sandwich, whatever, and I decide to swim across the lake. No big deal. The lake's only about a half a mile wide and I was a good swimmer. Piece a cake, right? So off I go. I get across to the other side. It's nice and quiet, peaceful. I rest a while 'cause the water's pretty cold, then I start swimming back. Don't you know I get this cramp. That's okay, I've had cramps before, like a Charlie horse, you know. Get it in my thigh, so I float a minute and while I'm floating I get this huge cramp in the small of my back. My God, it's like I've been whacked with a sledgehammer. Of course my first instinct is to double over, right? Which I did. And I was so startled by the pain that I gasped and breathed in all this water. I tried to straighten up, get my head above water, but I couldn't. It was like my back was frozen. I tried rolling over but I couldn't stay afloat, couldn't keep my head up. As I was turning back down into the water I caught a breath, only it was more water than air and I started choking. I'm breathing in more water and thinking, oh, my God, I'm gonna freakin' die out here. This is it. I mean, time stopped. Everything was getting gray and I couldn't get my head outta the water." Annie held a finger over the plate of onion rings. "Think I could have one?"

"Oh, sure." Frank pushed the plate closer. "Help yourself. So what happened?"

"So what happened is, I feel this whack on my arm, like it's in a vise, right? And I get yanked. I break the surface and look up into this old woman's face. She's got wrinkles, long gray hair, and she's draggin' me over the side of the boat. Haulin' me in like a prize catch. And let me tell you, I ain't no lightweight. Not back then, neither. I'm sittin' there doubled over, coughin' my lungs out, shakin' like a leaf. She wraps this scratchy wool blanket around me—it stunk to high heaven. Mold, diesel fuel, and let me tell you I've never been so grateful for anything in my life than that rotten old blanket—I point and cough out where I live and she takes me to the shore. Helps me out, watches me walk up the path toward the cabin we was staying in. I tell my mother and my aunts what happened and they're practically hysterical. They spend the whole night making food for this woman and the next morning we all set off to find out who she is and where she lives."

Annie sipped her wine. Frank was so engrossed in the story that it didn't bother her.

Wagging a finger, she continued, "We spent the whole day, I'm telling you the entire day, sunup to sundown, talking to people in town trying to figure out who this old gal could be. Some woman from the city staying at one of the cabins? A local? A hermit? Who was this broad? And you know what? And I'm talkin' a little town here. Out in the middle of nowheres. Everybody knows everybody and they know each other's business. But not one person had a clue who we were talking about. Everybody said no, there's nobody like that around here. And this isn't a huge lake, either. Way it's shaped, way the banks were, there's only really four places a person could get a boat in. At the third boat ramp, my aunt tells the story to an old man coming back in. He listens and when my aunt's done he breaks into a big smile.

"'Sounds like you met old Ruth,' he says. My mother's crying, 'Who's this Ruth? Where can we find her?' The old man kept smiling. He tilted his head toward the lake. 'Reckon she's out there somewheres,' he said. 'But you ain't gonna find her lest she wants you to.'

"'Well, we have all this food,' my mother said. 'We want to thank her. How can we get it to her?'

"The old man shrugged. 'Put it in the lake,' he said. 'That's where you'll find her. Old Ruthie's boat went down about two miles from here, oh, close on to twenty-five years ago.'

"My aunt said, 'You mean . . .' and the old man nodded. 'Pulled a little boy outta the lake 'bout six years ago. A woman before that. Pregnant. Heard she had twins.'"

Annie sopped her plate with a piece of bread. "Let me tell you. I never seen my mother cross herself so fast. Speed crossing. If you'd a timed her, she'd a broke a record. So do I believe in guardian angels? Damn right I do."

"If this old woman had saved so many people how come no one knew who you were talking about?"

"Oh, they knew all right. But the old man said they was afraid of Ruthie. Claimed she'd taken as many lives as she'd saved. Why she saved me, I can't say. Alls I know is, I'm freakin' glad she did."

"Me too," Frank said. "Is that why you do the Mary business? The praying and all that?"

Spearing an onion ring, Annie said, "That's one reason. I been lucky all my life, you know? But it ain't luck. I call it that, but it ain't. It's providence. I believe someone's watchin' out for me. Someone who's got plans for me. Drives my mother crazy but I tell her, when the bullet with my name on it comes for me there ain't nothin' I can do to stop it. On the other hand, there's nothin' I can do to make that bullet come until it's ready. That's all outta my hands. Meanwhile, I'm grateful for each day I get."

Frank snapped her fingers. "I got it. You know who you look like?"

Rolling her eyes, Annie groaned. "Anne Bancroft."

"That's right."

"Pretty slow for a detective. I get people askin' for my autograph all the time. I give it to 'em. I tell you, half a New York thinks Anne Bancroft's real name is Silvester."

"You're terrible."

"What? They go away happy, I get my fifteen minutes a fame, and everyone thinks Anne Bancroft's a nice lady. Who's hurt?"

The waitress cleared their plates and over dessert they swapped cop stories. When the waitress slid the bill folder between them Frank reached for it. She put her credit card inside and left the folder by her elbow.

"Give it here," Annie said, waggling her fingers.

"Nope. It's on me."

"Don't be ridiculous. Give me the bill."

"Uh-uh. Think how much money I'd be spending on a hotel. Least I can do is buy you dinner."

Annie protested, "You can't feed me every night."

"Why not?" Frank smiled. "Just accept it as a small token of my gratitude and let it go at that, huh?"

"Some small token. That's a hundred-dollar bill."

Frank shrugged. "One night at the Seventeen. Believe me, it's worth it for the company."

"Stop with the compliments already. And that goes both ways, you know. The company being worth it."

Holding the door for Annie on their way out, Frank asked, "If you want company, why don't you rent one of your rooms out? You're sittin' on a gold mine there."

"Psh. I tried that. I don't want just any company. Besides, this way Ben and Lisa got a place to stay when they come to visit. Other times I let some of the guys crash there. There's a couple of 'em live outta the city. It's nice for 'em if it's real late or we been working back-to-backs. Oh, yeah, that reminds me, I'm having dinner at my mother's tomorrow. You should join us."

"That's nice, but with any luck tomorrow we'll be interviewing a suspect and eating at McDonald's."

Touching Frank's arm, Annie cautioned, "Don't get your hopes up too high."

"I know. Wishful thinking. And thanks for the invite but I'll pass."

"Suit yourself, but you're gonna miss my mother's cooking. She's making spaghetti with my cousin Bill's venison sausage. I'm tellin' you, cookie, it's to die for."

"I'm sure it is, but you're about all the company I can handle lately."

"Whaddaya mean?"

Frank shrugged. "I'm just enjoying all this down time. The surveillance is easy, I've been reading a lot, and it's nice to come back to your place and not have to do anything. No files to work on, no reports due. It's like for the first time in my life I'm starting to unwind. It's nice. And it's about all I can handle at one time. So I appreciate the offer but I think I'll order pizza and finish my book."

"Rent a movie if you want. There's a Blockbuster couple blocks away. I'll leave you my card."

"You know," Frank said, avoiding the cars parked along the sidewalk. "I feel rotten I gave you such a hard time that first day. You've been nothing but great to me. I can't tell you how much I appreciate it."

Annie laughed. "You came on kinda strong. Then me workin' two homicides for two days straight. It's a miracle we're standin' here at all."

Frank ribbed, "Must be my guardian angel lookin' out for me, huh?"

Annie warned, "Don't you laugh, my friend. Don't you laugh."

CHAPTER 26

Despite telling Annie otherwise, Frank was excited on Saturday morning. Annie was still sleeping so Frank dressed quietly and slipped out to drop off her extra clothes at a Chinese laundry down the street. By the time she got back Annie was sitting in the kitchen. She had the *Times* propped in front of her and was talking on the phone.

Frank held up a bag of bagels and Annie said into the phone, "I got a friend from LA stayin' wit me. She's gone out for bagels already, can you believe it?" She laughed and said, "I'll talk to you later, hon. Bye-bye." Hanging up, she told Frank, "For Pete's sake, I'm gonna have to go on a diet when you leave."

Even in a baggy blue bathrobe Annie looked fit, and Frank answered, "Not from what I can see."

"Yeah, well, you can't see it all, cookie." Annie patted her tummy. "Believe me, it's there."

"Okay," Frank relented, laying the out the shmears. "More for me."

"How do you stay so slim?"

"Hardly slim. Gained fifteen pounds since I stopped drinking. I work out when I'm at home. I have a gym and a treadmill. Knees are startin' to bother me though. Can't run as long as I want to."

"Tell me about it. I used to run in the morning before the kids were up. Got shin splints somethin' awful. Had to quit. I been swimming for about six years now. I try to go three times a week. 'Course I don't always make it, but it's better than nothing."

"Anything's good," Frank agreed. "So if I need to call you today you'll be on your cell phone?"

Annie poured coffee for both of them. "Yeah. I'll be here working on reports I shoulda gotten to during the week. I'm going to my mother's about three. Offer still stands."

"No, thanks. Mind if I look at the sports section?"

"All yours." Annie handed it over. They ate in companionable silence until Frank got up to shower. Flattening the Metro section against the table, Annie said, "You change your mind, you call me."

Traffic was heavy out to Canarsie, worsened by a funeral procession as she neared the cemetery. She had to park a couple blocks away until the mourners left, then she claimed a space on the east side of the cemetery. There was another funeral that afternoon but by closing time no one had lingered near her father's grave. Frank returned to the city, mildly disappointed.

She stopped at the central AA office to pick up a meeting schedule. After eyeing her up and down the cute gay guy helping her pouted. "You just missed an absolutely fabulous gay and lesbian meeting in the Village. Oh, here's one! Gay, lesbian and transgender on West Thirteenth at eight thirty *and* nine thirty!"

"Thanks," she said. "Maybe I'll check it out."

"You do that, honey. And good luck!"

Downstairs in the Nova, Frank studied the meeting schedule, deciding on a seven thirty at Trinity Place. In the meantime, she picked up her laundry, then stopped at a breakfast joint, reading her Big Book over coffee and corned beef hash.

She was cool with Step One. Admitting she was powerless over alcohol and that her life had become unmanageable was a no-brainer. Normal people don't sit around downing quarts of whiskey and encouraging themselves to blow their brains out. Step One was simple. But Frank balked at Step Two, which stated, "Came to believe that a power greater than ourselves could restore us to sanity." She read the chapter dedicated to agnostics and left the restaurant chewing on more than a toothpick.

She called Mary but got her machine. Frank left a message that she was fine and headed for a meeting. She found Trinity Place but parking was nonexistent. Three blocks away she wedged the Nova into a space and jogged back to Trinity Place. Mary had strict guidelines and one of them was to not be late for meetings. It was distracting to others, it didn't give you a chance to introduce yourself, and worst of all, you missed the readings. She said practically everything you needed to know about getting sober and staying sober were read in the first five minutes of every AA meeting.

Frank got into the room just as the secretary cleared her throat to announce, "Hi. My name is Jenny and I'm an alcoholic."

As they finished conversations and fixed coffee, men and women, old and young, punk and square, responded, "Hi, Jenny!"

Frank slipped into a seat between a woman who looked like a stockbroker and a man who looked like he'd crawled in from out of the gutter. While Jenny read the AA preamble Frank marveled at the contrast between the drunks sitting next to her.

The wino smelled rank but the stockbroker hinted of very elegant perfume. She was immaculately dressed in a tailored wool suit and the wino wore what he'd found in a dumpster. He gripped his hands in his lap but they were still shaking. The stockbroker's hands were steady and clean with buffed pink nails. Contrasts abounded in the small room, reminding Frank to look for the similarities that made her part of the group rather than the differences that kept her apart, a nice idea for humanity in general.

When Jenny asked if there was anyone visiting from out of town or new to the Trinity Place meeting, Frank spoke up. "My name's Frank. I'm an alcoholic from Los Angeles."

There were welcomes around the room, then Jenny went on to announcements.

The stockbroker leaned toward Frank, extending her smooth, white hand. "Hi," she whispered. "I'm Margaret. Can I get you a cup of coffee?"

Frank took the hand and accepted the offer. "Black would be great."

Leaning around Frank, Margaret touched the wino's knee. "Mick? Coffee?"

Mick looked up with painfully red eyes and nodded. Margaret rose gracefully, returning with three cups. Frank took her cup and as Margaret turned toward the wino Frank took his cup for him. His hands were shaking so hard he could barely lift them. She settled the milky coffee between them. He smiled his thanks, managing with both hands to bring the cup to his lips.

Frank was struck by an awkward, teary gratitude, thinking that was how it worked in AA—steady hands being held out to those whose were still shaky.

Jenny turned the meeting over to the speaker, a doe-eyed waif who looked like she'd just given up the tit. For the next twenty minutes she told a story of escalating horrors that climaxed with kidnapping her sister for enough ransom to buy a key of heroin and a case of Jack Daniels. When her twelve-year-old sibling looked at her and asked why she was doing this, the waif suddenly took it all in—the stained mattress she was living on, the pain in her sister's eyes, the hole in her gut that she could never fill, and just as suddenly she knew a case and a key would never be enough. That she'd need another case and another key after they ran out until she died like her friend had, with a hot load in her arm.

She kept tears back as she continued. "My parents took the money they were going to give me for my sister and instead of just writing me off they put me into a ninety-day rehab. That was four years ago and I haven't used or drank since." Clearing her throat and swiping her knuckles across her eyes she said in a clear voice, "For those of you that are new, welcome. I hope you keep coming back. When I first started coming into these rooms I did the things that were suggested to me." She ticked off on her fingers. "I didn't drink or use between meetings. I went to a lot of meetings. I got a sponsor. I worked the steps with her. I got into service, and, well, eventually I trusted God. That was hard for me. All the other stuff was easy but I was raised in a Baptist household where there was only one, true God. And you can believe it when I say I didn't want anything to do with *that* God. So if you're new, don't worry about all the God talk. God is one force with many faces. It'll find you and present itself to you in a form you can handle. For me, God's in the sun. I know I can count on it to be there every day. Always. And even at night, just because I can't see it, that doesn't mean it's not there. It was there long before I was born and it'll be there long after I'm gone. I like that there's something more dependable and durable out there than just me." Everyone laughed when she chuckled. " 'Cause relying on myself just ended up with me thinking that kidnapping my sister was an absolutely genius idea. So I'm glad to be here, I'm glad you're here, and I'd like to call on our visitor from Los Angeles."

Mary told Frank to share when she was called on, and to share a feeling, not the weather or how nicely the speaker was dressed. Heart racing, as if someone had jammed a muzzle against her temple, she said, "My name's Frank. I'm an alcoholic."

The room responded, "Hi, Frank."

"Good to be in New York. I was born here. Great story. I didn't kidnap anybody, though."

There were a few chuckles.

"I just put a gun to my head one morning and was trying to convince myself to pull the trigger when I realized what I was doing. Called an old friend who's been sober a long time and he got me into these rooms. Gotta admit it's been an interesting ride so far. I liked what you said about the God business. I'm at Step Two and having trouble with it. Don't know that I can believe in a god but I have to admit that something stayed my trigger finger that morning. I like the idea that God will come to you in a form you can accept. Guess I'm still looking for that form. And I hope I find it because I like being sober and I want to stay that way. Thanks."

Other people were called on and when the hour was up everyone rose. They held hands in a circle and someone started the serenity prayer. Everyone joined in. Even Frank.

Mick immediately shuffled for the door but Margaret kept Frank's hand. She smiled. "Welcome home. Literally and figuratively."

"Thanks."

Giving Frank's hand a squeeze she said, "Don't worry about looking for God. If your heart's open, God'll find *you*. So just relax and have faith that He'll come when you're ready to let Him in. Or She or It or whatever God's going to be for you."

Margaret moved off and a few other people introduced themselves to Frank, some offering advice.

A big, burly guy said, "I been sober twenty-eight years and I don't believe a fuckin' word about God. But I believe in AA and the power of the group and that's what gets me through."

A heavy blonde offered, "Honey, God's always there. We turn our backs on Him but He's always there waiting with open arms. When you're ready to turn to Him, He'll be right there for you."

Frank nodded, anxious she'd get cornered by a rabid Christer. But in six months that hadn't happened yet. AA people seemed to have a very laissez faire attitude about God, passionate about what they believed in but never foisting their passions onto her. She appreciated that, because if someone had tried to force-feed her a god she'd have been out the door faster than the old wino.

Edging toward the exit, she bumped into Margaret with a cluster of women.

"We always go for dessert after the meeting. Won't you come with us?"

Frank sucked in a deep breath. Mary also advised her to accept invitations when offered. She said the meetings after the meetings taught you how to talk without a glass in your hand and helped keep you sober another hour or two.

Sucking in a deep breath no one could see, Frank answered, "Sure. That'd be great."

CHAPTER 27

Frank only had coffee with the ladies, and to celebrate having gone out with them when she didn't really want to, she brought another pint of Ben and Jerry's back to the apartment. Annie was on the phone when Frank let herself in. Curled on the couch in her fuzzy blue robe, hair wet and slicked back, Annie lifted her chin in greeting.

Scooping ice cream into a mug, Frank heard her say, "Awright, Carmy. Thanks. I love you."

The phone clacked against its cradle and Frank looked into the living room. Annie was fetal on the couch. "You okay?"

"I don't know. Who can do this job so long and be okay?"

"Would some ice cream help?"

"What flavor?"

"Wavy Gravy."

"Bring it here."

Frank stuck a spoon in the carton and handed it over.

Annie struggled to a sitting position. "I got called in after you left. Mother beat her baby with a hammer. Wouldn't stop crying. Not the first time I heard that excuse. I don't know. It just got to me tonight. All the time I'm bookin' her this woman's gripin' about her baby this and her baby that. I tell you, Frank, it was all I could do to keep from rippin' her tongue out and stuffin' it down her throat. I swear to God." Squinting at a clock on the mantle, Annie said, "Nine months, two weeks, five days, twelve hours and I'm pullin' the pin. I'm gonna retire in Florida and swim in the ocean. Eat whatever I want, whenever I want, get fat, and watch *Oprah*. I'm sick a this shit. You hear me? Sick of it. Absolutely sick of it. Day in, day out. I can't do it no more. Ain't enough gold in Fort Knox to keep me here." After a bite of ice cream she mumbled, "I'm sorry. I shouldn't take this out on you."

"No problem. That's probably how you stay sane, huh?"

Casting a sharp glance at Frank, she quizzed, "Do I look sane to you?"

Frank grinned. "From where I sit you look pretty well-adjusted."

Annie kept her tired gaze on Frank. "You miss the drinking?"

"Yeah," Frank admitted. "I do. It's like walking around with a big hole in my heart. My sponsor says the hole is God-shaped, that only God can fill it. But I don't get God. Can't wrap my mind around it."

Annie tapped her chest. "She's right. God lives in here. Not here." She tapped her head.

Frank put her feet up on the coffee table. "So let me ask you. Where's your Mary on a night like this? Why does she let a woman hammer her kids to death?"

"Psh. I can't answer that. Theologians can't answer that. There are mysteries we don't know. I can't explain evil. It's like porn—I can't explain it but I know it when I see it. I can't presume to know more than God. I just have to believe there's a reason for all this crap. Just because I can't see the big picture don't mean there isn't one. Like people thinkin' the world was flat, right? Just because they couldn't believe in a round world don't mean it didn't exist." The room was quiet while the women sucked on their spoons. "It's faith. I have faith there's reasons for this crap, much as I hate it. I believe it happens for reasons that are completely unknown to me. My job is just to clean up the mess and move on to the next job. Beyond that, I got no friggin' clue."

"And that helps you? To talk about it all? The dead babies and stupidity and senselessness?"

"You're damn right it does. My friend Bee—she works at the DA's office—we take turns unloading on each other. That was my sister Carmen I was talkin' to. God bless her, she listens to more of this than she should have to. And my friend Pat, too. We went through our rookie year together. We still get together every couple a weeks for lunch. I don't know what I'd do without 'em."

"I'm jealous."

"Yeah." Annie sighed. "Truth a the matter is, I'm damn lucky. I got my health. I got my family. I got my friends. At the end of watch, that's really all that matters."

"Miss having a man around?"

"Oh, yeah, sometimes. But not enough to do anythin' about it. I date now and then. It's kinda fun but it don't go nowhere. Maybe someday when I'm not so focused on work I'll want one around. But for now, I barely have time for the family I already got. Besides, I need any heavy liftin', I call my son, Ben. What else I need man for?"

"Open pickle jars."

"Psh." Annie waved. "Slam 'em on the counter. You ever do that? Hold the jar upside down and give it a smart crack on the countertop? Works nine times outta ten and I don't have to put the seat down on the toilet."

Frank laughed and so did Annie.

"Can you beat it? The lesbian's givin' *me* advice on why I should need a man around. Ah, brother. See what I mean? Another mystery. They're everywhere. Hey," Annie said, hefting the carton. "Thanks for this."

"No sweat."

"What I can't figure is, why don't you have a nice lady waitin' for you at home? You cook, you clean, you got a good heart, you're employed . . ."

"I used to. Gave her up for the bottle."

"Ahh, that's a shame," Annie said shaking her head, digging into the carton.

"Yeah. She's a good woman. She deserved better."

"You straighten up and fly right, cookie. You got a lot to offer someone."

Frank grinned. "Think so?"

"Hey, don't go fishin'. What are you doin' out so late anyway?"

"Went to a meeting then went out for coffee afterward. It was nice."

"Good for you. That AA thing's workin' for ya?"

"Seems to be."

"Good. You stick wit' it. Told you about my nephew, right? Worked miracles for him. I seen it work for others, too. Tougher nuts 'an you."

Ice cream and talk settled the women down and soon they headed for bed. For the first time in at least a year Frank slept straight through the night.

CHAPTER 28

Sunday, 16 Jan 05—Canarsie

Here I am. Sitting in a cemetery. Guess it beats lying in one. Grumpy sky. Looks like more snow on the way. Got to admit I don't miss the dirty slush plowed up against the curb.

Quiet yesterday. Couple funerals but no one near the grave.

Went to a good meeting last night and afterward went out with a couple ladies. I was of course the youngest one there. They had twelve, ten and seven years of sobriety on me. Felt like a four-year-old hanging out with her sister from Vassar. But it was nice. They're pretty serious about their sobriety. Talked a lot about the "G" word. They all reiterated that if I was willing to believe then eventually I would. That's the thing, though. Am I willing to believe in something greater than myself? Why am I so stubborn about this? Christ, that business at Mother Love's should be enough to convince anybody. Why not me? Self-reliance almost bought me a bullet to the brain. Why can't I just say, yeah, okay, uncle, there's something bigger out there than me?

All right. Bottom line is it's scary. Scary to think I might not be in charge here. How fucked is that? Not like I've done such a great job of it lately. You'd think I'd want someone else to be running the show. Like those ladies last night, Mary says I just have to be willing to believe. Fact I called her before I went to bed last night.

She said, "Just be willing to entertain the possibility. And that possibility can be anything. Jesus, Buddha, Allah, the London Bridge—whatever floats your boat. Just take one step toward God and he'll take five to you."

I said she makes it sound so simple and she countered that it is—I'm just making it harder than it has to be. Said I'm creating "paralysis by analysis." Told me to stop thinking about what God is and just hang with the idea that God is.

Smart ass that I am, I had to say, "So I could use the Empire State Building as my God?"

"Absolutely," she says—got a fucking answer for everything. A friend of hers who's been sober nineteen years walks the Golden Gate Bridge every morning because that's where she feels closest to God. Says it doesn't matter who we send our prayers to because they all go to the same address.

I said, "Like all those letters the post office gets for Santa Claus."

She laughed and said, "Yeah, but those don't get returned. Our prayers do. Not always the way we want them or expect them, but God always gives us what we need."

"Always?" I asked.

"Always," she answered. "Like it or not."

She said she thinks of God as a good parent. We're the kids always asking for something—the new toy, a candy bar, day off from school—and does a good parent give her kid everything she asks for? Hell, no. The kid would be sick as a dog if you let her eat everything she wanted. The kid can't understand that, of course, and gets frustrated, but the parent is taking good care of her by not indulging her every wish. A good parent is concerned with her kid's long-term health, not her immediate gratification for things she doesn't need. Mary thinks that's how God is. Might not always give us what we want but we always get what we need. Didn't Mick Jagger say that? Damn, maybe he's god. That'd work for me.

So I'm trying to be open-minded about this thing. Willing. I'm willing to be willing.

Think I'd be more willing if I hadn't watched my father bleed to death or my mom go crazy or Maggie drown in a sucking chest wound. Or Noah. Christ. Barely forty and his sternum gets crushed against a steering wheel, so three more kids grow up without a dad. What's that about? Kind of begs the question what kind of a heartless bastard would let this shit happen, but hey, what the fuck do I know? I was the one eating a nine mil, right?

And I can't ever get away from Marguerite James and Darcy and all that weirdness with Mother Love. No explaining that away. Definitely beyond mere coincidence there.

Shit. Feel like Thelma and Louise. *The FBI's behind me, wanting to throw my ass in jail, and in front of me, just a huge leap of faith. We don't know that they died, right? Like Butch and Sundance leaping over the cliff. Maybe they lived, right? Who knows? Skedaddled off to a quiet little corner of the globe and started new lives.*

But first they had to jump.

CHAPTER 29

Monday morning the sun shone pale but sweet. Perching her long frame against a headstone Frank faced east, absorbing what she could of the far candescence. It occurred to her in that moment of calm that she'd gotten sidetracked from the point of her trip. She'd come to apologize to her mother, yet in all this time she hadn't looked twice at her mother's grave.

A stone rolled into Frank's chest and settled under her heart. A sigh did nothing to move it. From a couple yards away she studied her mother's grave. She scanned the cemetery. It was deserted. She stepped the few feet to the grave. Considered the packed snow a moment. Squatted on her heels.

She squinted at surrounding stones, the hazy sky, crows squabbling on bare branches. She looked at everything but the granite slab in front of her. The flowers she'd left on her first visit were gone. Manny and Robert must have thrown them away. She was ashamed she didn't have an offering, some token of reconciliation.

"But you're dead," Frank said to the block of stone. "Dead people don't need flowers, right? Don't need anything. Not even apologies from daughters who let them freeze to death."

She winced. She sounded like a promo for the Jerry Springer show. She stood up, giving the stone her back. Under the delicate sun the snow had turned into a field of gems—fiery rubies and glinting emeralds, flashing sapphires and glowing amber, filaments of gold and silver. Frank closed her eyes against the twinkling beauty.

Her mother had loved the snow. She'd bundle Frank into layers of clothes and they'd run to the park to make snowmen and snow angels. Frank flashed on lying in the snow against her mother's chest, both of them panting after making a choir of snow angels. Her mother's arms were so tight around her that Frank could barely breathe. Smothering her in a flurry of kisses, her mother had whispered fiercely, "I love you *so* much. You're my very own snow angel that I get to keep forever and ever. You'll never melt or leave me in the spring."

Frank bit her lip. The snow jewels blurred and her throat ached. She looked up to the sky. "Why?" she asked, her voice a harsh whisper. "Why all this waste? Why me running and you dying? Crazy out of your fuckin' mind. God, you scumbag cocksucker, can you explain that? Huh? You got a goddamned point or do you just groove on suffering? Some sorta sick fuck or what?" She glared at the benevolent sky. "Fucking asshole," she growled. "What is your goddamned point? Crazy goddamned idiot. Can't even run a fucking planet."

Her rage degraded into sorrow, crumbled into the loss she could never admit, could never allow. She bowed her head. Great, fat tears melted through the snow.

"Jesus fucking Christ," she whispered.

Over and over she swore, the curse becoming a mantra. Crouched at her mother's stone, Frank felt the smooth granite, letting the hate drain from her. Sorrow and ruin and loss poured from her in twin rivulets, coursing down her cheeks, steaming through the snow to touch the ground at her feet, the ground that surrounded and cradled her mother, and through her tears Frank was connected to her.

A single cloud covered the sun and wandered on.

Trucks bleated backup warnings. A siren rose and fell.

Two women talked outside the cemetery, their words a steady purr as they passed.

Pigeons waddled and cooed. Crows fought over an empty potato chip bag.

Frank traced her mother's name. Bent her head to the flat rock.

At last she stood, palming her face dry. The cemetery was still empty. The sun had angled higher and Frank glanced at her watch. She rested a hand upon the granite, receiving the stone's cool touch as benediction.

CHAPTER 30

Frank sat in the Nova with a warm cup of coffee. When her phone rang she answered without looking at who the call was from.

"Hi," Gail said. "How are you?"

"Funny you should ask." Frank thought a minute, deciding she couldn't articulate an answer. Didn't want to. "What are you up to?"

"I just got out of a meeting and I'm walking back to the office. It's a beautiful day. I was thinking about you in the cold and the ice and snow. How are you?"

Damnably on the verge of tears again Frank sat up straight. She squinted into the snow. "Oh," she said, fighting to keep the quaver from her voice. "I'm a lot of things. Mostly right now I'm awful damn glad to hear your voice."

"Are you crying?"

Frank swallowed hard. "Not yet. But I seem to be doing a lot of that lately. Weirdest thing. Just about anything can set me off. Hold on."

Grabbing a napkin from under the seat, Frank blew her nose. She gave her cheek a not so gentle slap.

"There we go," she said into the phone. "All better. Christ. My cheeks are gettin' raw from all the salt on 'em lately. But I guess it's good. S'all good to the gracious."

"Is this LA Franco I'm talking to? *The* Lucifera Angelina Franco?"

"Hey, come on." Frank kidded. "This isn't a secure line. You swore to secrecy about my name. So no, it's not LA Franco you're talking to."

"Well, tell me who I am talking to."

"Christ, I wish I could. She's a damn crybaby, for one thing. Guess that's just the way it's got to be for a while. There's a lot that's got to come out. I'm reading *The Da Vinci Code*—probably the last person in America to read it—and there's a great line. Something to the effect that men will go to greater lengths to avoid what they fear than to obtain what they want. And that's me. I've spent my whole life avoiding pain rather than facing it and getting what I want."

"What *do* you want?"

You, Frank almost answered, but she knew it was a cheap answer. She took a big breath, finding the truth there. "I want a quiet heart. A quiet head. I don't want to be scared all the time, wondering what I'm going to lose next. Wondering which corner the next bombshell's coming around. I just . . . . I want to live and not be afraid. Just take each moment as it comes and not spend so much time trying to protecting myself. Trying to anticipate where the next blow's coming from and heading it off. Shit happens. Much as I hate it, all the running in the world hasn't kept me from it. If anything, I think it's been running right alongside me, getting even stronger and faster. So what I want is to quit running. To quit looking over my shoulder trying to see what's coming after me. I just want to be still. I want to be quiet inside."

151

The phone sounded dead.

Frank asked, "You there?"

Gail sniffed. "Now you've made *me* cry."

"Why?" Frank gave her time to answer.

"Because I always knew you were brave. Not the knock-down, drag-out kind of brave, but brave in your heart. Do you know when I first fell in love with you?"

"Nope."

"Remember that night you came by to get Placa's tox report? We had dinner at the Grill and I asked if you were ready for a real date. You said you weren't, remember? That you were cleaning up your past and weren't ready for anything new yet. And that's when I fell in love with you because I could see that you were honest and brave. That your heart was strong and that I'd wait you out. And I did. Even through Noah's death and even after you left I couldn't believe that was really you. It was like you were possessed by an evil twin. She looked like you and sounded like you but she couldn't act like you because she forgot the best of you. She forgot your heart."

"Hey, cut it out. I'm gonna start crying again, too. Know when I fell in love with you?"

"Uh-uh."

"The night you told me about your mastectomy. I wanted to tell you then how beautiful I thought you were. I wanted to kiss you but I'd barely had the thought before I talked myself out of it. See how brave I am?"

"You were brave enough to keep dating me."

"Ah, that wasn't brave. That was easy. Like falling off of high heels."

"It's funny. I know how much you cared for Placa so I don't mean to sound callous, but if it hadn't been for her murder I wonder if we'd have gotten together. You spent a lot of time on that case and a lot of time at the morgue."

"Yeah. We spent a lot of time together."

152

"Before that I rarely saw you. You were usually content to let someone else do the posts."

Frank nodded. "I wanted everything firsthand with Placa."

"I know. And thank God. It's a selfish thing to say but thank God for her. Is that awful?"

"No. I was just thinking, you know, all these things in my life— these things I've always hated—they're not all bad. To stretch the cloud with the silver lining analogy, my dad dying and my mom being nuts made me capable and self-reliant. That pain made me strong and hard—granted, to an extreme— and his death made me want to be a cop. By then, after taking care of my mom so long, taking care of strangers was second nature. I can look back and see how the path was laid. If he hadn't been killed and if I hadn't been forced to rely on myself I might never have been a cop. I wouldn't have met Maggie or partnered with Noah or known Placa and probably not you. It's like you said, I can look back at each one of those events and almost be grateful for them, awful as they were. And that night with the gun, bad as it was, it got me here, sober and talking to you. I'd go through it all over again just to get another shot at you. No pun intended." When there was no reply, she asked, "I do have one, don't I?"

"Oh, Frank. I want to say yes and tell you to come home and we'll be together and happy and it'll all work out, but there's a part of me that needs time. I know alcoholics have the best intentions. I know you can mean to stay sober and not do it. I grew up with those sincere promises and they were broken every time. I want to believe you're different, Frank. I hope and pray that you are. But I'm not willing to fall head over heels for a sincere promise."

Frank ate her disappointment. "I understand. You deserve more than a promise."

"Yes, I do. And that's not to say I don't love you. I do. But I don't love you enough to live with your drinking. I won't go through that again. I can't."

"I know. And I can't make you believe this, but I won't go

through that again either. And that's a promise for me. Not for you or anybody else. I have to vow that to myself because I'm pretty sure if I drink again I'm gonna die. Sooner or later, one way or another. And I don't want to do that just now. That night with the Beretta convinced me. I'm just not ready to go yet."

"I'm glad to hear that."

"Yeah. Me too. Look. I'll let you go. I didn't mean to put you on the spot. I was just hoping . . ."

"Hoping what?"

"Nothing. I'm pushing. I want more than I can have right now. Probably more than I need. Just tell me we're still friends. Can you do that?"

"Yes. That I can do. And I'm not ruling you out, Frank. If what you say is true then maybe we have a chance, but that's going to take time."

"I know. I'm just suddenly hungry for it all. For you, for everything. I feel like I've been trapped in ice for forty years and I'm thawing out. I'm like a kid in a candy shop. I want it all right now. But I know I can't have it all now, and that's okay. What I have is good."

She wanted to say she had to go, to end the moment's painful vulnerability, but she rode it out. Gail asked how it was going at the cemetery, if there were any nibbles.

"No, not yet. I'm gonna give it through Sunday and if I haven't seen our friend by then I'm gonna hire a P.I. to watch the place for me."

They finished lightly, promising to talk soon. Hanging up, Frank reached for her coffee through a shaft of sunlight. She had the oddest sensation that her mother was sitting next to her, calm and not crazy.

Frank studied the empty passenger seat. Lifting her cup, she said, "What the hell, huh? To possibility."

Frank smiled, sipping the cold coffee.

154

CHAPTER 31

As usual, Annie was on the phone when Frank got back to the apartment. The women waved at each other and Frank went to her room with a pint of Vanilla Swiss Almond. A few minutes later there was a knock on the door.

"Yeah?"

Annie leaned in. "Hiya."

"Hi."

"No gourmet dinner tonight?"

Frank lifted the ice cream. "This is it."

Annie whined, "Why don't you weigh five hundred pounds?"

"Keep eatin' like this and I will. But my sponsor says I can do whatever I want the first year, long as it's not drinking. Besides, I could barely eat when I first got sober so I'm making up for it."

"Psh. Hey, I got a question for you, 'bout your pops."

"Shoot."

"Funny you should say that. You was livin' in the East Village at the time but he was killed in the Ninth. What were you doin' over there?"

"My uncle was a cop. He worked outta the Ninth."

"No kiddin'?"

"No kiddin'. Sergeant Albert Franco. At end of watch on his day shifts my dad and I would meet him at Cal's. We went there a lot. It was only a couple blocks away and they could drink cheap. Feed me cheap. We were walking home from there. Stopped at a deli to get some milk and cereal for breakfast. We got oranges too. For my mother. She loved fruit. I can still see 'em. After he dropped the bag and it broke, the milk spilled onto the sidewalk and the oranges were so bright against it. So orange. Like a still-life in my head that won't ever fade."

"Some things . . ." Annie said. "They never go away." Then she smiled. "Cal's was closed by the time I got to the Ninth, but they still talk about it."

"Yeah. The bar legends are made of."

"So your uncle and your pops, they just drank and hung out?"

"Pretty much. They'd talk to other cops, some of my uncle's friends. I think some of the cops resented havin' a kid in the bar but they got used to me. We were there a helluva lot. They played cards sometimes, arm wrestled when they were really loaded. That's how I knew they were in the bag. One would challenge and the other'd accept. But mostly they talked and drank. Why? What are you thinkin'?"

"Nothin'. Just gettin' a feel for who he'd know there."

"Cops." Frank shrugged. "It was a cop bar."

"Yeah, okay. Anything today?"

Lots, Frank thought, but answered, "Nah. Quiet. Could you leave Charlie Mercer's number for me? I want to call him tomorrow, see if I can hire him next week. Unless we get a hit by Sunday I'm going home Monday."

"Yeah, okay, I'll leave it for you. He's a good man, Charlie. You could leave your surveillance in worse hands."

"I'm takin' your word on that. How was your day?"

Annie flicked a shoulder. "Nine months, two weeks and *four* days."

"You hate it that much?"

"I don't hate the Job. I'm just tired, is all. So much crap, and most of it internal. Like we don't get enough on the street, the captain comes in this morning all bright-eyed and well-rested, waving a memo. Says he gonna dock us fifteen minutes every time he sees us with our feet up on the desk. Says it's unprofessional. Doesn't look good to citizens. So you know what our loo ordered us to do?" Annie laughed. "He *ordered* us to sit around with our feet up all morning. Everyone. The captain was havin' a walkin' coronary, I kid you not. About lunchtime Loo said the memo had disappeared and we could get back to work. Helluva waste of a day, huh? But God bless Loo. He's a good man. Reminds me of the first cop I ever rode with. You remember your first day?"

"Christ," Frank replied. "Like it was yesterday. My training officer was an asshole deluxe. He was about to rape this pregnant girl in an alley, invited me to watch or leave. I didn't do either. Took out my night stick and swung at him. Didn't warn him or anything, just swung with all I had. He went down but he got up pissed. We sparred around that alley for what seemed like hours. We were both tired. His shoulder wasn't working too well where I'd hit him and he was swingin' his stick at me with his left. We got a radio call and he had to grab the portable with his left hand. When he switched his stick from his left to his right that's when I knew I had him. I walked back to the unit and got in. He came a minute later and we responded to the call like nothing had happened. He talked shit behind my back until he got transferred to a cushy assignment in a white-collar division but I never had trouble with him again. Stupid how much time you have to waste defendin' yourself against people who're supposed to be on your side."

"You said it, sister." Looking at the ice cream, Annie wondered, "You got anymore of that?"

"Whole other pint in the freezer."

157

Annie shook a finger at Frank, calling as she left, "You're evil, cookie. Pure evil."

She came back, eating out of the carton like Frank, saying, "Let me tell you 'bout my first day. I was workin' the Twenty-Third, up to Harlem. We get this call. Domestic disturbance, right? Could be anythin'. We get to this fallin' down tenement, climb twelve flights 'cuz the elevator's broke and besides, my partner says, elevators are like roach motels for the police—cops go in but they don't come out. We get up there and there's all this commotion in the hallway. Neighbors say the woman's ex-boyfriend's in the apartment cuttin' on their three kids. He found out she had a new boyfriend and he's gonna kill the kids before he lets another man raise 'em. We knock and the guy won't open. The girlfriend's screamin' inside that he's killin' the babies and the spooky thing is, the kids aren't crying, so we call emergency services. But meanwhile the woman stops screamin'. My partner's tryin' to talk the guy into opening the door but for nothin'. Damn it."

She looked for the ice cream she'd dripped onto the floor. Frank wadded up the paper towel from around her own carton and called, "Catch."

Annie grabbed it, mopping up the spill. "Thanks. So here comes EMS runnin' up the stairs and they ram the door in. My partner and me we charge in behind 'em. I never seen such a mess. I'm just standin' there in shock. There's blood everywhere. On the ceiling, the floor, the walls, the furniture. It's like someone's almost finished painting the place red. The boyfriend, he's red too, just rockin' on the couch next to the woman. Her throat's slit to her neckbone. EMS cuffs the guy and my partner gives me a poke. I follow him into the bedrooms. We find the kids back there, all three of 'em, their throats cut. We go back to the living room just as this itty-bitty old lady charges through the busted door, screamin' 'Sweet Jesus Almighty.' I'm thinkin' oh shit, it's the kids' grandma or somethin'. I'm thinking how the hell am I gonna calm her down, get her outta here, right? Then she turns and looks me square in the eye, this sweet little old lady, and she demands,

'Who's gonna pay to clean up this fuckin' mess?' I shoulda known right then what I was gettin' into, huh?"

Frank grinned. "Do you regret it?"

Annie considered her spoon. "I wish'd I'd had more time with the kids. I was selfish, I guess. Back then I wouldna given this up for nothin'. I loved it. Never knowin' what you were gonna get into that day, who you were gonna meet . . . but my kids paid the price. I missed a lotta things. Things they still remind me of to this day. My mother, too."

Frank chewed an almond. "Hypothetical question. What if you'd walked out on your husband and left him with the kids? He was a cop too, right? And let's say he raised the kids as well as you did. What would your mother say about him?"

"I don't know."

"Guess."

"She'd probably say he was a saint like my cousin Henry. His wife run off with a car salesman—after she stuck him for thirty large for a new Buick—and he's raisin' his baby daughter, goin' to school nights and workin' in a bank."

"He's a saint, right?"

"Yeah. He can walk on watuh."

"So your husband walks out on you, leaves you with two kids, and you manage to raise them and hold down a good job at the same time. Your cousin does that with one kid and he's a saint, but you do that with two and you're selfish? What am I not seeing?"

"What you're not seein', cookie, is a long line of Italian mothers who sacrifice for their kids. I shoulda found a nice man, remarried and settled down. Quit all that crazy police business. This may be the twenty-first century but my mother's still living in the nineteenth. Nah. The way she sees it, I'm selfish."

"Then if that's the way you see it, you got a foot in the nineteenth century, too."

"So? What's wrong with that?"

"What's wrong with that is you're a saint, too. You're not selfish. You raised two kids all by yourself, doing a man's work, and

159

you should be givin' yourself a pat on the back, not a kick in the ass."

Annie gave Frank a hard stare. "You don't know the whole story, cookie. It was selfish. Thanks for the ice cream."

Swinging the door closed, Annie left Frank puzzling what the whole story could be.

CHAPTER 32

Annie had become Frank's alarm clock. A light sleeper, Frank got up when she heard her puttering around the apartment.

"Hey."

"Mornin'. Ya sleep good?"

"Like a baby. You?"

"I had better nights. Shouldna eaten all that ice cream. I'm gonna have to spend an extra hour in the pool today."

Dropping bread in the toaster Frank asked, "You want me to make you a real meal tonight?"

"I want you should stop bringin' home pints of ice cream for me, that's what I want."

"All right. Let me cook a good dinner for you. I'll make something healthy."

"You don't have to cook for me, Frank."

"I know, but it gives me pleasure. Keeps me distracted. Makes me feel useful."

"Well, if you want. I'd never turn down a meal."

"Any requests?" Frank said, sitting at the table.

"Surprise me. It's all been good so far. Just no sweetbreads or liver. I don't like organ meat."

"Makes two of us."

Frank took part of the paper and the women ate in silence. Still looking at her paper Annie reached for her coffee and said, "I'm gonna miss you, ya know. Gotten spoiled coming home to food and company."

"Maybe this is all prep for findin' yourself a nice man in nine months, two weeks and three days."

"Listen to you with the nice man, already. Some lesbian, always pushin' men on me. You ain't earnin' no toasters, cookie."

Frank laughed as Annie smoothed the paper on the table and went to dress for work. Frank cleared her dishes and brewed a pot of coffee for the Thermos. She read the rest of the paper and as Annie headed out Frank reminded, "Don't forget to give me Charlie's number."

"Oh, yeah. Lemme get that for you."

She rummaged through her phone book and wrote the number on a Post-it. Frank stuck the note on the Thermos, watching Annie go through her routine with the Virgin.

Later, as Frank was on her way out the door, she winked at the Madonna. "Wish me luck, Baby Muvuh."

She ran through her usual morning routine at the cemetery, then settled in the Nova to make a shopping list for dinner. Annie called in the middle of it.

"Hi. I been tellin' my daughter what a good cook you are and she wants to come over for dinner. Is that all right with the cook?"

"Sure," Frank answered. "What does she like?"

"Psh. My kids, I tell ya. You'd think they was raised like royalty. Ben won't eat nothin' that's not organic or free-range and Lisa won't eat nothin' with a carbohydrate. They're not my kids. I think the stork brought 'em."

"No problem. Ben and Lisa or just Lisa?"

"Just Lisa, thank God."

"What time?"

"Anytime after seven, Job permittin'."

"All right. See you then."

"Sure you don't mind?"

"It's an awnuh," Frank teased.

"You're a doll. See you later."

Frank crossed out the menu she'd been playing with and started over. It wasn't like she had anything better to do.

She ended up making roast beef in a Dijon shell, steamed kale drizzled with Hollandaise sauce and baby lettuces with a mustard vinaigrette. Lisa had her mother's appetite and vibrant dark looks. She was duly impressed with Frank's mastery of the kitchen and spent the evening pumping Frank for Hollywood celebrity sightings. Frank had met dozens of rappers and a few actors from the 'hood, but when she compared South Central to Upper Harlem Lisa was disappointed.

"All the glamorous places you could be working and you're both in the pits. What's up with that? Are you masochists or somethin'?"

Annie and Frank exchanged sheepish grins.

"Anyway, I've gotta run. I've got a mock trial at seven a.m. Dinner was gorgeous, Frank. Thanks for havin' me."

While Annie walked Lisa out of the building Frank put the leftovers away. She missed her music. If she were home she'd put something jazzy on the stereo, but Annie never seemed to play music so Frank let it go. Maybe the silence was just as well. Bending old routines was probably good for her. And the music would always be there.

Annie walked into the kitchen, crying, "Whaddaya doin'? Get out! You made dinner. Go sit! Watch TV or somethin'. Shoo!"

"All part of the service, ma'am."

"I'm serious. Get outta here." Shoving her sleeves over her elbows Annie ran water in the sink.

163

Frank sat at the table with last night's ice cream. "She's a nice girl."

"Yeah, despite me, huh?"

"Yeah," Frank kidded. "Despite how selfish you are."

Annie grunted, swirling her hands in the soapy water. "Ya miss not havin' kids?"

"Nope. Never wanted 'em. I didn't get a maternal gene. I mean, I like 'em if they're somebody else's, but talk about selfish. I could never give that much time to somebody else, especially when I was drinking. That was a full-time job in itself."

"I can't imagine you drunk."

"Good. It's not pretty." Frank scraped the bottom of the pint. "So let me ask you somethin'. What's the whole story?"

"Whaddaya talkin' about?"

"Last night. When I said you weren't selfish you said I didn't know the whole story."

For a second Annie was still. She said nothing, but started washing the dishes again. Frank waited and was rewarded.

"I had three kids. Ben, Lisa and Brian. Brian was six when I got a call from the school saying he was in the hospital. You know those playground carousels the kids push and then jump on to? Well, he went to jump on and misjudged his step. He tripped. His chin hit the metal floor and he bounced his skull into the foot of one of the bars. Bruised his brain. Contrecoup injury. They couldn't get the swelling down. He died next morning. Never regained consciousness."

Annie rinsed the roasting pan, searching for a place to put it. Frank took the pan, drying it as Annie continued.

"I made sergeant after that. Left Ben and Lisa with my mom as much as possible. Or with their aunts. After sergeant I went for my shield. I worked hard for it. Took me three years to make gold. I worked twelve, sixteen, eighteen hours—whatever it took—every-day. Whenever the Job needed me. I didn't think about Brian when I was workin'. Ben and Lisa either. So it was selfish. Very selfish."

Annie passed Frank a pot. She toweled it and put it away. "You must have done somethin' right. It seems like you have pretty good kids."

Shrugging, Annie replied, "It kinda all came to a head when Ben was in seventh grade. The detective's son was caught peddlin' dope in the boys' room at school. I didn't know how to deal with that. I was floored. A cop's son, right? He should *know* better. My mother, my sisters, they ganged up on me. Said they weren't gonna help with the kids anymore unless I got into counseling. Oh, let me tell ya, I was steamin'. What did I have to go to counselin' for? It was Ben with the problem, not me. But I went. Turned out a large part a Ben's problem was not havin' a father *or* a mother. I got better after that. Put in for days whenever I could get 'em. Brought work home instead of stayin' at the House. Got involved with their lives. Poor kids. They was bein' passed around like orphans. Half the time I didn't know if they were at their grandmother's or their aunt's."

Frank wagged her head.

"What?" Annie asked.

"Nothin'. I was just thinking this morning, the paths our lives took. I was feeling bad about all the running I've done, running from my past, but this is where it's brought me. Here tonight. Sober. Helping with the dishes. Talking to a friend. Full belly. Warm bed. Laying ghosts to rest. Hard as a lot of it's been, I guess I wouldn't trade any of it. Even the bad stuff."

Annie offered a wan smile. She nodded. "I haven't told that story in years." Pulling the drain plug, she added, "Thanks for listenin'."

"Thanks for tellin' me. I got bad news, though."

"What's that?"

"While you were talkin'? I ate all the ice cream."

"No." Annie chuckled. "That's good news."

CHAPTER 33
Tuesday, 18 Jan 05—Canarsie

Mary Catherine Franco.
Sounds so churchy. So Boston Irish. Neither of which my mother was.
She was born Mary Catherine Stenthorst. Good Swedish name. Sounds
like stamping your feet in the snow and ordering your horse to stand.
Nothing churchy about that.
Mary Catherine Franco.
She loved snow and daisies and sugar cookies with lemon icing. She
was young once and pretty. Beautiful even. She turned men's heads. She
was slim and tall, very Nordic. A blonde Julie Newmar, only not so jaded.
Or stacked. I got her height and her flat chest. Better than being barrel-
shaped like Dad. She had gorgeous cheekbones. She could hang clothes on
them. But she hated her eyelashes. Called them stumpy. I'd sit on the
toilet watching her curl them, a cigarette dangling from her mouth,
swearing at them as she layered on coat after coat of mascara, an old-
fashioned sweating on the sink. They always drank old-fashioneds before

they went out. Dad showed me how to make them. I forget now, but something about muddling sugar and bitters—that's what he called it, muddling. Critical step—you muddle the sugar and bitters in a teaspoon of water, add ice, bourbon and a maraschino cherry. I loved the cherries after they'd been soaking in the booze. Sure sounds good right about now.

See, that's how I know I'm an alcoholic—it's ten in the morning, the middle of winter and my toes are frozen yet an icy, dripping, old-fashioned sounds like heaven. And I don't even like sweet drinks. I'm a rummy, just like Hemingway's drunks. Sounds so much more genteel than alcoholic. Alcoholic is so clinical. Has no charm. Rummy sounds quaint, amusing. If a rummy sticks a gun in his mouth and almost pulls the trigger it's amusing. If an alcoholic does it it's desperate. There's a lot in a name.

Like Mary Catherine Franco. Lace Irish, Catholicism, white dresses. But not my mom. She was Cat. Always Cat. Never Mary Catherine, and Catherine only when my dad was frustrated with her. He called her everything starting with "cat"—catawampus, cataclysm, catamaran, Katmandu—he'd come home from work and sweep her into his arms, singing, "How do you do, Katmandu?"—catapult, katabatic. When she was in a down cycle, all depressed and lethargic on the couch, he'd hold her head in his lap and stroke her hair, calling her "my catatonia."

He loved her. He loved her so fucking much. Through the ups, the downs, the in-betweens. There couldn't have been another woman. Yeah, okay, so maybe he knocked off a piece here and there. My mom wasn't exactly available when she was depressed but as far as loving another woman, I can't see it. Not enough for her to still be prowling around his grave after all this time.

And the lows just weren't that bad while he was alive. They were more spread out. Seemed like she was more manic while he was alive and then afterward more depressed. Lucky me. But sometimes the highs were as bad as the lows. Like the night she decided we needed new dishes. She took every plate and bowl we owned and smashed them against the wall. My father tried to stop her but she was just laughing and hurling china. Neighbors called the cops. Thought someone was getting killed.

Crazy cat. Katzenjammer. Cat Ballou. Catamount.
Mom.

CHAPTER 34

Frank snapped out of a doze to see an elderly white woman walking from the direction of her father's grave.

"Oh, shit." Rocketing from the car, Frank trotted up to the departing woman. "Excuse me. Are you here for the Deluca funeral?"

The woman stared with wide, rheumy eyes. "The Deluca funeral? Oh, no."

"Oh. Which one then?" Frank pressed.

"I'm not here for any funeral. I was visiting my brother."

"Oh. Your brother." Frank made a show of looking beyond the woman. "Is there a funeral goin' on here?"

"Not that I know of." The woman turned, searching too.

"Shoot. I hope I got the right day. Maybe I got the time wrong. I coulda sworn it was this mornin'. Well, thanks anyways." Frank pretended to move away but stopped to ask, "Say, who's ya brother? You're a dead ringer for Frankie Ford."

"Oh, no." The woman smiled. "My brother's Samuel Abrams. He died of cancer two days past Thanksgiving."

"Aw, geez. That's terrible. I'm sorry for your troubles."

"Yes, well, thank you. Maybe you could ask about your funeral at the office."

"Hey, that's a great idea. I'll do that. Thanks. Sorry to bother you."

"Oh, it's no bother."

The woman waved and Frank headed to the office. From a corner of the building she watched the old lady leave, relieved she caught her and disappointed she was nobody.

Inside the office, Frank said, "Mornin'. Can you tell me where Samuel Abrams is buried?"

"One minute," the receptionist told her. "I check for you."

Frank followed his directions to Abrams' plot, satisfied with the fresh prints and flowers at Abrams' stone. She checked her father's grave. No prints that weren't her own.

Returning to the Nova she poured coffee and fidgeted. She remembered to call Charlie Mercer and arranged for him to take over surveillance. After talking to him she dialed the squad.

"Homicide, Detective Lewis."

"Sister Shaft. S'appenin'?"

"LT, that you?"

"S'me. S'up?"

"Da-amn, girl. Where you at?"

"Sittin' in a rusty Nova, freezin' my ass off outside a cemetery in Brooklyn."

"Yeah, whassup up with that? When you comin' home?"

"I'll be back Monday. That's the plan. How's things goin'?"

"Let's see. Bobby's in court. Diego's at the morgue. The new guy's weird."

"How so?"

"Kept callin' me Queen Latifah."

Frank laughed.

"Yeah, funny, right? I got in that home's face and told him if he

169

called me Queen Latifah one more time I was going to fuck him up so hard make Queen Latifah look like Pee Wee Herman."

"Great." Frank cringed. "How'd that go over?"

"Let's just say *Larry* be givin' me some space now."

"Try not to kill him before I get back, okay?"

"Yeah, maybe. We'll see 'bout that."

"Just ice, Joe Louis. He's not so bad."

"Skinhead best not be gettin' in my face again. That's all I gotta say."

"What else? Anyone doing any actual police work or ya'll just hanging out playing kindergarten?"

"We're working," Lewis huffed. She filled Frank in as she absently registered the street. There were faces she'd become familiar with, regulars catching the bus, the old man walking his Airedale, another old man with an obese poodle, a dark woman her age that limped by every day around noon.

Even Frank had her routine. She checked the graves in the morning, then returned to the Nova, content to take in the neighborhood and drink coffee. When she tired of that, she spent the obligatory time on her journal, visited the bathroom and walked around the cemetery. She dawdled, reading names until lunch. If it was nice she ate in the cemetery, and if not, she'd eat in the car and listen to news. After lunch, she'd pour her last cup of coffee and read. She usually nodded off a few times, jerking herself awake. Then it was time for another walk around the cemetery, bemused by both her dreams and the quality of light as the winter sun descended.

It went that way Thursday and Friday, with Frank's second Saturday at the cemetery fast becoming as fruitless as her first. Warm in the heavy wool coat she'd borrowed from Annie, Frank admired a sculpture of the Virgin Mary holding her crucified son in her lap. The Mary looked so pained and the Jesus so dead. Frank was amazed that stone could be so vivid. She studied the epitaphs of the family beneath the monument, deciding she didn't want to be buried. Who would visit and why waste the space?

Wondering if she could arrange for her ashes to be put in a dumpster, she eyed a man hurrying by on her right. He was about six feet tall, weighed around one-seventy, maybe black or Latino. She couldn't tell from the way he was hunched into his jacket. He wore John Lennon glasses and seemed to know where he was going. In one gloved hand he clutched a grocery sack. Yellow chrysanthemums poked from the edge.

Frank followed discretely.

Her heart jumped when he stopped at her father's grave. The man searched the ground. He looked behind the headstones and at the surrounding markers, then knelt and crossed himself. He appeared to pray for a moment. Done with that, he took the flowers from the sack and propped them against the carved letters *Francis S. Franco*. Then he took a glass candle from the bag. Stuffing the empty sack into his jacket he fished in a trouser pocket. He struck a match and lit the candle. Arranging it at the base of the flowers, he bowed his head.

Frank edged closer. She drank him down like whiskey. Kinky short hair flecked with gray above a furrowed, walnut-colored face. The skin under his chin bunched under his bent head and she put him in his mid-fifties. He wore black trousers over black lace-ups. The pants and shoes were worn but clean. The down jacket was navy-colored, no brand.

He stood but didn't leave, his gaze rarely straying from her father's headstone. Frank watched, making herself crazy with the possibilities. Could he be the perp? Maybe. Frank tried to see him almost forty years younger. Couldn't. Maybe her father's illegitimate child? Maybe a half brother from somewhere? Maybe he'd been bisexual and this was his old lover. Hell, after Annie's bombshell Frank was ready to accept anything.

The man looked toward her. Frank checked the monument at her feet, crossing herself like she'd seen Annie do. From the edge of her vision she watched him do the same thing then hurry toward the gate. Frank went after him, keeping half a block between them. He stopped at a bus stop and Frank ducked into a grocery. She watched from there, getting a couple dollars worth of change. Five minutes later a bus pulled up and Frank got on behind him.

The bus zigzagged north through Brooklyn. When the man got off Frank did too. She maintained her half-block trail. He seemed oblivious to her. Various people greeted him as he walked. A few times he stopped for a brief talk. Frank strained to hear but couldn't. She twisted and turned with him until he abruptly crossed the street and entered one of half a dozen entrances into a large brick building. Frank crossed too. Reading a sign on the door listing Rectory Hours, she paused.

A young Hispanic woman came out and lit a cigarette. She quickly puffed half of it and as she stubbed it out against the building Frank approached her.

"Excuse me. Who was that man that just walked in to the rectory? Tall guy, glasses, dark coat."

"You mean Father Cammayo?"

Frank hid her surprise. "Is that who that was? I lived here a long time ago. I thought I recognized him but I didn't want to go up and say hello to a total stranger."

Flashing a nervous smile the woman nodded, then returned inside.

Frank walked around the corner and dialed Annie, but she didn't answer. Frank told her voice mail, "It's Frank. I got him. Call me." She pressed end and read the name scrolled above a large set of wooden doors.

Our Lady Queen of Angels.

She climbed the steps to the doors. She pulled a large iron handle and the door gave easily. But she dropped her hand, letting the door close in a whisper of incense. Above her, three stained glass windows stretched to the sky. One panel looked like Mary ascending to Heaven in the company of angels. The second was a mournful, El Greco-style Christ and a third appeared to be Adam and Eve. While grappling with the significance of the triptych her phone went off. It spooked her and she checked the number, relieved.

"Hey," she told Annie. "I got him."

"So I heard. Where are you?"

"Brooklyn. Williamsburg, I think. I'm at a church." Frank tilted her head back. "Our Lady Queen of Angels. On Eighth Street."

"Is that where he's at?"

"Yeah. He's a fuckin' priest."

"Hey, hey. Watch your mouth. A priest? How do you know? Did you talk to him?"

"No. He went into the rectory and a minute later a woman came out. I asked who the man was that just went in and she says, 'You mean Father Cammayo?' A priest. Go figure. When can you talk to him?"

"I just got outta the pool. I was on my way to Mom's but I guess I'll come over there instead. What's the address?"

"Uh . . ." Frank looked around. "Corner of Eighth and Havemeyer. The rectory's around the back. I'm gonna keep an eye on it, see if he comes out again. How long you think it'll take you to get here?"

"I dunno." Annie sighed. "Gimme a half-hour."

"All right. There's a pizza joint across the street. I'll be waiting in there."

Frank ordered a slice and picked at it, too excited to eat. She scoured her memory for a priest. Her father was raised Catholic but except for an occasional Christmas Mass she'd never seen him inside a church, and certainly never with a priest. Although her mother dabbled in practically every known dogma, cult and creed, the woman was adamantly opposed to Christianity in all guises, a backlash from her rigid Lutheran upbringing.

Frank would have liked to talk to her mother. She wished she could be here now to share the excitement. Frank reflexively thought to order a beer. Realizing she couldn't, she concentrated instead beyond the window, one eye on the rectory door, the other searching for Annie.

173

CHAPTER 35

After an agony of time, Annie finally appeared. They made a quick plan inside the restaurant, and Annie ordered, "You just be quiet, okay? Let me do all the talkin'."

Frank nodded, impatient to get started.

Glancing at the cold pizza, Annie asked, "You gonna finish that?"

Frank pushed the plate toward her.

"This father, he look old enough to have known your pops?"

"Maybe. I put him in his mid-fifties."

"Any way your pops coulda known him?"

"I been racking my brain, but I'm comin' up blank. He didn't go to church except for a Mass now and then, but my mother made such a stink I doubt it was worth it. She hated the Catholic Church. Said it was the second largest corporation in the world and it got that way by burning women at the stake and keeping the rest barefoot, pregnant and in the kitchen. Sorry, but she was no fan of Catholicism. My father wasn't much of a fan either, from

174

what I remember. I think he just went outta guilt. He always looked sad in church. I asked him once, why he was sad. We were at a Christmas Mass and he just said 'Hush.' He was quiet all the way home. I never asked again."

"Your pops, what sorta temper did he have?"

"Temper? Hardly any. He was an easy-going guy. Had to be to live with my mother. She was the one with the temper."

"Didn't get into fights?"

"No. Twice I saw him swing at someone and both times it was because the other guy pushed him."

"What do you mean pushed him?"

"I mean got in his face."

"Your pops knew how to fight?"

"He knew some moves."

"Where'd he learn 'em?"

"Look, why are we talkin' about this when Cammayo's across the street?"

"Humor me. Where'd he learn to fight?"

"Christ, I don't know. His friends. The street. His brother. How the hell should I know?"

"What streets?"

"Chicago."

"He grew up in Chicago?"

"Where are you goin' with this?"

Dusting pizza flour from her hands, Annie said, "Guys learn to fight interestin' places. Prison, the army, boarding schools. Just trying to figure where your pops was comin' from."

"You couldna asked me earlier? Before we had a potential witness waiting across the street?"

Annie stood and leaned over the table. "You didn't tell me earlier your pops was George Foreman."

Frank followed her outside. "He wasn't George Foreman, for Christ's sake. He just knew how to defend himself."

Crossing the street Annie asked, "He ever swing at a man of God?"

"Why would he? He wasn't a loose cannon. I told you. Twice I saw him fight. Both times it was in a bar."

"And the night he got shot."

"How do you know that?"

"It was in your statement. You said he swung at the perp and that's when he got shot."

"Yeah. So three times. And each time he was defending himself. End of story. Jesus, Annie. He wasn't some loony vigilante."

"Awright, I'm just askin'."

Opening the door to the rectory, Annie was all silken politeness to the woman behind the desk.

"Hi," she said, displaying her ID. "My name's Detective Silvester. NYPD Homicide. I hate to bother him on Saturday afternoon, but we need to speak with Father Cammayo. Where might we find him?"

The woman looked back and forth between Annie and Frank. "Um, he's not here. He left just a couple minutes ago."

Frank glared at Annie and held back a curse. Unruffled, Annie continued, "Oh, that's too bad. See, we need to talk to him as soon as possible. We believe he might have some very important information about a parishioner we're looking for. This is a very time-sensitive matter—we're talkin' lives hangin' in the balance—and I'm sure you wouldn't normally do this but we need to ask you for Father Cammayo's address and phone number. It'd be a huge help."

The woman bit her lip. "Could I see your ID again?"

Placing her shield and ID on the woman's desk, Annie assured, "Absolutely, miss. You're right to ask. Copy the numbers for your records. CYA."

"What?"

"Cover yourself."

Having written Annie's information on a slip of paper the woman consulted a printout. She wrote Cammayo's information on a pink memo slip, handing paper, badge and ID back to Annie.

"You're a doll. Let me ask you one more thing. What's his schedule for the weekend?"

The woman checked another list. "Father Cammayo has the eight a.m. and the five p.m. masses tomorrow."

Annie extended her hand. "Thanks, Miss . . . ?"

The woman took Annie's hand. "Mrs. Perez."

"Thank you, Mrs. Perez. You've been a *tremendous* help."

Outside the rectory Annie warned, "Don't even say it."

Frank's jaw bones bunched.

"Hey, thirty-six years, right? What's another couple hours? Come on." Annie unlocked the passenger side. "We'll find him. Where's the Nova?"

"Canarsie. I followed him on the bus. Where we going?"

"East Flatbush." After passing through a couple lights on Broadway. Annie posited, "Best case scenario, the priest is your junkie. Turned to God after he killed your pops. After all these years of carryin' this horrible burden he wants to come clean. Confesses everything."

Frank muttered, "Aren't you the fuckin' dreamer?" A few blocks later she groaned, "Christ. You're probably right. My dad *was* having an affair, only with a Catholic priest."

Annie wagged a pointed nail. "I doubt it. Don't believe every-thin' you hear, huh? Sure there's bad priests, but there's a lotta good ones, too. All in all, more good than bad. It's a cryin' shame the way the rotten ones undermine the good work of their broth-ers. I hate all these scandals. And I hate the priests that commit these abuses—don't get me wrong—but what good does it do to tro' the bat' watuh out widda baby, huh?"

"I'm just sayin' I'm ready for anything."

"Well, it probably ain't gonna be nothin' like that. Just relax. Don't get ya knickers in a twist."

"They been in a twist thirty-six years. Why untangle 'em now?"

Annie ignored her, scanning building numbers. "Figures he's in a church. They got so many churches in Brooklyn they call it the borough of churches. This is it." Slipping her NYPD plate on the dash she double-parked. "You ready?"

"Yeah," Frank said, not ready at all.

177

CHAPTER 36

Pedaling up the street on a bicycle a lean black man glided to a stop in front of the building Frank and Annie were watching.

Frank said, "That's him."

"The guy on the bike?"

"Yep."

"Let's go." Just as he hoisted his bicycle onto his shoulder, Annie called, "Father Cammayo?"

He turned to look. "Yes?"

She waved her ID, introducing herself. "May we talk to you for a moment?"

"What about?"

Annie smiled warmly. "Could we go inside, Father? It's kinda chilly out here."

Cammayo held the lobby door open. Silently he led the women up three flights of stairs.

His apartment was small and clean. A black man in his late thirties-early forties looked up from the couch.

"Al, these are homicide detectives. They'd like to talk with me."

"Oh." The man put down the paper he'd been reading. "I'll leave you alone."

He retreated down the hall and entered a room. Leaning his bike against the wall, Cammayo asked, "What's this all about?"

"Father," Annie replied, "what is your relationship to Francis Franco?"

The priest froze. His gaze shifted between the detectives, stopping on Frank. "You were at the cemetery this morning."

She nodded.

"What concern is this to the police?" he asked. His English was correct and formal, like an immigrant's, Frank thought.

Annie smiled. "How do you know Francis Franco?"

"Am I under investigation for something?"

"Not at this point, no."

"Not at this point," he repeated. "Meaning I may be at a future time?"

"It's possible," Annie parried.

"May I ask for what?"

Annie thought about it, suddenly blurting, "For his murder."

Cammayo's firm gaze weakened. It wandered from the couch, to the floor, around the room.

Annie pressed, "How do you know him, Father?"

He flapped a lifeless hand. "I don't. I never knew him."

"So tell me why thirty-six years later you're bringing flowers to his grave."

"You wouldn't understand."

"Try me."

The father gave the women his back. "When I was a young man I lived near where he was killed. The morning after he died I heard some neighbors talking. I found a paper and read about it. There wasn't much, just a paragraph that said he'd died in a mugging. I went to the spot where he was killed. There was still blood on the sidewalk. The paper said his little girl had been with him."

Frank was impassive under Annie's quick glance.

"My father was killed too. When I was six years old. I barely

179

remember him. I felt sorry for the little girl but I suppose I felt sorrier for me. I think it was on the sidewalk that morning, standing there, that I knew I was going to be a priest." He faced them, clarifying, "For less than pure motives, mind you. I decided to join the church that I may never again be attached to corporal flesh. Neither wife, nor child, nor lover. I was done with entanglements. I wanted only to attach myself to God, who I knew would never desert me. And that is why I visit that man's grave even after all these years. To pay homage. To remember where I came from. To fortify my will when I feel weak. I talk to God. It's quiet there. Peaceful. I get ideas for sermons when I'm there." He shrugged. "It's not a crime, is it?"

"Not at all," Annie allowed. "How often do you visit?"

"Every few weeks, time permitting."

"And you've been doing this thirty-six years?"

"Off and on. It's more convenient now that I live closer to the cemetery."

"Father, forgive me, but thirty-six years is a long time. I remember the day I decided to be a cop, believe me. I was at Brooklyn College sitting out under a tree studying for a final when two cars crashed in front of me. I went over to help but within seconds, *whoop-whoop-whoop*, here come the police. They call an ambulance, get the drivers separated, calm 'em down, get all the details sorted out, and as I'm watching these guys I know right then and there this is what I want to do with my life. I want to be the one that people call on in an emergency. I want to be that first responder, right? Let me tell you, I remember that moment vividly, but the thing is, Father, I don't go back to that street in Brooklyn every couple weeks and leave flowers, you know what I mean?"

The father offered a patronizing smile. "I dare to say our callings are vastly different."

"How so?"

"No disrespect, Detective, but I don't think being a policeman compares to devoting your life to God."

"Maybe so," Annie said into his gaze. "Still and all, an epiphany's a pretty powerful thing, huh?"

"It is indeed."

180

Annie continued, "An epiphany sets you on a path and you move ahead. You grow from that moment on and move out from the epiphany. You don't keep clinging to the moment. Pardon my language, but it's like getting a kick in the pants. It pushes you forward. It doesn't keep you tied to the past."

The father blinked.

A lock of hair fell across Annie's eyes and she tossed it back, asking, "How old were you when Franco was killed?"

"I was seventeen."

"Where'd you live?"

"Lower East Side."

"Whereabouts?"

"Delancey Street."

"That's a rough neighborhood. A lotta kids don't make it out."

"I take no credit for it. God gave me the strength and the faith to succeed."

"Where did you go to school?"

"Seward Park."

"Are you a diocesan priest?"

He nodded once.

"That must keep you pretty busy."

"The Lord's work is never done."

"Amen," Annie replied, crossing herself quickly.

"You're Catholic?" he asked.

"For all of my fifty-four years." Annie smiled. "Father, I know you're busy, but if I could trouble you with just a few more questions, what exactly was it you heard your neighbors talking about the morning after Mr. Franco was murdered."

He waved a hand as if chasing a fly from his face. "Talk. That a man was stabbed while walking home on Ninth Street. What a shame it was. What sort of place were they living in where a man loses his life for three dollars. That kind of talk. Nothing concrete. Just the idle chatter of women and old men."

Annie said, "Well, thank you, Father. I'm sorry we've taken so much of your time." She slipped him a card. "If anything comes to mind, maybe you could give us a call, huh?"

Cammayo read the card. "Of course."

Heading out the door Annie stopped to ask one more question. "Father"—she smiled—"pardon my ignorance, but why do you burn a Niño de Atocha candle at the grave?"

She and the father locked eyes. A small smile tipped his lips. "Much of my work is related to prison ministry. Saint Niño de Atocha, my child, is of course the patron saint of prisoners. And as I told you, I get much of my inspiration at Mr. Franco's grave."

Appearing satisfied, Annie said, "Thanks again for your time, Father."

She and Frank didn't speak until they were back in the car.

"Don't forget the Nova," Frank told her.

"Right."

"What do you think?"

"What do I think? I think it's funny that considering the Lord's work is never done Father Cammayo makes time every two weeks to visit the grave of a stranger dead thirty-six years. I think that dog's not runnin' on all fours."

"It's kinda odd."

Checking traffic over her shoulder, Annie said, "I think we need to do a little background on the *padre*."

CHAPTER 37

"Hey. It's Frank. Just wanted to say hi. I'll try you later."

Frank wondered where Gail was on a Saturday evening. Her jealous streak itched but she didn't scratch it. Instead she reached for her journal. She got a paragraph written before Gail called back.

"Hi. I got your message. How are you?"

"Okay. How 'bout you?"

"I had a lovely day. Trina's here and we went for a walk on the beach and had a scrumptious dinner. It was really nice."

Trina was Gail's sister and Frank answered, "How long's she staying?"

"Just tonight. She's going home tomorrow."

"I'm glad you took a whole day off. You're not working too hard."

"I know. I've got a stack of paperwork I brought home and I'll get to it tomorrow but today I played. How about you? Are you about frozen to death?"

"Yeah. Ready to come home and thaw out."

"When's that going to be?"

"I'm not sure. I got a bite today."

"You're kidding!"

"No. The mystery visitor turned out to be a goddamned priest. Imagine my surprise. Didn't know I could still be surprised. Anyway, I tailed him to this church and called Annie. We lost him while I was waiting for her to show but a secretary gave us his address. We tracked him down—Annie did all the talking—but his story sounds pretty hinky. Some bullshit about how my father's murder changed his life. It was an epiphany for him and he's never forgotten."

"Well, how did he know your father?"

"He didn't. The man was a total stranger to him. He claims he heard about it the morning after it happened and he went and visited the spot and practically ascended. His story holds water like a leaky bucket. Annie and I went back to the precinct and worked the computers for a couple hours. Nothing unusual apart from the fact that he is *Monsignor* Roberto Cammayo."

Frank summarized from the notes she'd been jotting down in her notebook.

"Born nineteen fifty-three, in Colon, Panama. Mother Rosalia Pretto, father Romeo Cammayo. Mother's remarried. Name's Calderon. The guy does prison ministry so there was a lot of DOJ background on him. He was arrested twice for public protest. Has a sister with a rap sheet half a mile long, mostly prostitution and possession. Sister's name is Alvarez. Flora Alvarez. Last known address was Baruch Houses, where the mother lives. So guess where I'm going tomorrow. Of all the places to live in Manhattan she's got to live there."

"What's Baruch Houses?"

"The last place my mom and I lived."

"Oh."

"Anyway, the padre's story smells. He spends an inordinate amount of time paying homage to a thirty-six-year-old memory.

184

Just doesn't make sense, so we'll pump the mother tomorrow. See what she remembers." Frank reached for the bottle of Perrier by her bed. "Another thing. Why would my dad's death in particular stand out? This was the seventies. The city was in the middle of a huge crime wave. People getting killed—especially where Cammayo lived—would have been an everyday thing. So why the sudden epiphany for a murder that one, he didn't even witness? Supposedly. Two, for a man he didn't even know? A complete stranger. And three, my dad was popped up on Ninth Street. If Cammayo was living down on Delancey at the time, like he claims, then that's not even his neighborhood. It all stinks like a week-old fish. I'm not buying it. I don't know what he's hiding but we'll figure it out."

"Well, it's great you have a lead."

"Yeah. It is."

"You don't sound happy about it."

"No, I am. It's just . . . weird. Standing in this guy's apartment and listening to him talk about my dad. I felt like I was watching a movie I'd already seen. I gotta admit I'm a little numb. It was exciting following him, but it's still weird. Half of me really hopes he knows something but the other half wishes this would all go away. Half the time I'm sorry I opened this whole can of worms, then half the time I can't wait to dig deeper. Guess the cop and the daughter in me are duking it out."

"Who's winning?"

"I don't know. Doesn't matter, I guess. Either way, it won't bring him back. Even if Cammayo did it, even if he turns out to be a hope-to-die junkie turned priest who killed my father, it still won't bring him back. Nothing can ever change that and I still hate that.

"I guess that's the bottom line. I hate all this. And I want to find the hype that started all this shit and make him hurt, too. Priest or not. Whoever he is I want him to hurt as bad as I do." Frank sighed. "But I know hurting him won't fix the hole my dad left. Nothing can change that. So then I start arguing, why am I doing this if nothing's going to change? I can't fix all those years without him so what the hell's the point? Then Lieutenant Franco chimes in—'It's the law. Justice. Man committed a murder he should be caught and punished. The fact you can't bring your father back is irrelevant. It's a matter of law and order. Period.' I just wish it were that simple. Sorry. I'm rambling."

"You're right. You've become practically loquacious since you quit drinking."

"Ah, there's my English professor. What's loquacious mean?"

"Talkative."

"Ah. Sorry."

"No, I like it much better than your characteristic reticence. That means silence."

"I knew that one." Frank smiled at the wall.

"I like it a lot. I like knowing what's going on in your head. It makes me feel like you trust me enough to tell me. I hated when you were drinking and you'd just shut down. I always felt so left out."

"I know. You were. Everybody was. Including me."

"So talkative is much better."

"Good. 'Cause that's what I've got to learn to do. Talk, talk, talk. I've even started a journal. Can you believe it?"

Gail laughed. "No, I can't. My God, you really are changing."

"I'm trying, doc. Trying like hell."

"Well, it sounds like you're doing a wonderful job. Tell me more."

"Let's see." Frank stretched on the bed, reveling in Gail's voice. "It's been a helluva couple weeks. For that matter, a helluva last six months. I wonder what I'd be doing right now if I hadn't called Joe that night."

"I can guarantee you wouldn't be talking to me."

"Or sleeping in a cop's guest room in New York, and certainly not tracking down leads in my father's murder. It still sounds weird saying that. My father's murder. It's almost like having an out-of-body experience. I think I'm still kind of numb around it. And

186

that's okay. I need some distance to be able to do this. But you know what? I didn't call to hear my own voice. Tell me about Gail."

"Gail's all right. It's nice to see Trina. I miss her. I should take a weekend off and go up to my mom's to see everybody."

"You should. It'd be good for you to get out of the morgue and spend more time in the fresh air. How much of that shit can you breathe before it gets to you?"

"Oh, come on. I'm lucky if I spend a couple hours in there. You know I'm always in a meeting or at the university or in my office. I'd love to be in there more."

"Well, I'm glad you're not. Can't be good for you."

"Hey, congratulations. When did you get your medical degree?"

"Same time you went into stand-up comedy." Gail laughed, making Frank smile again. "Think when I get home you can squeeze me in for dinner? Sometime between your day job and your night job?"

"I'll check my schedule," Gail assured.

"You do that. Let me know."

"I will."

To postpone hanging up, Frank asked how Gail's co-workers were, her boss, even her cats. When the clock on the nightstand flicked to midnight, she said, "I'd love to talk to you all night but I should let you get back to Trina."

"Yeah. We're going to watch a video. Romantic comedy. You'd hate it. You should get to bed. It's late there."

"Yeah, I know. See you when I get home?"

"You bet. Get some sleep, copper. Good luck tomorrow."

"Thanks. Say hi to Trina for me." There was a pause at Gail's end. Frank had seen the women in Gail's family close ranks around each other and she guessed they hadn't been happy about Frank dumping Gail. "Or don't," she added.

"Yeah. Maybe later."

"Right. Well, have fun."

"Okay," Gail answered softly. "Sleep tight."

Frank hung up, too wired to sleep. She paced the small room, sipping Perrier and pausing to write in her notebook or check her father's file. In between, she tried not to read too much into why Gail wouldn't say hi to Trina for her.

CHAPTER 38

After Annie went swimming on Sunday morning she and Frank headed for the Baruch Houses. Frank asked, "Was that true what you told Cammayo yesterday, about wantin' to be a cop?"

Annie offered a crooked grin. "Let's just say I went to Brooklyn College and one day there was a car crash out front, okay?"

Frank tried not noticing the familiar sights outside her window. "So why did you?"

"Steady paycheck. Good benefits. Good pension. Somethin' different happenin' everyday. You?"

"Same," Frank fibbed.

Crossing Canal Street Annie asked, "You ever been in Baruch?"

Frank nodded.

"It's the largest public housing project in Manhattan. Got twenty-four hundred apartments."

"I know."

"How do you—? Don't tell me you lived in Baruch, too."

"Last two years of high school."

"Where else?"

"That's all. East Village, to Masaryk, to Baruch."

Annie went quiet and Frank liked it that way. Her eyes skimmed the skyline, refusing to dip to street level. Even after Annie parked Frank averted her gaze.

"What?"

"What, what?" Frank countered.

"Whaddaya lookin' for up there?"

"Nothin'." Frank got out. She let Annie lead the way even though nothing had changed in twenty-seven years.

A man in torn clothes started toward the detectives. Recognizing the car and making them for cops he retreated. The women climbed to the fourth floor and found the apartment they wanted.

"You okay?"

"Peachy."

Annie shrugged and rapped hard on the metal door.

"Who is it?"

"Police."

"Police?"

"NYPD. Open the door."

There was grumbling but after a series of locks tripped, a thin, ashen-skinned woman opened the door. Unkempt and red-eyed, she bounced in her own skin. A crackhead.

Holding her ID out, Annie asked, "Rosalia Calderon?"

"She ain't here."

"Are you Flora Alvarez?"

"Yeah."

"Can we come in a minute?"

"For what?"

"We'd like to ask you some questions."

"I ain't done nothin'!"

"Not about you. About an old homicide, when you would have been about five."

"Five?" came the shouted reply. "Don't know nothin' 'bout no *homicide* when I be five."

"You might be surprised how much you remember. Can we come in?"

"I don't know." The woman looked over her shoulder, pulling at a twist of hair. From inside the apartment a television and a radio blared.

"I promise we'll only be a minute."

Flora pulled the door open.

"Do you live here?"

"Don't it look like it?"

As Frank took in the blankets on the couch, empty Rheingold cans and full ashtray, Annie asked, "How long have you lived here, Miss Alvarez?"

Flora raised a hand over the floor. "Since I was dis big."

"Would you have been livin' here in nineteen sixty-nine?"

Struggling to make the calculations, Flora finally agreed, "Yeah, I'd a been here."

"Who else was living here then?"

"My mother. My father was dead. He was a electrician. He got shocked to death when I was four. My brothers woulda been here." She scowled, reaching for a cigarette. "Pablo woulda still been here. Maybe. No," she decided, lighting her smoke and inhaling deeply. "He be gone by then. I remember he left in winter."

"Who's Pablo?"

"My brother."

"How many brothers do you have?"

"Two. Well, three, maybe. I don't know."

"You don't know how many brothers you have?"

Alvarez scratched under her hairline. "Pablo he took off in 'sixty-nine and we ain't seen him since."

"Why'd he take off?"

Alvarez shrugged. "Berto said a dealer be lookin' for him and he had to go. Owed the man lotta money is the story I always heard."

"Who's Berto?"

191

"Roberto. Roberto and Edmundo my brothers."

"You're sure Pablo took off in 'sixty-nine?"

"Yeah."

"And it was winter?"

Alvarez bobbed her head without hesitation. "Pablo had his own bed and when he left, I got one of his blankets."

Annie and Frank looked at each other.

"And no one's heard from him since?"

Alvarez blew smoke. "That boy prob'ly been dead a long time now."

"Why do you say that?"

"He a junkie," the woman stated wistfully. "A junkie ain't long for this world."

Alvarez's foot bounced and between drags she beat a steady *tap-tap-tap* with her cigarette on the ashtray.

Frank told her, "Describe Pablo for us. The last time you saw him."

"That was a long time ago," Alvarez answered, gazing back into the past.

"Try. How tall was he?"

"Taller than Berto, by a little. Skinny. He was always skinny but he got skinnier after the junk. He wunt light like me. He was dark, like our daddy. And handsome, too. Before the junk, I remember dat. He used to swing me 'round 'til I be dizzy. He made me laugh. He made me a doll oncet. Outta wood. He liked to carve things. I remember dat. He be always carving some'tin'. He was nice. I liked Pablo."

"How much older than you was he?"

The question confounded Alvarez. Her face frizzled up. "I don't know. Maybe twelve, t'irteen years."

"Did he use for a long time?"

"All my life."

"Any of his friends still around? Anybody he woulda used with?"

"I don't know." Alvarez jumped up and started pacing. "Why all dese questions? Why you wanna know 'bout Pablo? You t'ink he done somet'in'?"

"We think he mighta seen somethin'," Annie said.

"Well, he be dead now. I tell you. What he seen, only God know now."

"What was your brother's full name?"

"His full name?" Alvarez struggled again. "Pablo. Maybe he have middle name. I don't know."

"Pablo Cammayo?"

Alvarez bobbed her head. Loosing another cigarette from the pack she lit it off her stub.

Annie asked where her mother was.

"To my aunt's." Flora pointed with her chin. "She in da next buildin' over."

Done with Flora, the women crossed to the next building in the complex. Rather than take their chances in a project elevator, they climbed eight flights to the aunt's apartment. Both were breathing hard when they got to the landing.

"All that ice cream," Annie gasped, but Frank didn't answer. She was trying hard to ignore the smell of frying onions and old piss, the drone of music and *noticias* and babies, the scrawled graffiti and stripped light fixtures.

She'd lived two floors below. Sixth floor. Below the bug line so mosquitoes and flies still found her on sweltering summer nights.

"Ready?" she asked Annie.

Annie nodded and they knocked. The apartment number was painted on the door in glitter and Frank's hand came away speckled in gold.

A broad woman, her gray hair in cornrows, opened up. Annie flashed and asked for Rosalia Calderon.

"Rosa," the woman called without taking her eyes off the cops, "look like your girl in trouble again."

CHAPTER 39

Rosalia Calderon confirmed what her daughter had said. She had, might have, didn't know, a son named Pablo Arturo Cammayo, born in 1949 in Panama. She and her husband moved from Panama to New York in 1956. She did laundry and ironing, he took day labor. She eventually got secretarial work and he found electrical jobs. He died when Pablo was twelve.

"Hard times for everyone," she remarked, a quiet woman with sullen eyes. "I lose my husband. I lose my son. Soon my daughter . . ."

Annie said, "You have two other sons. Tell us about them."

"Edmundo, he's a mechanic for Ford. He's a good son. Given me t'ree grandbabies. And Roberto, he's a priest. That bwoy." She nodded with grave solemnity. "He was *called*. He *always* knew he was gwan be a man of the Lord. Even from a teeny bean of a bwoy."

Annie and Frank shared a glance.

"Always?" Annie asked.

"*Always*," the mother insisted.

"Didn't decide it later in life, in his teens?"

"No. Always he knew. My second husband, he called him *Padrito*, Little Fat'er."

"How was Roberto after Pablo disappeared?"

"He was always a quiet bwoy. Not joking all the time like Pablo and his father. Berto's more like me. He knows there's much pain in the world. He missed his brother, anyone can see that, but he just prayed more. All the time, Berto was prayin'."

"Did Roberto ever use drugs?"

Calderon looked disgusted. "Never. Not him. Not oncet. I tell you, he was a man of the Lord, even from a small bwoy."

"How did you find out Pablo was gone?"

"Berto. He said Pablo come to him in the night. That he was in trouble wit' a man over drugs. That the man wanted to kill him and he had to leave for a while. Bobo told me he stole money from my purse for him. I cried more for the money than that bwoy, I can tell you. I long since used up all my tears for that bwoy. My firstborn."

"Who's Bobo?"

A faraway smile flitted over Calderon's face. "Berto. When Flora was small she couldn't say Roberto. It came out Bobobo. We called him Bobo back then."

"Thank you, Mrs. Calderon."

Frank stood quickly.

Walking downstairs Annie smirked, "Still leavin' Monday?"

Eyes straight on the step in front of her Frank gave a joyless smile.

"Well," Annie said, "I think we better talk to the Father again."

"Let me ask you something. Can you be objective, Cammayo being a priest and all?"

Annie whirled. She lifted the ID around her neck. "I didn't get this sellin' Girl Scout cookies, Frank. You askin' whether I can do my job or not?"

"I just need to know."

"You just worry 'bout yourself, cookie, and keep outta my way." Annie brushed past and Frank let her stomp ahead.

Back in the car, Annie gunned into traffic.

Frank explained, "It's just you being Catholic and him being a priest, it made me wonder."

"Yeah, well, don't wonder no more. You maybe let your personal life interfere with your work. Me? I got twenty-six years on the Job. You don't think I've ever worked a priest before? I could work the Pope if I hadda, cookie, so don't you worry about a chump like Cammayo."

"All right. Sorry."

Annie shook her head and grumbled. She fished through her purse and chomped on espresso beans. "It's Sunday, you know. I could be home, but what am I doin'? Runnin' around chasin' down a cold one for you, that's what I'm doin'. And what do I get for it? 'Annie, can you interview a priest?' No, this I do not need."

Staring out her window, Frank let Annie rant.

Annie parked at the precinct and Frank followed her upstairs. Annie flipped on her computer. Frank sat and watched.

"Think you could make coffee while I work?"

"You runnin' Pablo Cammayo?"

"Yeah. Wanna tell me how to do it?"

Frank bit off a smile and made the coffee.

After she brought Annie a "regular," meaning with a regular amount of cream and two sugars, Annie told the monitor, " 'Fraid we ain't gonna get much, this being 'sixty-nine and prior. Got somethin', though."

She hit the print button and Frank retrieved the paper. Lifting a brow she read, "Nineteen seventy. Busted in Kansas. Armed robbery. Did half a nickel in Leavenworth. Paroled early."

Annie scrolled and typed. Her coffee got cold. At last she sat back, whipping off her reading glasses. "After that, nothin'. Probably shot a hot load and is pushin' up daisies in a Podunk Potter's Field. You know that's the odds, right?"

"Yeah," Frank agreed. "I still want to talk to Cammayo."

"He's got a five o'clock mass. It's one thirty. Ya already ruined my Sunday. Wanna ride to Brooklyn?"

"Thought you'd never ask."

CHAPTER 40

Father Cammayo was at Our Lady Queen of the Angels. Obviously dismayed to see the women, he checked his watch. "Sunday's a busy day for me."

"It's my day off," Annie countered. "Surely you can spare ten minutes."

Cammayo looked at his watch again. "No more."

"Good. You tell us the truth, Father, and it shouldn't even take that."

"What truth might that be?"

"We talked to your sister Flora this mornin'. And your mother. Very nice women, both of 'em. Very helpful. Very fond of you. Very respectful of how you've always wanted to be a priest. How you had the callin' since you were this high," Annie said with her hand over the floor. "So enough already with Franco's murder and your sudden epiphany. And tell ya the trut'," Annie confided, "your story wasn't that good the first time ya told it."

"What else did they tell you?"

"You're pressed for time, Father. We don't need to go into that. So tell us again why you're still takin' flowers to this man's grave."

"They wouldn't understand," he told his folded hands. "It *was* an epiphany. A vision, if you will. I'd always known I would be a priest, yes, in my head. But standing on the sidewalk that morning I knew it in my heart. That was when I truly felt touched by God, when Christ became real for me, a man of flesh and blood as I was, who *suffered*. But as I admitted, I was weak. I didn't want to suffer like Christ—choosing to follow a life of the spirit seemed less a trial than following a life of the flesh. And that morning I felt as if God had touched me personally, had approved my choice and offered His grace even though I felt it was a coward's way out. So it was an epiphany. And I still am grateful after all this time."

Frank clapped. "Nice, Father. Maybe it'll play in the pulpit but I'm not buying it."

"That's your choice," he conceded. Looking at his wrist again, he added, "Now I really must go."

Frank looked at her watch too. "Aw, you said ten minutes, Father. Don't tell me you're not a man of your word."

"If you don't believe me what else can I say?"

"Well," Annie responded. "You could tell us about Pablo."

Cammayo blinked. "Pablo."

"Yeah. Pablo."

"What about him?"

"When was the last time you saw him?"

"Nineteen sixty-nine."

"Yeah, winter, right?" Aiming in the dark, Annie added, "The night of February twelfth, to be precise. What happened that night?"

Cammayo's Adam's apple rose and fell. "I don't know where my brother is."

Annie shot an eyebrow up. "I didn't ask ya that. I asked what happened that night."

"It was a long time ago. I was young. I don't remember."

Annie was crestfallen. "No disrespect, Father, but you're killin' me here. All my life a Cat'lic, and here's a Father *lyin'* to me. You're breakin' my heart here."

Frank interrupted. "Thing I wanna know is, how'd you know Franco died for three dollars?"

"What are you talking about?"

"You distinctly said yesterday that it was a shame a man had to die for three dollars. How would you know how much the killer took from him? You couldn't unless you were the killer or the killer told you, right? So how do you know that?"

Cammayo stood like a marble statue.

Frank stepped forward. She pulled her ID. "Do you remember my name?"

"No. I can't recall."

"You know it," Frank urged.

"I don't think I do."

"Sure you do." Frank lifted the plastic holder. "Franco. Just like my daddy."

She let that sink in while Cammayo read her face.

"I was there that night and matter of fact he did have three dollars. I know 'cause we'd just got groceries. The bill was sixteen and change. He paid with a twenty. Got three bucks back. Just like you said." Frank stepped closer to the priest. She put her hand on his chest and he stiffened. She leaned into him, speaking softly. "I know you got a heart in here. I know you lost your daddy. You and me, we both know how that feels. Know how I know you got a heart? Because you bring flowers to a dead man. A man dead thirty-six years. Only a man with a heart would do that." She patted his chest. "Not only did you lose your father, you lost a brother, too. And if Pablo was my brother, I'd do everything I could to protect him. And you've done that, Berto. But it's over. You did the best you could all this time and now it's over. You don't have to keep a secret for a dead man. I hate to say that, but you and I both know, being the junkie he was, Pablo's probably dead. You're lying for a dead man. Lying in front of your God and for what? How's he gonna feel about that come Judgment Day? Is he gonna be pleased with you, Berto?"

She plied his weakness with the tender family diminutive.

"I don't know much about God but even I gotta think he's not gonna be too happy with you. But it's not too late, right? You can come clean. To us, and more importantly, to yourself and your God. It's time, Berto. None of us are gettin' any younger. It's time to tell the truth and put the past behind us, to bury it and let it go. What happened that night, Berto? It's time to tell. You're safe now. We don't care what happened after the fact. All we care about is seeing this through. For thirty-six years, you, me, even the taxpayers of New York been carryin' this corpse around. Let's bury it. Right here. Right now. Let Pablo go with full honors. He deserved that. You deserve that. Tell us what happened that night, Berto."

Cammayo broke away and turned his back to her.

Frank went around him. "Go ahead," she whispered the demand. "Tell the truth. You've protected Pablo long enough. It was a good hard fight but it's over. You did your best. Now finish it. Cleanly and with grace. Truly. For God's sake."

She could tell from the way Cammayo slowly wagged his head that he was breaking, that he was fighting the telling. And she knew that great secrets were hard to tell. The greater the secret, the fewer the words for it.

"It's okay," Frank urged. "It's not a secret anymore. It's time to let it go."

When Cammayo spoke he was barely audible. "He was sick. He needed to score. I was afraid he was going to wake everybody up and scare the little ones. He was my oldest brother. Pablo. You'd have had to known him before the dope. He was kind and funny and he took care of us. He'd discipline us when we needed it and he'd protect us when we needed that. And I guess it was too much for a boy. He shouldered all the responsibilities of a man and at some point it became too much for him. I can understand that. After he left it was my turn to bear the load. But I was older then. And I had God to turn to. Pablo never had that. All he had was that false god in the needle. I tried to get him off it. Sometimes he'd be clean for months at a time but he'd always go back to it. He was scared that night. Scared like I'd never seen him. He made me scared. He thought he'd killed a cop. He said he needed the money. He had to fix and get out of town. I scrounged up what I could for him and he left. I never saw him again. Never heard from him. I heard the talk next morning, and later, in the paper, there was a paragraph about a man that had been robbed and killed in the East Village that night. There was no suspect. Anyone with information was asked to contact the police."

When he finally looked at Frank, the priest's eyes were wet. "I couldn't do that. I fought with my conscience, but blood won. Pablo was my brother. I loved him. I couldn't betray him. All these years . . . I've always wondered what happened to him. I think of him every time I visit your father's grave. It keeps me connected to him."

Frank had heard enough. The urge to hurt Cammayo was a throbbing red pulse throughout her body. She stepped to Annie's ear. "I'll be outside if you need me."

"Yeah, sure."

As Frank's hand hit the knob, Cammayo pleaded, "Forgive me."

Frank stopped. She took a deep breath and held it. Felt it turn scarlet inside her. She walked out the door.

CHAPTER 41

"You okay?"

Frank moved her head in the affirmative.

"I gotta bring him in for a statement."

"You do that. I'll catch a taxi."

Annie rubbed Frank's shoulder. "I'll see you back at the apartment, okay?"

"Yeah."

Frank walked away from Our Lady of the Angels. She walked blocks and blocks, ignoring taxis. She seethed. Passing bars, she noticed each one, fully aware that what was inside them could dampen her fury into a dull and manageable anger. She kept walking. One foot in front of the other. Over and over she thought, he knew. All this time, he knew. The lying, hypocritical bastard knew. He knew.

The accusation became a chant. She walked, each step being the next thing to do. She reiterated her mantra, concentrating so brutally on Cammayo that she forgot the liquor stores and bars. By the time she walked her rage into a simmering, bruised anger, it was dusk. She had no idea where she was. Except on a corner. Near a bar.

Daley's Bar.

It sounded so welcome. The outside was brick, the door worn wood. Small signs in opaque windows blinked *Bud* and *Open*. A working-class bar. She bet it was dim inside and smelled like centuries of beer. She imagined the sour, malty smell, the way the bartender would draw the beer from the tap, the thick glass against her lips, how the beer would bubble over her tongue in a sharp gush.

She pulled on the door handle and stepped inside. She was right. It was dim and smelled of generations of smoke and sweat and ale. Three men at the bar turned to stare. She walked in their direction. Her eyes tracked the bartender.

"What'll it be?" he asked.

She leaned into the smooth, slick wood. Rows of bottles beckoned. She considered each one. The bartender shifted his weight, sighed.

"Phone book," she finally answered.

The bartender glared. He slapped the book on the bar and continued his conversation with the men.

Outside, Frank hailed a cab. The drive to Tribeca was short. Annie had the door open before Frank could turn her key in the lock.

"Where were you? I was gettin' worried."

"Walking."

Behind her Annie bolted the door. "Walkin'? You walked here from Brooklyn?"

Frank sighed. "I walked. I stopped. I took a cab."

"Oh. You hungry? You must be starvin'. I bought pizza. It's in the oven. I'll get you a slice."

Frank waved her off. "I'm not hungry."

"You sure? You had dinner?"

"No."

"You should eat. I'll get you a slice."

"I'm not hungry, Annie."

"Forget hunger. You should eat anyway."

Giving in seemed easier than fighting. Frank dropped into a kitchen chair. "Get your statement?"

"Yeah. You worked him nice," Annie said, sliding a plate onto the table.

Frank picked at an olive, wishing she had a beer chaser.

"The thing I don't get is why Pablo thought he'd killed a cop. What made him think that?"

Frank shrugged. "Ask his brother."

"I did. He couldn't say."

"Must've seen us coming outta Cal's."

"But how dumb is that to jack a cop?"

"Cop with a little girl's a different story. Cop's gonna protect the kid, so they'll probably just hand the money over and not make a fuss. Besides, it was winter. It was cold. Not like there were a lot of good marks out. And for Christ's sake," Frank snapped, "we're talkin' about a junkie, right? It wasn't fuckin' Einstein that jacked my pop. How fuckin' smart is a junkie? Especially one lookin' to fix?"

Frank pushed away the pizza. Annie watched from against the sink.

Frank apologized. "It's just . . . a lot to take in. That this bastard—this pious man of God, right? That he knew the whole time and never told anyone. All the time I was looking and wondering, he knew. All the time my Uncle Al spent looking and wondering, Cammayo knew. All the hours my uncle spent trying to find this bastard. He retired still looking. Died two months later. Liver failure. Drank himself to death. Never got over he couldn't find his own brother's killer. Pablo didn't kill just one person. He took a lot of other lives with him. So forgive me if I'm a little bitter, huh?"

"There ain't nothin' to forgive. You got a right to be angry."

"A priest, of all people. A guy you're supposed to be able to trust. That's the part that burns me. Pure and holy and all that crap." Frank ran her fingers through her hair. "Man of God, my ass. How can you believe what these people tell you, Annie? You're a bright woman. How can you believe that crap the church feeds

204

you about truth and virtue and honesty? It's a ration of shit. How can you believe what they tell you out one side of their mouth when they're lying out the other side?"

"It's not a man I believe. It's an idea."

"Yeah, well, what fuckin' idea is that?"

"I understand you're upset but I don't think attackin' my belief is gonna make you feel better."

"No. I'm serious. I want to know. You don't believe in a man but an idea. So, enlighten me. What's the big idea? Let me in on the secret."

Annie pursed her lips and folded her arms. Frank was pleased with the conversation's distraction despite feeling guilty about needling Annie into a defensive posture.

"You really wanna know or am I just handin' you more ammo?"

"I really wanna know."

Annie pulled out the chair opposite Frank. "The big idea," she started slowly. "It's hard to put into words. It's more a feeling than an idea. It's a conviction, a certainty that someone is watchin' out for me. Like that story I told you about the lake. When that old woman fished me out, I was shook, but I felt absolutely safe. I felt rescued. Somethin', someone was takin' care of me. All that stuff about Mary and Jesus and God"—she crossed herself—"habit. It's all nice but in my humble opinion it's not the truth. For instance, Mary over there. I love her dearly. I cherish her, but she's not the big idea. Neither's Jesus or even God. They're just avenues to something much bigger, to a mystery, to a spirit so huge we can't even begin to imagine it. But for all its immensity that mystery permeates every cell of our bodies. It's there all the time, but I *forget*. I get caught up in paperwork, traffic, meetin's, a run in my stockin', everything, and I forget I'm part of somethin' much bigger 'an all that. I forget I'm a part of the mystery, of the immensity of it all, and Mary's my way of reconnectin' to that feelin'. She's the path I take to the mystery, to that absolute conviction that everything's right with the world no matter how messed up it looks from my miniscule perception. And there's lots of paths, but again, in my opinion, they all lead to the same the place."

205

"To the mystery."

"Yes. To an infinite . . . indefinable conviction that rests in the marrow of my bones."

"That's a paradox. Infinite and indefinable yet sitting in the marrow of your bones."

"That's the thing!" Annie slapped the table. "It *is* a paradox. It's cellular yet it's immense. It's indefinable yet it's absolutely knowable. That's the mystery of it all. It's why one face, one name, can't start to describe it. So I have my faith, I have my Mary, but I know they're limited. I know that priests and nuns and popes are limited. They're only human. All they can do is tell the stories that might get you to the mystery, but *they're* not the mystery. They're just spokesmen, the pitch men."

"PR for the unknowable."

"Exactly." Annie leaned over the table. "You ever tell my mother we had this conversation and I'll cut your tongue out, ya hear me?"

"She believes the story?"

"God bless her." Annie nodded. "The story's more important to her than the meaning of it. That's how you get your fanatics, your zealots. It's easier to believe in the stories than to seek the mystery behind them. Dogma's for people too tired to think. But faith, that's trickier business. It requires work and effort, especially when things aren't goin' your way."

Frank probed, "When your son died, did you have faith?"

Annie sat back. She smoothed the creases in the tablecloth. "I was angry. I was mad. But under it all I think I always knew it was the way it had to be. I didn't know why—I never will—but you and me, we see it every day. People die every day. Kids, good people, people that got no business dyin'. Like your father. It's just all part of life, part of the mystery, much as we hate it and much as it hurts. That's when I started turnin' away from the church I was raised in and leaning more on Mary. She was comfortable. Her story reassured me I wasn't the only one to suffer, that people suffer all the time, for reasons we don't know why. And we endure and we go on and life goes on. And there's joy again and pleasure. It's all cycles and we take each day as it comes."

"One day at a time."

"Exactly," Annie affirmed. "One day at a time."

Frank pulled the pizza toward her.

"Want I should warm that up?"

"Naw. It's good. I guess it's all good, huh?"

Annie nodded. "All part of the mystery."

Frank chewed. The pizza was good. She got up for a Coke. "You mind if I talk to Cammayo?"

"'Bout what?"

"His brother. Just some things I want to know. I wanna put a face to the man who killed my dad. I been trying to see it for a long time."

"You okay with talkin' civil to him? I don't want you harassin' him."

"I'm not gonna harass him. I just want to ask a few questions. Come with me if you want."

"Nah. I got all the answers I want. Just be respectful, huh?"

"'Cause he's a priest?"

"No. Because he lost somebody, too. You're not the only one lost somebody that night. You even said so yourself."

Frank agreed. "I'll behave."

"Better." Annie pointed a sharp nail. She pushed out of her chair, rising with a yawn. "I'm bushed."

"Yeah. Long day. Hey."

Annie looked at her.

"Thanks for everything."

"Forget about it. I'm happy. I closed a case, right?"

"Right. Sleep well."

"Yeah, you too. Sweet dreams, huh?"

"Back at you."

Frank was left with dinner as cold as her anger.

CHAPTER 42

"I know you've got a busy day but I need five minutes of your time."

Cammayo protested, "I've already told you and Detective Silvester everything I know."

Frank squashed her irritation. "Telling me everything I want to know would take months. All I want is five minutes."

Cammayo bowed his head. He opened the door and Frank entered the familiar apartment. Seeing her, Cammayo's roommate retreated from the living room. Cammayo switched off the TV.

Frank said, "Tell me about Pablo."

"What about him?"

"Anything. Everything. What was he like? What was his favorite color? Did he have a nickname? Did he like baseball? Football? Everything."

"He liked baseball. He was a Yankees fan. I don't know his favorite color. I do know he was good boy and I wonder every day what kind of man he would have been. If he could have kicked the dope."

"You say that like you know he's dead."

"I'm under no illusions, Detective. I know the kind of junkie my brother was. I know the odds of him being dead by now. But you asked what he was like. He was kind. That's what I remember most. He could be stern and sometimes he hit us but never without a reason. He punished to teach a lesson. But mostly he was affectionate. I remember my sister hugging him all the time. My younger brother, too. He'd sit with them on either side of him, an arm around each child. He smiled a lot and laughed. Pablo laughed like birds singing. I always envied him. I never saw humor in the world the way Pablo did. He was kind. He had a gentle soul. That's why it was easy to keep his secret all these years. He was easy to help. If you knew him, you'd want to help him. He was like that. A very kind young man. Very giving."

Frank took an unoffered chair and Cammayo perched on the sofa.

"How old was he when he started using?"

Cammayo frowned. "I was twelve so he must have been sixteen. I tried to get him to stop but he'd just laugh and tell me not to worry. Which of course I couldn't do, so I prayed for him. I prayed for all of us. With our father passed on, Pablo was the head of the household. My mother worked two, sometimes three jobs, so you see, it was Pablo who raised us. Until the drugs became more important and then it was my turn to wear our father's shoes."

"Is that why he came to you that last night?"

"I suppose. And he knew I'd help him. I loved Pablo. I'd do anything for him."

"And you did. For a long time."

"Yes."

"I never had a brother or sister," Frank volunteered, "but if I loved them I'd have probably done the same thing."

"Maybe, maybe not. We're all different. I wrestled with my conscience a long time. For me, in the end, blood was thicker than water. It's ironic."

"How so?"

"I wanted to be a priest so I would be freed from all corporal attachments yet I am bound to my brother by this invisible chain."

"And you never told anyone?"

"Only God."

"Why didn't you tell?"

"The better to protect him. I chose the lie that he owed a dealer money. It was certainly believable. It explained why he left in such a hurry and it protected him from harmful speculation. It was easily assumed he was in trouble over drugs and that was what I wanted everyone to think."

"Where do you think he might have gone?"

"He didn't have any money. I managed to find a little over twenty dollars but I imagine that was quickly used on dope. He couldn't have gone far. I remember he said he might go to Panama and that he'd call me. But of course he never did."

"What's in Panama?"

"Our grandparents were there. Our mother and father were from Panama City. They came to the United States when Pablo was seven. My mother always talked of going back . . ."

"Of everyone in your family, who do you think Pablo was closest to?"

"My mother. Well, before that, my father. I know it was hard on him. He didn't laugh a long time after my father died. None of us did, but with Pablo you noticed such a thing."

"So if he was closest to his mother why didn't he go to her that night? Why didn't he ask her for help?"

Cammayo shrugged, stared at the carpet. "Because he knew I'd help him. That I'd do whatever he asked. I don't think he wanted to hurt my mother any more than he already had. The drugs hurt her. He'd beg money from her and when she finally realized where it went each time, no matter how elaborate the story, she finally stopped giving it to him. Then he'd steal it. She had to hide whatever she had from him."

"He was still living at home with you and your family, so what was he doing in the East Village that night? Why so far away?"

"I couldn't tell you. There were many nights Pablo didn't come home. More nights than not."

210

"Did he have a girlfriend?"

Cammayo smiled for the first time. "For a while he went with a beautiful girl named Alma. She was very quiet, very shy. Everyone called her Conejo—that means rabbit in Spanish. She was just like one. Soft and shy." His smile faded. "She started using when Pablo did. I heard she died about a year after he left. She was pregnant and went into premature labor, but the baby was crooked or something. It wouldn't come out right and she died in labor. Her heart stopped. I heard she weighed eighty-five pounds when she died."

Frank couldn't help comment, "For such a kind young man your brother sure spread a lot of misery."

"Satan comes in many guises, Detective. For our family he came in the form of white powder. I wish you could have met him before the drugs. You couldn't have helped but like him. Ask anyone. He was a good person until the drugs took him."

"Drugs don't take people. People take drugs." Hearing the hypocrisy in her anger she changed the subject. "What did he take with him when he left? Besides money."

"Nothing. He came in through the fire escape. I knew because the window was open and all the cold air was blowing in. Then he left the same way after I gave him the money."

"Why didn't he use the door?"

"I don't know. Maybe he heard the TV on and didn't want my mother to see him."

"Who was watching TV?"

"My mother had it on. She was asleep on the couch with my sister."

"So who else saw Pablo that night?"

"Nobody. Just me."

"What did he look like?"

Cammayo closed his eyes. "Scared. Sick. Junkie sick. He was sweating and shaking. He smelled. He was dirty. He was sick."

"What was he wearing?"

"I don't know. Dark clothes, maybe. I can't remember. Nothing stands out."

211

"How was he wearing his hair?"

"I don't know. He had a cap on. A ski cap."

"Anything unusual about his face?"

"Yes," Cammayo answered right away. "His eye was swollen almost shut."

"Which one?"

Cammayo touched his face. "The right one."

"From top to bottom, tell me everything you remember about that night."

Cammayo cooperated. His story was consistent with his statement. Unwavering. Frank had hoped to find some inconsistencies and her frustration turned to anger.

"Do you think your brother loved you?"

"What does this have—"

Holding up a palm, Frank interrupted, "Yes or no. Did Pablo love you?"

"Yes."

"And his mother?"

"Yes."

"And his sister and his other brother."

"Of course."

"Then explain to me, how in all this time, your brother hasn't once contacted you or Flora or your mother or Edmundo. Can you explain that?"

"No. I can't."

"You must have wondered about it."

"Every day," he admitted.

"So what's your best guess?"

"I already told you. My brother was a junkie. He's probably been dead a long time. I hate the idea but I take a pitiful comfort in it."

"How so?"

Cammayo shrugged. "I hate that his life was wasted on poison. He was a wonderful young man. He was kind and generous and he loved to make people laugh. I hate to think the gift of his life was taken so early. But then I find comfort in that as an explanation for his absence

212

and silence. Surely death could be the only thing keeping him from us. If he were alive he would certainly have reached out to one of us by now. I like to think it would be me. That he trusted me before he left, and that he would trust me again. That he would know how well I'd kept his secret. For all these years. Until you came along."

"Tell me about Leavenworth."

"Leavenworth," Cammayo repeated.

Frank lied, "Pablo called you from there. We have the phone records."

"You have phone records of Pablo calling from *Leavenworth*?" She nodded. "What did he want?"

Cammayo was either completely dumbfounded or a great actor. The way he held Frank's stare indicated the former. "Pablo was in Leavenworth?"

"What did he want?' Frank asked again.

Cammayo sputtered. "When was this?"

"You're telling me you don't know?"

"Of course I don't know. He never called me from *anywhere*. I've told you! I haven't heard from him since he left. When was he in Leavenworth?"

"You tell me."

"*I don't know!*" Cammayo bolted off the couch. "Why are you doing this? For God's sake, woman, when was he there?"

Frank relented. " 'Seventy to 'seventy-three. On possession. Busted in Topeka."

"*Topeka?*" Cammayo marveled. "He said he was going to Panama. What else do you know?"

Cammayo had come alive, hungry for more than Frank could provide, and suddenly she felt sorry for him. "That's it. Paroled in 'seventy-three and then he disappears off the face of the earth."

"What about before that?"

Frank shook her head. "Nothing between here and Topeka."

"What about cellmates? Surely you can get records of that. We can talk to them. Maybe he told them where he was going."

"Yeah. Maybe. But this is hardly a high-priority case for anyone but me. It'll take time. Mostly my own."

213

"I can help," Cammayo insisted. "I have connections in prisons. Surely between us we can find him."

Frank nodded. "He's gotta be somewhere. Even if it's in a shallow grave at least we'd know, right?"

Cammayo crossed himself, dipped his head. "Yes. I'd rather know even that than not know. Please. Help me find him."

"I will," Frank said. "One more time. Tell me everything about the last time you saw him."

Cammayo retold the story, but this time with animation. Frank saw him grasp for each detail but his story was identical to the others.

He finished with a sigh. "You'd have liked him. I know you would. Everybody did. He was just that kind of boy."

Crossing the room, Cammayo offered one of his rare smiles. He pulled a wooden crucifix from the wall and handed it to Frank. It was heavy.

He explained, "Pablo made that for me. For my thirteenth birthday. He hid it from me, working on it when I wasn't home and late at night. He was brilliant with a knife. He could make anything. My mother has a collection of statues he made for her. Over twenty saints. Twenty-two, I think. He had so much talent."

"Who taught him?"

"My father. He carved, too. He taught Pablo the basics, but Pablo was better than our father ever was. God definitely gave that boy a talent." Cammayo burst out with vehemence, "I hate drugs. I hate how they cut down God's flowers just as they're blooming."

"I know," Frank commiserated. "I know."

She admired the forlorn Jesus carved into the cross, handing it back to Cammayo.

"Let me ask you, you being a priest and all, why is that good people like your brother get taken so early? Why does God do stuff like that?"

"No one can know God's ways. He is a mystery and none can fathom mystery's reason. We must accept what God delivers, having faith that His reason is just, though to our simple human eye it appears anything but."

"The Lord works in mysterious ways and all that, huh?"

"And all that, yes."

Cop and cleric stared at each other.

"Thanks for your time," Frank finally offered. To her surprise, Cammayo placed a hand on her arm.

"You're not going to stop looking for him?"

"No."

"Let me help."

"We'll see."

"Please."

Frank nodded. "I'll be in touch."

She turned but Cammayo clamped down through her coat. "On your word?"

She held Cammayo's gaze. She owed him nothing.

"On my word," she vowed.

CHAPTER 43

"Well? So? How did it go?"

Frank let Annie wait on her cell phone. "How did what go?"

"Hello? Did you talk to Cammayo or not?"

"Yeah, I did."

"And? If I wanna talk to him am I gonna find him in a hospital somewhere?"

"I told you I'd be civil and I was. I don't think he knows anything. I think he's on the level."

"Yeah?"

"Yeah. I told him a bullshit story about how we knew Pablo had called him from Leavenworth and he went apeshit. Had no clue what I was talking about."

Annie chuckled. "I'd a liked to seen that. So now what? I can't spend much more time on this, you know."

"Yeah, I know. I appreciate what you've done so far. I'll follow up on Leavenworth, his cellies. Told Cammayo he might go to

Panama. Who knows? Maybe he got there. Probably a huge dead end but it's my time I'm wasting. Not the taxpayers'. I'll let you know what I get."

"Yeah, all right. You gonna stick around to do that?"

"No. I'm gonna take a late flight home. Surprise 'em at work tomorrow morning."

"Oh. Yeah, sure."

After a silence, Frank asked, "Can I take you out to dinner before I go?"

"Nah, we caught a stabbin' last night. Captain's got us all on it. I'm probably gonna be lookin' for this mutt all night."

"Then I won't see you before I go?"

"Not likely. So, you take care, Franco, huh? I gotta go."

"Wait." Unsure how to express her sincerity, Frank blurted out, "I don't know how to thank you for all you've done."

"Aw, shut up. I was just doin' my job."

"A bit above and beyond."

"Hey, it's no big deal. You take care of yourself, cookie."

"Yeah, you too, Annie."

"I'll do that."

Holding the dead phone, Frank already missed her friend. Without enthusiasm she found the Leavenworth number. She was passed through half a dozen numbers until she hit a dead end with an answering machine. She left her message then paced the apartment.

She was anxious. Something wasn't finished. She was clean with Annie—it was nothing there. And Cammayo felt done too. She still vacillated between anger and acceptance, but her anger was hollow. More habit than real. And although Cammayo might have missed a detail or two she was convinced he didn't have much else to offer. She stopped to look out the window, craning to see the skyline the World Trade Center used to fill.

Everything changed and nothing changed. Tower's rose and fell but there were always buildings. Weather changed but there was always sky. People came and went but there were always people.

"Yeah." She tapped the windowpane. "That's it."

Frank got into Annie's old coat one more time. She fired up the protesting Nova and drove east. She made a quick stop before parking in front of the Canarsie Cemetery, following the familiar path to her parents' grave. There were visitors scattered throughout the cemetery, but none were close.

Frank hunched between her parent's stones. She cleared her throat, looking at her father's name. "The good news is, I'm pretty sure who killed you. Bad news is, he's probably dead. But it doesn't matter anyway. You're all dead. Who knows? Maybe you already know each other. Playing cribbage on a cloud, I don't know. Anyway, I'll keep looking. Just in case. Mom, the good news is . . ." She placed a flamboyant bunch of flowers at her mother's stone. "I know you liked pansies." She swallowed. "But they didn't have any. Winter, I guess. So I just took one of everything the florist had. I know you like color . . ." Frank ran a hand across her mouth. She stood, looking around, part cop, part distraction. She squeezed the back of her neck. Glanced up at the bloodless sky.

"The thing is," she whispered, "I'm sorry. Sorry I left. Sorry I ran away. Sorry I wasn't there for you." Fighting the rising pressure in her throat, she tacked on, "I'm sorry you died alone."

The tears came anyway. Frank let them. She bowed her head. "I'm sorry for all of it. Sorry to the core of my bones."

Hot drops splashed on her mother's stone. She thought of them as liquescent offerings and choked on a small laugh.

"Big word, liquescent. I wish you could meet Gail. You'd like her. Both of you. She has your kind of politics. Very correct."

Frank pulled in a deep lungful of the wintry air.

She felt done. Until she had an idea.

Without daring to see if anyone was watching, Frank sat in the snow. She lay down, waving arms and legs, then rose carefully. Looking at the angel on her mother's grave, Frank concluded, "The good news is I love you. Very much. No bad news."

With a nod to the angel, Frank left the way she came.

CHAPTER 44

Frank landed in LA at two in the morning. She got a cab to Figueroa and crashed on the skinny couch in her office. Up at five, she took a French shower and changed into the fresh outfit in her locker. She'd finished half a pot of coffee by the time Darcy came in at five-forty.

"Hey." He plopped the *Times* on his desk and poured a cup. "Good trip?"

"Good enough. Glad to be home. Fill me in."

He did, as the rest of the squad trickled in.

They assembled for the morning brief, and afterward, cocking a hip on Bobby's desk, Frank praised, "Nice job holding the fort down, Picasso."

"Thanks."

"There's a lieutenant's exam coming up. You taking it?"

Bobby sat back and clasped his hands under his chin. He smiled. "I was thinking about it."

"Do more than think about it. Study up. Take it. I'm not gonna be here forever."

"What's that mean?"

"Just means you should be ready to take over a unit. Here or anywhere else." She picked up a six-inch statue on Bobby's desk. It was an intricate carving of a man with wings and a sword. "Who's this?"

"St. Michael. Patron saint of policemen."

Frank studied the dark wood. "Where'd you get it?"

"Irie." Bobby grinned. "Another sideline. He's pretty good."

She put the statue down. "What's Irie's real name?"

"Oh, man, I don't know. I'd have to look it up. John-John or something like that."

"Find it for me."

Frank didn't move and Bobby asked, "Right now?"

"Yeah."

"Why?" he asked, sliding open a drawer.

"Nothing. Just curious."

Obsessively tidy, Bobby found a specific folder in his tabbed and cross-tabbed files. He flipped through to an indexed page and read, "Romeo. John-John Row-*may*-oh."

"Row-may-oh," she repeated. "Huh."

"What?"

"Nothing. Did we ever fill out a package on him?"

Bobby shook his head. Detectives were supposed to register confidential informants. Irie, like a lot of other CIs, had balked at becoming an official snitch but the detectives used him anyway.

Frank edged off the desk. "Anyway. Good job. Get to studying, huh?"

"Roger that."

Before getting tangled in the whirlwind of running a homicide unit Frank closed her office door and called Gail. "Hey," she greeted. "How about lunch?"

"Where are you?"

"Work."

"When did you get in?"

"Late last night. Figured you wouldn't want to give me a ride home at three a.m."

"You figured correct, copper. Welcome home."

"Thanks. It's good to be back. So whaddaya say? Lunch?"

"I can't. Not today. It's too busy. But how about dinner? Maybe Saturday?"

"Dinner it is."

"Did you find anything else before you left?"

"You mean Cammayo?"

"Yeah."

"No. I gotta chase a couple leads down from when he was in the can. I'm pretty sure they'll just go to ground, but still and all, it's nice to have a name after all this time. Even though he's probably long dead."

"Are you sure it's him?"

"Certain."

"Well, good. That must feel satisfying."

"I don't know about satisfying," Frank mused. "More like done. Just over."

"I'm happy for you."

"Thanks. Me too. How you been?"

"Okay. Tired. Exhausted really. I fall into bed and wake up exhausted. I think I need another vacation."

"I read about the Bentley case. Sounds like it's the Sheriff's nightmare now."

"Yeah, thank God."

"So . . ." Frank danced around her question. "When was the last time you had a checkup?"

"I'm going in on Friday. I'm sure it's nothing. I probably just need to take my iron. I've been getting home too late to eat dinner and then I don't want to take vitamins on an empty stomach, so I don't, and this is what happens."

"Sounds like you need someone to cook for you."

"Does this mean you're making dinner Saturday?"

"Lady's choice. I'll take you out, cook at home, whatever you'd like."

"I miss your cooking. Why don't I come over?"

"What would you like?"

"I don't know. Steaks? Up my iron intake?"

Frank already missed the red wine she'd drink with a steak, but answered, "You got it. See you around six?"

"That'll be perfect. I'll see you then."

" 'Kay."

"I'm glad you're back."

"Me too. Saturday."

"Saturday."

Frank nestled her pleasure close to her heart, keeping it there like a small warm bird.

CHAPTER 45
Tuesday, 25 Jan 05—Home

Tired. Easy day but boring. Had to sit through one of Foubarelle's bitch sessions and then the supervisors' meeting. Cleared up a lot on my desk though. Hit the downtown meeting after work. Really like that one. Missed it. Always a lot of cops, law enforcement types there. A couple people missed me. Bull thought I'd gone back out. He's a good guy. Retired from the Santa Monica PD, been sober twenty-one years. Pretty inspiring character. He's got some hairy stories—stopped drinking after he'd called in sick three days in a row, on a bender. Sitting on his couch, throwing up blood into a crystal vase, he saw himself in the mirror over the mantle. Death warmed over, sitting in his living room, holding a vase full of bloody puke. Gave me the willies. Like seeing me in the TV with the Beretta in my mouth.

Had a nice talk with Gail. She's coming over for dinner on Saturday. Yeah, okay, I'm excited. I know anything can happen between now and

Saturday but just the fact that she wants to have dinner is encouraging. I miss her. Miss talking to her everyday, going to bed together, waking up next to her and everything in between. Even miss her clothes all over the floor and dishes piled in the sink. Small enough price to pay for love.

Had a good talk with Mary too. Told her about making the snow angel. She cried. She's so cute. She asked how the willingness to believe was going. I told her it was going well. I'm too tired to fight it. If there's something out there, great. If not, oh well, me and billions of others have been duped. And no way to tell either way. So whatever. I'm willing to be willing to believe there's something out there. Maybe that's who made Bull look in the mirror that morning or made me glance at the TV.

Speaking of weird, I was talking to Darcy and guess who walks into the squad room? Marguerite, of all people. All five-two and a hundred-twenty pounds of tightly packed flesh. Still a bomb, which made her appearance interesting enough, but given how much she dislikes poor Darcy I was surprised to see her there. He was too. While he was recovering, she says to me, "Hello, Lieutenant. You're looking well."

I thank her, tell her I am well.

"Yes," she says. "I can feel that."

I kind of nod, make to leave, but she shakes her head and says, "Still unconvinced, aren't you? What a waste."

"Waste of what?" I ask.

"You have a gift, Lieutenant. Like my ex-husband. The gods gave you both a talent and you both choose to squander it. It's a shame."

Darcy growls, "Marguerite, if you came to berate us maybe you could at least wait until end of watch."

She gives him a sour look and says she's come to talk about Gabriela, if he can spare three minutes for his daughter.

I say, "Good to see you again, Ms. James," and start for my office.

She tells me, "Likewise, Lieutenant," and before I can even see it she's taken one of her business cards—from out of nowhere—maybe she was holding it in her hand, but it felt too cool and smooth to have been held there for long—and she says, "Come see me again, Lieutenant. Soon."

I smile, ask, "Why soon?"

She laughs—gorgeous woman, frankly stunning when she laughs. I *swear she glowed, like chocolate backlit by sun—and she says, "You of all people should know. Our time here is short, unpredictable, and there is much to be done."*

Strange chick, I know, but she gets to me. I feel naked around her, like I couldn't keep a secret from her even if I wanted to. Which I don't. Weird, huh? I kept the card.

This is kind of interesting too.

Noticed a little statue on Bobby's desk this morning. He's had it a while but I never paid any attention to it until this morning. It's a pretty intricate carving of St. Michael. Struck me because Cammayo said his brother carved a whole series of statues for his mother. Bobby said Irie carved it for him. When I asked him Irie's real name, he tells me Romeo. Romeo was Cammayo's father's name. Romeo Cammayo. Then I remember Cammayo's mother saying "bwoy." Didn't think much of it at the time but she has a bit of an island lilt like Irie's.

See? That's how tired I am. Irie did it. He killed my father then came cross-country to settle in LA and snitch for me.

I was thinking I'd get him to carve a mini Madonna for Annie. A pocket pal she could keep in her purse. Little token of my appreciation.

All I'm knowing now fuh sure is dat some crazy white gull need fuh to get her some sleeps.

Later.

225

CHAPTER 46

For lunch the next day Frank grabbed a burrito from the bodega down the street and tracked Irie to his usual corner on Slauson Avenue. She parked and crossed the busy street.

"Off'cer Frank," the old man grumbled. "Twicet in one week. You gwan git me in trouble."

"Don't worry," she answered, waving off his concern. "I don't want to talk shop. I want you to make something for me."

"Yeah? What dat be?"

She spread her thumb and forefinger. "Little statue, 'bout this big, of the Virgin Mary. Can you do that for me?"

Irie's face split and he padded back to his crate. "Can I do dat," he boasted. "On'y wid my eyes closed!"

Frank studied the battered face, the rough scar under his right eye. "Irie, mon, you look like you been rode hard and put away wet."

"Ha, ha. Dat de trut'. So you wan' it 'bout six-inch big?"

"More like four. So you could carry it with you."

"Ah, like fuh put in you handbag."

"Yeah."

"What kind wood you want? Light? Dark? Middle?"

"I don't know. Dark, I guess. Heavy. I want it to be solid. Have some weight behind it."

Irie pulled at the stubble on his chin. "I gotta see what I got to home. Gonna cost you t'irty-five, maybe fifty dolla'. 'Bout dat."

"That's fine. I saw the Saint Michael you made Bobby. I want it like that."

Irie grinned. "I make you pretty Madonna. No worries."

"You're good. Where'd you learn to carve to like that?"

He dismissed the question. "Is a easy t'ing for me."

"Someone had to show you though, right? Who was that?"

Shaking his head, he answered, "No one. I jus' pick it up on me own."

"Pretty amazing." She tipped her head to the oranges. "May as well give me a bag as long as I'm here."

Irie handed her a bag and as Frank searched her pockets for money, she pretended to drop her penknife. Irie stooped to retrieve it.

" 'Ey. Dat's a nice knife," he said, opening the blade.

"I never do anything with it except cut food," Frank replied. "It's not like the knives you have."

"No, dat's still a good knife dere. Sharp," he said, running a thumb along the edge.

"Think I could start carvin' wid it?"

"Sure." He laughed. "Sure you can. It's easy t'ing." He folded the knife and handed it back.

Frank dropped it in her pocket. "Call Bobby when you get the statue done, all right?"

"Sure t'ing. Like a week or so."

She nodded, swinging the bag of oranges back to her car. As she eased into the flow of traffic she pulled on a latex glove. She felt silly, extracting the knife from her pocket and dropping it into an evidence bag. Running prints on John-John Romeo was doubtlessly going to be a waste of money. But it was her money and she'd sleep well at night.

The rest of the day was followed by more meetings downtown. Late that night, more like early on Wednesday morning, the squad caught a beating death. It was a merciful slam dunk in a bar full of witnesses, but then they caught a shooting Thursday evening. Their likeliest suspect, Armando Diaz, was the dead woman's husband but he'd gone to ground.

Friday night Frank told the squad to go home and get some sleep, come back first thing in the morning. She did the same, greeting her crew at six o'clock with doughnuts and fresh coffee. After getting them organized on the Diaz murder she left to shop for dinner and clean house. It didn't need cleaning—Frank had a housekeeper—but she dusted and vacuumed anyway, glad for the distraction. She was apprehensive about dinner, worried about where she and Gail stood, concerned she might trample their tender rapprochement.

She sorted through music, selecting albums that were romantic but not blatant, familiar but without memory. Arranging fleshy, pink roses she wondered if they were too flagrantly labial. She decided she didn't care—subtleties didn't count as pushing. A good thing because she was grilling a dozen oysters along with the steaks.

The semi-tropical winter day was cool enough for her to soak in a steamy tub. She read from the AA Big Book, sinking after a while up to her chin and reflecting. She found her hand coming out of the water, groping for the glass she habitually took into the bath with her.

"Jesus," she whispered, alarmed at the treachery of corporal memory.

She dried off and rifled through her drawers until she found a tiny vial of oil. Wrinkling her nose, she daubed her temples with it. The woodsy scent reminded her of search-and-rescues deep in sweltering canyons, but Gail loved the stuff.

Naked, Frank stood in front of her closet. Casting a side glance at the mirror, she noted the loss of her alcoholic bloat and the transition of flab back into muscle. There was still a little belly and pockets of cellulite she couldn't get rid of but she looked healthy.

228

Not ropy and wizened like a gym rat trophy wife, but firm and fleshy. Healthy.

Patting her belly, Frank told it, "Forty-five-year-old woman *should* have some droops and dimples. Shouldn't be mistaken for a walking stick of jerky."

She grinned, dressing in snug jeans and a black turtleneck. Her heart sank when the phone rang and she saw Gail's number.

"Hey."

"Hey, yourself. Are we still on for dinner?"

"Absolutely."

"Great. I'll be over in about half an hour."

"Good," Frank breathed. "Good."

She fired up the grill and the oven, popping potatoes into the latter and tonging oysters over the former. As she worked she sipped apple juice on ice. She didn't particularly like the stuff but the glass satisfied her hand, the color tricked her eye and the rattling cubes calmed her ear.

Gail was closer to an hour getting there and Frank kicked herself for starting the oysters so soon. She knew when Gail said half an hour it meant at least three-quarters and that an hour stretched close to two. But her irritation vanished when Gail walked in.

"Good timing. I just pulled oysters off the barby."

"Oysters?" Gail arched a meaningful brow.

"They're full of iron," Frank answered over her shoulder. "And they were on sale. Plus we gotta plump you up. You're looking skinny."

"Skinny? Me? You must be looking at somebody else."

"I'm looking at you, lady. You've lost weight."

Gail fluttered her eyelashes. "I haven't had anybody to cook for me."

"We're gonna change that. Sit. Get comfortable."

Frank produced the oysters, arranged on a platter between mounds of horseradish and lemon wedges.

"Now, I know these would be great with a beer or an icy Fumé but maybe I can interest you in a faux wine cooler instead?"

Gail laughed, the dry, throaty chortle that made Frank's crotch ache. "That would be lovely."

Frank mixed white grape juice with club soda and they slurped oysters as Frank grilled the steaks. The doc chatted through dinner and Frank listened happily. She missed her red wine a couple of times, but briefly and without intensity.

After they pushed their plates away Gail noted, "This is when you'd bring out the port or the brandy. How has it been going through all this sober?"

"You mean New York and all?"

"Yes."

Gail's eyes were shadowy, flecked with candlelight. Frank had an immediate glib answer, but she checked herself.

"Parts of it were difficult. But in going through all of it I'm starting to see just how numb I've been. For as long as I can remember. And truth to tell, even the pain feels good. Well, not good, but at least *real*. Honest. I feel like I'm coming out of the deep freeze. It hurts when limbs start defrosting but I can hear again and see and taste and feel everything. So, if that's the price . . . that's the price. Something I should have done a long time ago, but you know, I just couldn't. I wasn't ready. Everybody has a bottom. I hit mine. Had to go as low as I did. And now I don't ever have to go there again. So yeah. Parts are hard, but there are more parts that are beautiful. Overwhelmingly so. Like sitting here with you." It sounded like a throwaway line but Frank was suddenly close to tears. Gail reached for her hand and Frank said with a small laugh, "That happens a lot lately. I just . . . I don't know. I get moved easily. It's like this . . . I don't know . . . this realization how sweet life is. How *good*. Even when it hurts. Makes me all weepy. It's fucking weird. Downside is I get angry a lot easier too."

"I think it's lovely."

Frank was wordless. Rather she was full of what she feared were the wrong words, so she concentrated on Gail's hand in hers. Before she could say something stupid she gave a little squeeze and let go. "I got some movies. Took the liberty of hoping you'd stay for one."

"What did you get?"

Frank listed them and Gail frowned. "You hate romantic comedies."

"I don't *hate* 'em. Just don't want to spend eight bucks on 'em in a theater."

Gail wagged her bob. "The oysters, the candles, the sweet music. If I didn't know bet—"

A cell phone rang and they both got up. Gail's was on the table near the door, next to Frank's. They checked their messages and Frank swore.

"Franco," she answered.

"Frank, it's Lewis."

"S'up, Sister Shaft?"

"We got word Diaz is in La Quinta. Probably at a friend's house. Me and Darcy want to go get him."

"Whoa. Slow down. Let's call La Quinta PD, see if they can find him. If they do, they can pick him up, then you can go get him."

"Naw, Frank, I got it *deep* that he's there. I don't want no jake bustin' my play and losin' my boy for me. I want to get him myself."

"Lewis, I can't authorize OT to go get a suspect that might or might not be there. Call the locals, let 'em do their job. Then you can go."

"What if I went on my own time?"

Frank sighed. "Why you want this so bad?"

"You saw what he did to his wife? I want that mo-fo locked up and put away! You can't do shit like that in my 'hood and walk away. Nuh-uh. And I don't trust them Palm Desert cops to do the job right. I want it done right, I gotta do it myself. See it through. And it ain't no skin off the department's nose if I go off the clock. So what's the big?"

"No big," Frank admitted. "One thing though. Two. I'ma call Palm Desert and arrange backup for you. And you *will* use it, is that clear? You're not to go in alone."

"Yes, ma'am," Lewis replied sweetly. "And the second thing?"

"Call me. Keep me in the loop. Call me when you get him and if you don't get him call and tell me why. Clear?"

"Crystal, LT."

"A'ight. Be careful."

"I will."

Lewis banged the phone down and Frank winced. Gail was clearing the dishes and Frank called, "Hey, don't do those. I'll just be a sec."

But it took a while to get hold of someone at Palm Desert PD who could authorize Lewis's backup and by the time Frank was done Gail had finished the dishes.

"I thought I told you not to do those."

Gail leaned back against the sink, drying her hands.

Frank couldn't help but cup her hand against the doc's cheek. "You look beat. We'll save the movie for another night."

"No." Gail smiled. "I'm fine. You don't have to go in?"

"Nope. Just arranging for Lewis to pick up a suspect. She's a regular Stakhanovite." Frank grinned. "Reminds me of me when I was her age."

"What's a Stakhanovite?"

"Hey," Frank said, surprised. "Not often you ask me what something means. Stakhanovite's a hard worker, real industrious person. See, when I got my medical degree I got a linguistics degree, too."

"So I see." Gail laughed. She touched Frank's face. "I liked that. What you did with your hand."

Frank held Gail's cheek again. "That?"

"Yes."

Then it seemed that the next right thing to do was to kiss her. So Frank did. On the lips, slowly, mouths lingering.

Gail pulled back. She smiled but said, "How about that movie?"

"How about it?" Frank returned the smile.

CHAPTER 47

Gail nodded off about forty minutes into the movie. Frank tried to stay with it, waiting for Lewis to call, but she dozed off, too. The DVD defaulting to menu woke her. Gail was still out. Frank remoted the TV off.

For a while she watched Gail sleep, lulled by the doc's breathing. She still didn't wake when Frank got up for a blanket. She draped it over the doc who muttered, twisting against the pillows. Frank smoothed Gail's hair, whispering a "shh." Instead of sending Gail into a deeper sleep it roused her. She looked at Frank, dazed.

"Hey. You fell asleep during the movie."

Gail righted herself, looking around.

Frank knelt and took her hand. "Let me put you to bed. In the guest room. You shouldn't be driving home."

Gail nodded and Frank helped her up. She kissed Gail's forehead, steering her toward the spare room.

Frank turned lights off and double-checked locks. She looked in on Gail, calling through the bathroom door, "Want a tooth-brush?"

"Please."

Frank brought her a new one, and a clean T-shirt. "Thought you might like to sleep in this."

"Mm. Thanks. Sorry I flaked out on you."

"That's okay. I did too. Not the best movie in the world."

"Do I even have to ask how it ended?"

Frank shook her head. "Exactly as you'd imagine."

"Well, you were sweet to get it."

"Get some sleep. Lewis is supposed to call. I might not be here when you get up, but stay as long as you want, okay?"

Gail nodded.

"There's coffee, grapefruit, eggs, cereal . . . help yourself."

"I will. Thank you."

Frank turned to go, but Gail touched her arm. "Why didn't you invite me to sleep with you?"

"Thought about it." Frank grinned. "Figured that would defi-nitely constitute pushing. Should I have?"

Gail blinked, debating.

Frank tried to sway her. "It's not too late."

"I'd like that. Very much."

The answer was so ingenuously vulnerable that Frank blurted, "I love you." She offered her hand. "Come on. Let's sleep."

Expecting nothing more than the pleasure of Gail's proximity, Frank offered a chaste good-night kiss. Gail returned it eagerly and Frank offered another. It too was hungrily accepted. Frank gave and received more kisses, as their hands roved the familiar terrain of each other's bodies. Their lovemaking was hot and ardent, wordless, their passion speaking for itself.

After their desire had spent itself to a whisper, they lay in a tangle of limbs.

Frank swore, "Christ, but I've missed you."

"Mmm. Me, too."

Gail's breathing quickly evened out and Frank basked in the

simple pleasure of Gail against her. She wondered why Lewis hadn't called yet, then her thoughts shifted to Irie. She'd felt absurd dropping his prints at the lab, justifying to herself that it couldn't hurt to have background on him. There was a reason Irie wouldn't register as an official CI and odds were high it was a criminal reason—probably nothing worth the price of a private print check but Bobby'd be pleased with the extra info.

Checking the night clock Frank thought about Lewis again. Until Marguerite James snaked into her thoughts. Even with her arms wrapped around her lover, Frank had to admit a potent attraction to the *mambo*. It wasn't an emotional pull, or even intellectual, but completely physical. The woman wore her sexuality like strong cologne.

The phone rang and Gail woke but Frank told her to go back to sleep. She picked the phone out its cradle and took it into the living room.

"I got him!" Lewis crowed.

"Good. Where are you?"

"We found the bastard in Indio. Got him locked up in the back of the car."

"Good job. I'll meet you at the station at . . . six?"

"Make it six thirty." Lewis laughed. "I been up all night and I'm *starving!*"

"Six thirty it is."

Frank went back to bed to salvage a couple hours sleep. She half-heartedly tried rousing the doc but Gail didn't respond. Just as well, Frank decided, dropping hard into sleep.

Only a few hours later, Diaz broke in the box. Lewis was happy but tired. She headed home, leaving the booking and reports to her well-rested partner. It was Sunday morning and the squad room was empty except for Frank and Darcy. Frank cocked her head at him. "Hey."

He grunted at his paperwork.

"You told me you had a gift and chose not to use it. But why does Marguerite think *I* have a gift?"

"Because you do," he answered, still not bothering to look up.

"How so? What kind of gift?"

He stopped abruptly, pinning her with cool blue eyes. "You should talk to her about this."

"Why can't I talk to you?"

"This is her area of expertise. Remember? I gave it up."

"But you know what she's talking about."

He flicked a heavy shoulder.

"That whole business with Mother Love, you finding me . . . all that?"

"All that and more. That's the thing, Frank. There's always more. What you went through, what you experienced, that's not even the tip of the iceberg."

"That was plenty for me."

"It's hard," Darcy agreed. "Gifts like these aren't free."

"Is that why you walked away?"

Darcy spit tobacco juice into an empty soda can. "Partly that, partly Gabby. I considered her the greater responsibility. I couldn't see devoting myself to Marguerite's lifestyle and providing for my kid at the same time. So I took the easier route. Every now and again I take my talents off the shelf, dust them up and show them off like a parlor trick. Like telling Jill where that forty-four was, or finding you. Marguerite hates that. It drives her crazy that I don't respect what's been given me."

Frank chewed that over. "Ever regret your decision?"

Darcy swiveled back to his report. "I got a kid costing me a thousand bucks a month in medical bills. I don't have the luxury of regret."

Retreating to her office, Frank called around, reaching Gail at her apartment. "Hey."

"Hey yourself."

"Get some sleep?"

"Yes. Thank God. I was exhausted."

"Didn't act like it around midnight."

"That was my second wind."

"If that was your second I can't wait to see the first."

Gail laughed. "Are you working all day?"

"I'm done. Outta here. Wondering if you'd like to do something."

"We-ll," Gail stalled. "I'd love to do something outside. I've been cooped up all week. I need to get out and get some fresh air into my poor oxygen-depleted bloodstream. Are you up for a hike?"

"Sure. Where?"

"Why don't you come pick me up and we'll decide then."

" 'Kay. I'll pick up some lunch. Make it a picnic."

"You're spoiling me, copper."

"Indulge me."

"Consider it done."

"All right. See you around noon." Strolling through the squad room, she told Darcy, "I'm going home. Holler if you need me."

He tossed his head. "May the tutelary gods be with you."

Frank stopped. "That another voodoo thing?"

Darcy spit into his can. "The tutelary gods?"

"Yeah."

"Not quite. *Tutelary* is Latin. Tutelage, guardianship. The tutelary gods were lesser deities, spirits charged with protecting certain people and places. Python, he was the tutelary god of Delphi until Apollo slew him."

"I thought Apollo was Greek."

"He was. The Romans co-opted all the Greek gods and goddesses, then Judaism borrowed them, turning the spirits into seventy guardian angels that watched over the seventy nations. But at some point all the angels went bad. The only one to stand uncorrupted was Michael, the guardian angel of Israel."

"Who must have been adopted by Christianity," Frank interjected, "because he's the patron saint of cops."

"Correct."

"Alrighty then. Now that I've had my Sunday school lesson, may I take my leave, Professor? Me and my tutelary gods?"

Darcy saluted.

Frank saluted back. She was almost out the squad room door, but she had to ask. "Professor. If you were me, would you call Marguerite?"

Darcy's answer was almost wistful. "In a heartbeat."

Frank pursed her lips, leaving her cop with his paperwork and his past.

CHAPTER 48
Monday, 31 Jan 05—Work

All right, all right. Got a little distracted over the weekend. Missed two days. I'll make up for it. So here I am and what the hell, maybe there is a god. After this weekend I'll believe just about damn near anything.

Gail came over for dinner Saturday. Ended up spending the night. We made love. Fireworks, earthmoving—the whole shebang. No pun intended. All praise to Allah. I had to go in Sunday for a couple hours but then we had a picnic up in the San Gabriels, went for a hike, held hands. It was magic. Felt like I was under a spell—"that old black magic that you weave so well"—thank you, Marguerite James, my favorite mambo, *but this is the only hoodoo I'm interested in.*

Went back to her place to wash up before dinner—ended up in bed again. Sweet and slow and oh so lovely. Ate at Fox's. Took her home, left her there after a hundred kisses good night. Wanted to stay but she had work to do and has an early day this morning.

239

Life is good.

Talked to Mary. She warned me not to get too excited. Says it's nice that we've reconciled but sobriety has to remain my first priority. No sobriety, no Gail. Simple as that.

Agreed.

Went to the eight o'clock meeting last night. Bev led. She's an AA Nazi but has a life too. Some of these people, that's all they have is AA. They go to meetings all day and sit on panels at hospitals and institutions and that's all they do. Which is fine for them but I want a fuller life. Like Bev. She's great—gets to about five meetings a week, sponsors at least half a dozen women, works full time, has a husband and two kids . . . all that because she puts sobriety first. If she drinks again, sooner or later she'll lose the home, the kids, the husband, the job, everything. Even herself. So why risk it, she said.

Why indeed. I've been given a second chance. By who (whom?) I don't know, but I'm grabbing it by the horns and running with it. I know where I'll go if I drink. I don't know where I'll go if I stay sober. So far sober looks a whole lot better. Might go to the downtown meeting at lunchtime. Got to be down there anyway. Fubar had a fit about—

CHAPTER 49

A knock came on Frank's door. She slid the journal into her drawer and answered, "Come in."

Bobby swung half his body in. "Sorry to bother you. Irie called. Said your statue's ready. And I'm going for sandwiches. Want anything?"

Frank checked her watch. "No, thanks. I'm heading out. I'll be downtown."

She signed out and drove toward Slauson. In the stop-and-go traffic she indulged her inane fantasy about Irie, hoping his prints would come back soon and put an end to her wasteful and wishful thinking.

He was hustling oranges on his usual corner and as she parked, Frank said, "That was fas', mon."

"Irie need de money." He produced an oily cloth bundle and gently unwrapped the dark Madonna inside.

Frank picked it up. The wood was slick and heavy, fragranced with a spicy polish. It was a familiar smell but Frank couldn't place it. She traced the Madonna's delicate features, the fold and drape of her gown. "Jesus, Irie. This is beautiful."

"You like 'er? She wha' you want?"

"Yeah. And then some. This is great work."

Irie exposed his remaining teeth, basking in the compliment.

"Fifty, right?" He nodded and Frank gave him three twenties. "Call it good."

" 'Preciate it, Off'cer Frank."

"You should be havin' shows, Irie. You got some serious talent."

"Shows." He laughed. "Gull, listen at you."

"I'm serious. I ain't no art critic for the *Times* but this is talented work, mon." She inhaled the rich, citrus polish, then jerked her head up. "What kinda polish is this?"

"Bee'wax and orange oil."

"Where do you get it?"

"To de hardware store."

"No shit. Can you get it anywhere?"

Irie shrugged. "I suspec'."

Frank tried a wild gambit. "I was in New York a couple weeks ago. Friend of mine had a cross—a crucifix I guess. I don't know the difference—but it was dark like this and heavy. It was big, about eighteen inches long. Had a beautiful Jesus carved on it, real striking detail, you know—the suffering expression, the wrinkles in his skin, even had fingernails and toenails." She grinned. "Not every day you see Jesus's toenails. But it was a gorgeous piece, a lot like this. Smelled like this too. Belonged to a friend of mine, a priest. Nice guy. I told him it should be in a church somewhere, or a museum, like this one, but he said, 'Oh, no.' His brother made it for him for his birthday, a long time ago, then a couple years later he disappeared or something. Never saw him again. Real sad story. But that cross, it was beautiful. Just like this."

Irie slumped onto the plastic crate.

Frank watched like a cat on a mouse. She casually asked, "You ever been to New York, Irie? It's a beautiful city."

The old man shook his head, prodded a callous. "Dat priest," he asked gravely. " 'Im white devil like you?"

"No. Panamanian actually. Nice guy. His dad died when he was little   ."

Irie glanced at her.

She concealed her excitement, blandly continuing, "His mama raised him alone. He had a sister, too. And two brothers. Until the one disappeared. I think he was a hype or something. Still rips my friend up to talk about him. Gets tears in his eyes even after all this time."

"And he neve' 'eard from 'is brot'er again?"

"Never. Figures he's dead. The only reason he can think of that he wouldn't have called or been in touch. He loved his brother. Thought his brother loved him."

"Sad." Irie breathed. Then, "Wha' you friend name?"

"Roberto," she answered slowly. "Roberto Cammayo."

Irie became as stiff as his statue. Frank crouched next to him. She didn't believe this was happening. Was certain she'd wake up any second to sharp disappointment.

"His brother's name is Pablo," she whispered. "Pablo Cammayo. Got into trouble and disappeared one night. Got into more trouble in Kansas. Did time in Leavenworth." Frank guessed from here. "Got out and cleaned himself up. Moved to California. Got a new name, new life. Gets by talking to the police now and then, selling oranges, carving really good statues on the cheap. Doesn't want to draw attention to himself. Turned his back on his family. They hope he's alive but they think he's dead. Probably junked out somewhere a long time ago. Else why wouldn't he have called or come home? Sent a letter, a postcard. Something. Why do you think that would be?"

"Don' know." Irie leapt from his crate. He grabbed his sacks of oranges.

"Where you goin', Pablo?"

The old man spun. He sprayed spit, shouting "I ain' Pablo!"

"Jesus Christ." Frank gaped, shaking her head. "Pablo Cammayo."

"Stop sayin' dat! I tol' you I ain' him!"

Irie pushed past Frank but she clutched his arm. "Where you gonna run to now, Pablo? Huh?"

The old man stared, eyes wide and white, spit bracketing the corners of his mouth.

"Remember that knife I dropped? You picked it up. Got your fingerprints all over it. I took it into the lab." She lied, "Prints came back to a Pablo Cammayo. Now whaddaya got to say?"

"Why?" he moaned. "Why you fuh do dis?"

Frank stepped within inches of the haunted face, glorying in the moment and slightly repelled at the same time. She shook him. "Look at me. Do I remind you of anyone?"

Irie shook his gray head. "No."

"Think back," she ordered. "Way back. The night you left home. The night you shot my father. For three lousy fucking dollars." She smiled. "I know you're a new man. John-John Ro-*may*-oh. But still, you can't forget that night. You'll never forget that night. You *dream* about that night. You know how I know? Because I do, too."

She let that sink in. Irie continued shaking his head, as if he shook it long enough she'd disappear.

"You can' be," he stammered. "You can' be dat lil gull."

A wild, improbable laughter took Frank. "Oh, man." She cackled. "What are the fuckin' odds, Irie? Huh? What are the *fucking* odds?"

She laughed again, feeling slightly hysterical, the laughter veering closely to tears.

"Oh, man," she gasped, wiping at her eyes. "Wha' hoppnin', mon? Irie, 'im look like he seen duppy."

"You duppy," he agreed, his face ashen. "You mus' fuh to be ghost. Can' be 'er. Can' be."

"Can be her. Am her. Touch me." She held her arm out. Irie scuttled back. The scary laughter bubbled out of her again. "Jesus,

Irie. Of all the dumb fuckin' luck. How the hell did you end up snitchin' for the daughter of the man you killed? Huh? Can you tell me that, mon? Huh? Can you explain that?"

He stepped backward. Frank followed.

"Can' be," he whined over and over. "Can' be."

"Wouldn't think so, would you? I've spent most of my life wondering who the hell you were . . . I waited so long I gave up. Then I went to New York, visited my father's grave—first time since he died—and who's there but your brother. Berto—Bobo—"

"No." Irie sobbed.

"Yeah." Frank nodded. "Bobo. He's a priest. Was always gonna be one. Well, he is. Still has that cross you made him. For his thirteenth birthday, right? Was that it? Hmm?"

Irie stabbed a finger at her. "You lyin'! Why he at you fat'er's grave?"

"Excellent question, Irie. Pablo. Whatever the hell your name is. And I'll tell you, he goes to pray. To get inspiration. And to remember you. He says a prayer for you every time. Every time for the last thirty-six years. And what have you done for him? Nothing. Broke his heart. Broke your mama's heart. You ran like a baby. Like a coward. Like a weak, gutless *bwoy*."

"No." Irie cried, tears dribbling over scars and wrinkles. "You can' say dat! You don' know wha' it take to stay away, fuh to try and forget and never forget. You can' know."

"You *asshole!*" Frank twisted the cloth at his neck. Irie dropped his crate and oranges. "You're telling *me* I can't know? You have the fucking *balls* to tell me I don't know what it's like to try and forget my father and never forget him? You have the fucking *nerve*? I oughta make you eat this fucking sidewalk, asswipe. I oughta make you eat until it comes out the other side of you."

She whirled him around. Dropping a hand to pin his wrist against his back, she propelled him toward the Honda. She yanked the door open and fumbled for her cuffs. Slamming them onto his wrists, she shoved him in.

Pulling into traffic she almost hit a truck. The driver leaned on his horn while she glared at Irie in the rearview. He sat slumped and quiet, breathing through his mouth, his corrugated face shiny with snot and tears.

Frank was suddenly sick. She stamped the brakes and threw the door open in time to puke onto the street. Behind her, the guy in the truck repeated his honking, adding obscenities screamed from his window. Frank threw up again before closing the door and continuing onto a side street. Weak and trembly, she got out to pace, gulping shallow breaths until she could get back into the car.

Irie stared dully out the window. They rode in silence until he muttered, "I can' fuh believe you dat lil gull."

"I can't fuh believe you dat fuckin' junkie."

"I ain' 'im no more. You know dat. I been clean long time. I no dat bwoy no more."

Frank caught Irie's reproving stare in the mirror.

"'Im die one mornin' on a prison floor. Dat bwoy gwan. Pablo Cammayo gwan. When he wakes up, John-John Romeo done took his place."

Frank glowered into the mirror. "Yeah. If only it were that fuckin' easy."

Irie shook his old gray skull. "Not easy. Never sayed it was easy."

Neither spoke again until they got to the station.

CHAPTER 50

Frank put Irie in one of the interview rooms while she collected statement forms and a tape. Jill and Diego were in the squad room. She told them not to interrupt her.

"What'd he do?" Diego asked.

"Don't ask. If anybody's looking for me, take a message. I'll get back to 'em."

Opening the interview room door, she changed her mind. She came back a minute later with two Cokes. She pushed one to Irie, popped the tab on the other. Took a long swallow, pretending it was beer.

"I'ma tape this, Irie." She paused. "Or Pablo? What do you want me to call you?"

His face screwed up. "It gwan be strange but call me Pablo."

Pablo repeated the name as she got the tape ready. For the record she described the time and location, her name and rank, Pablo's various names and the reason for the interview. She read him his rights.

"You understand you don't have to talk to me?"

He nodded.

Frank pointed at the recorder.

"I unnerstan'."

"Let's start on February twelfth, nineteen sixty-nine. What happened that night?"

Pablo wobbled his head. "I can still see it, like it happen one night ago."

He told the story just as Frank remembered it. When he was done he put it to paper. She checked the statement, got his signature and concluded the interview.

She pushed back from the table but didn't get up. "Couple things. Off the record.

"Why him? You saw us coming out of Cal's. You knew it was a cop bar. Why jack a cop?"

"You remember? It was cold dat night? Wunt a lot of people out wit' money in dey pockets. I seen a white guy, lil gull, t'ink he make easy pigeon. I wunt gonna kill him. Just wan'ed his wallet. T'ought he'd hand it over easy like, 'cause a the gull. 'Cause a you. Den you go inside dat deli, and I t'ought, 'Damn, I fuh fool!' Shoulda got money befuh 'im spend it. But it cold. You bot' walkin' fast. I had hard time fuh keep up."

"It was cold," Frank agreed. "So you bounced around after Leavenworth, but how'd you end up here?"

"Warm, fa' away. Sunny like I imagine Panama to be. Nobody know me."

"No, I mean why Figueroa? Why South Central?"

"Met a Dominican lady lived here. I stayed wit' 'er a couple mont', t'ree maybe. 'Ere I was jus' anot'er poor nigger. No one see me."

"Then why snitch? Doesn't make sense if you were trying to be invisible."

"No," he admitted. "But I do it once or twicet. For money. No bad trouble come. So Irie keep his eye and ear open, mout' shut. Money come easy for jus' payin' attention."

"Jesus." Frank shook her head. "And you had no idea who I was?"

"How could I?" Irie asked. "You suppose' be in New York, not here like me."

Frank collected her tape and statement. Irie watched her. "A detective's gonna come and book you."

"Off'cer Frank," he implored. "You gotta fuh do dis?"

"I have to."

"You known me long time . . ."

She nodded.

Palms wide, he appealed, "Maybe for dat . . . ?"

"Can't."

He slumped farther into his chair, dropping chin to chest. Frank stared at him. She tried to conjure hate, even anger, but all she could dredge was sorrow.

"Romeo," she mused. "For your father?"

"Fuh 'im. I try, but I couln' fuh to give ever'tin' up."

"Why John-John?"

A sad smile deepened his wrinkles.

"Fuh John-John Kennedy. I see 'im fuh standin' dere, doin' dat salute like a brave lil sol'juh. I ne'er forgettin' dat. 'Im lose 'is daddy, jus' like me." He paused. "Jus' like you."

Frank hardened her stare as Irie leaned toward her.

"I di' not mean fuh to kill you daddy. I jus' nee'ed to fix. I jus' wanna money. No dead daddies." He sucked his teeth and sat back. "Too many a dem already. Too many."

Frank opened the door.

Behind her he accused, "Dat was a lie, dat Berto's you frien'."

"That was a lie," Frank agreed, turning. "But the rest was true. He's a priest. He ministers to prisoners. Hoped maybe someday he'd find you that way. Your mother—"

"You saw 'er?" Irie cried.

"I talked to her." Irie asked how she was before Frank could explain, "She's fine. Edmundo's a mechanic. Got three kids. You're an uncle. Your sister, Flora, she's pretty strung out on crack."

"No-o-o," Irie moaned. "No-o. She a sweet gull."

"Not no more," Frank said. "Ain't none of us sweet no more."

She trudged back to her office, bone tired and desperate for a drink. She gave Jill quick instructions, then looked up a number in her office. She dialed, finally got connected.

"Annie, it's Franco."

"Hey, cookie! How are ya?"

"Been a long, strange day."

"How so?"

"Got a CI here, I've known him nine years. Good snitch. Good guy. You're not gonna believe this. I still don't believe it. I put two and two together, it made four, so then I put four and four together and got eight. Annie, this guy is Pablo Cammayo. One of my detectives is booking him even as we speak and I'm holding his confession."

"*No freakin' way.*"

"I know. It sounds impossible. I mean, what are the odds, right? But he spilled everything. Everything. He's been running for thirty-six years, just like me. Shoulda seen it when I called him Pablo. It was like I was talking to a ghost. He denied it for a couple minutes but I told him I ran his prints and he folded like a bad hand."

"I can't believe this."

"I know, neither can I. Keep thinking I must be in some very lucid dream, but so far, I haven't been able to wake up."

"Well, let's extradite him before you do."

"You gonna come get him?"

"I'll talk to the captain, see if he'll cut me loose."

"All right. You'll have a room and a hot meal waiting for you."

"Deal. But tell me, what was the two and two you added together after all this time? You said you've known this guy, what, nine years?"

"Didn't know then what I knew after talking with his brother, with Roberto. A lot of little things clicked. The scar under his eye, no history. He's a carver—makes beautiful statues. Didn't know that until I talked to Roberto. He was going by John-John Romeo—his father's name was Romeo. And the Jamaican accent—remember, his mom had a trace of one? After he got out of the pen he drifted around with a Rasta for a while and figured that would be a good identity. His parents were Panamanian but the grandparents came over from Kingston. Assuming a Jamaican identity was a way to stay connected to his past."

"What happened between now and Leavenworth?"

"He got clean in the can. He was brought in pretty beat up and went to the hospital unit. He detoxed there. Knew if he went back out he was gonna die, and knew he couldn't go through another detox again so he walked away from the junk. There's a switch, huh, go to jail and get clean? He got out, bummed around, took odd jobs, drifted west. Figured the farther from New York he got, the safer he'd be."

Frank took uneasy note of the irony.

"He's pretty much a street person. He's got an old lady that has a regular job. He gets by peddling oranges, hawking tips, selling his carvings now and then but I know he gives a lot of 'em away. He's a nice guy, Annie. I've always liked him. I hate that it's him. I always thought it'd be such a relief to find the man who killed my dad, but there's no relief in this. None at all."

"I'm sorry for that."

"Yeah, well. You'll give me a call? Let me know when to expect you?"

"You bet, sister. Let me go track the captain down, get the ball rolling at this end."

"Roger that. Talk to you later."

Frank distracted herself with forms and reports. She slid a drawer open, groping for paper clips but fingering the journal she'd stashed earlier. She drew it out, took a glance at the clock. She dialed Gail at all her numbers, to no avail. She sighed, stared at the clock again.

Five-ten. Happy hour was well underway in every watering hole around the city. Frank started to rise. Changing her mind, she sat and drew the journal close. When she was done, she called Mary.

"Hey. Figured I'd better check in."

"Good. What's goin' on?"

Frank told her sponsor everything, including the part she'd admitted to Annie. "On the one hand here's the asshole who murdered my dad, right? On the other, I've known this guy a long time. We've got a good working relationship. He's a decent guy. Aside from the fact he killed my dad. So it's weird locking him up. I didn't want to do it. Thought that would be the happiest day of my life and it's anything but."

Frank traced the grain on her chair arm. The worn wood was smooth as glass, but warmer, softer. She thought of Gail under her hand.

"You know, it feels kinda like locking myself up. Yeah, okay, we're different color and different gender, but me and this guy, we're cut from the same cloth. When I was done interviewing him I asked, 'So all this time you had no idea who I was?' and he said, 'How could I? You're supposed to be in New York, just like me.' I had to leave the room, Mary. We both ran away. We both abandoned our families. Both lost our dads. Both tried to ignore the past and ended up here. It was like we couldn't run any farther. Like we've been running parallel all these years and finally crashed into each other at the end of the road. Now there's nowhere left for either of us to run."

Mary suggested, "Maybe that's a good thing. You can both stop running now."

"Yeah, but I don't have to go jail."

"Don't you think he's been in jail all this time anyways?"

"Spare me."

"No. Think about it. You didn't like putting a gun to your head, Frank, but it sobered you up. And you don't like *getting* sober but you like the relief it brings. Yes or no?"

"Yes."

"Maybe this man will too. I'm not saying he *wants* to go to jail but maybe this will be the gun to his head. Maybe now he can drop the load he's been carrying, just like you're doing, and who are you to deny him?"

"I'm not denying him anything. He's going."

"And that's the way it has to be. My point is, we never know who our angels are. Did I ever tell you about my last day?"

"Nope."

"I was done. I'd had it. I'd left my husband, abandoned the kids. I had nothing left but my car. I was living off five-dollar blow jobs. Five bucks was just enough for the vodka it would take to get me through another day. And I was done. I didn't want another day. I'd had all I could take. So that morning I blew the clerk at the gas station for a quart of vodka and a gallon of gas. I was gonna drink the vodka, drive up the Coast Highway and turn left over the ocean. I stumbled out to my car and a man filling up next to me said, 'You look like you're having a rough day.' I told him he didn't know the fucking half of it. He said, 'I bet I do,' and took a card from his pocket. He gave it to me. He was an insurance salesman and I though he was hustling me, but he went on. 'If you decide you want to stop doing what you're doing, give me a call. Anytime. Day or night.' I said something rude and drove off.

"But I kept the card. Thought he might be good for a twenty-dollar blow job. I drank the vodka. Drank it straight down and headed north. That's all I remember until I came to in a phone booth. It was dark and foggy and I had no idea where I was but I was talking to this man and he was listening. I told him everything. About the blow jobs, leaving my kids, how I couldn't control my bladder anymore—I mean everything. He stayed on the line with me for what seemed like hours, until finally these two women drove up in a warm, shiny car that didn't smell like piss or booze. They put me in the backseat and covered me with a blanket. I woke up the next morning in a recovery house. I never saw that man or those women again. I have no idea who they were. But I do know they saved my life. That's why when Joe called that morning and asked me to pick you up I was only too happy to do it. Because

253

someone did it for me. So don't beat yourself up, Frank. You could be this man's angel."

"Oh, yeah, that's me. Got a seat in the tutelary god squad."

"The tootle who?"

Frank explained what Darcy told her.

"Sounds like you're working the second step."

"Hey, that's his theory, not mine."

Well, so how's it coming?"

"It's coming."

"Geez," Mary griped. "Give me a for-instance or two."

"Let's see," Frank reflected. "'Came to believe a power greater than ourselves could restore us to sanity.' Well. For starters, I'd kill for a drink right now—quiet the banshees in my head—but I'm not gonna do that because I have faith that the desire will pass. That if I talk to you and go to a meeting and have dinner that feeling's gonna change and I'll get through another day without a drink. And I have faith that's gonna work because you tell me it does—that if I tell the truth and go to meetings the desire will pass. And I have faith that's true because I've seen it happen. In the beginning I could barely go a few minutes without thinking about a drink. Now it's hours. I have faith that at some point in the future it'll be days, then weeks, maybe even months or years. But that's getting ahead of myself. Gotta take it one day at a time, right?"

"That's the deal, kiddo. That's how it works."

"Yeah." Frank nodded. "So there's my faith."

"Good enough," Mary said. "And think about those tutelary gods. You never know where they are."

"Roger that."

"Okay, kiddo. Anything else?"

"Nope. Just thanks, as usual."

"No, the thanks are all mine. You helped keep me sober today. One alcoholic talking to another."

Frank grinned into the phone. "Were you in danger of going out?"

"Probably not, but only because I get to talk to you and *my* sponsor and go to a meeting tonight. And because I never forget that, even after twenty-five years sober, my next drunk's only as far away as the end of my hand. You been getting to meetings since your love life picked up?"

"One a day."

"Atta girl. Don't drop your guard just because life suddenly gets good again. You're an alcoholic, you're always going to be an alcoholic, and you need to always remember that. This is a disease and you need to treat it like you would any other. Keep doing what you're doing even when the ride's smooth, because I can promise you there are bumps ahead, and when the ride gets rough you want to be able to reach into your toolbox and pull out the tools that'll help you through. Okay?"

"Okay."

"Good. Stay close, kiddo. I'd hate to lose you."

"I'd hate to be lost. I'll call you tomorrow." Frank hung up.

Talking to Mary always made her feel like she had dumped a heavy pail of rotting trash. Not only dumped the trash but scoured the pail as well. Frank slid into her coat and switched the lights off. If she hurried she could get to the downtown meeting. She jogged down the stairs and stopped halfway across the parking lot. She went back inside, to the holding cells. Pablo sat in the last one.

"Irie," she called, shook her head. "Pablo. Come here."

He shuffled to her. Bringing her head close to the steel Frank spoke quietly. "I'm sorry it had to end this way. You're a good man. I know you didn't mean to kill my father. I knew it then—that look on your face when you shot him—I'll carry that to my grave. You were strung out. Junkies, drunks . . . they do things they never meant to. I know it was the junkie that killed my father, not the man standing here today. So for what it's worth, if it means anything to you, I forgive you."

Tears spilled over red-rimmed eyes and Pablo said, "I never mean' to hurt nobody. All dese years, dis time I hadda t'ink about it. If I coulda taked back dat one minute, jus' d'at one *second*, evert'ing be differen'. You know? Evert'ing."

"I know."

He lifted his hands to her. She glanced around and violated the rules by putting her hand through the bars. Pablo grasped it, shedding tears. Frank checked again, grateful there were no cops.

"Hey. It's gonna be okay, mon. It's gonna be all right. You get to see your family again. Think how happy they're gonna be."

He yanked his head up. "You t'ink?"

She took the opportunity to extricate herself. "I *know*. You can call Roberto if you want. Tell him you're alive."

"'Im be mad. 'Im 'ate me now fuh sure."

"No," Frank assured. "He doesn't hate you. He might be mad, but he doesn't hate you. Your mother either."

"My mot'er," Pablo marveled. "Wha' 'er look like? 'Er still pretty?"

"She's old, mon, but yes, still pretty."

"Old," he repeated, twirling a finger around his head. "In my mind 'er still t'irty-six!"

Frank smiled. "I'll give the guard your brother's number. It'll be a short call though. Tell him you're coming home and to call Detective Silvester. She'll know when you're coming back. All right?"

"I'm goin' 'ome?"

"You're goin' home, mon. I don't know what'll happen once you get there, but you're goin' home."

"'Ome." Irie tasted the word, then seemed to find it bitter. "You sure Berto won't be mad?"

"Not a chance." Lifting a hand to the man who'd killed her father, Frank walked away.

Outside the station, under the balmy Los Angeles dusk, a sickle moon winked over the freeway. Frank stopped to look at it. She thought about Noah, how many times they'd said good night, right here, under this same moon. She thought about her mother and father. About Mary in a midnight phone booth. About Annie's angels and Darcy's tutelary gods.

256

Ridiculous tears sprang up again. Frank blinked them back. She nodded at the blurry moon.

"Yeah, okay," she whispered. "Maybe so."

Slipping her key into the Honda, she realized she didn't want that drink anymore.